THE HORSES

'...the world ended, Jo, and we missed it...'

ELAINE WALKER

Rolling Olive Press

Published by Rolling Olive Press
7518 Bayside Road, Franktown, Virginia 23354-2106, U.S.A.

Print ISBN-10: 0-933316-82-8
Print ISBN-13: 978-0-933316-82-9

Cover and interior design by Naia E. Poyer.
Cover photo of horses © Neil Lockhart / Dreamstime.com.

eBook ISBN-10: 0-933316-85-2
eBook ISBN-13: 978-0-933316-85-0

Previous edition by Cinnamon Press
ISBN-10: 1907090096

CONTENTS

Dedicated to JB—
the original Poppa Horse

CHAPTER 1

The horses came the day my father died. That was the worst day and yet also the best. He always said that loss and gain went hand in hand.

My mother woke me early. It took all day to forage enough food and fuel, so getting up with the birds was usual. Except that there weren't any birds left, or at least so few that they were something to cause excitement.

'I saw a sparrow!'

'No. Where?'

'Over there – by the gate. Quick. There – oh, it's gone.'

Early mornings were as common as birds used to be, so when Moth called me, I was already waking. She didn't sound urgent, only quiet, same as always, so I stretched and assumed the fire had gone out or the goats had escaped again. I sat up, yawning, scrubbing my hands though my hair, starting as the door opened suddenly and Ginny looked in.

'Moth's calling.'

'I heard. I'm on my way. What's up?'

Her blue eyes were fearful. 'It's Dad.'

I moved then, fast, throwing back the covers and reaching for my jeans. I stepped out of bed and straight into them, heading for the door as I pulled on a sweatshirt. Dad hadn't been the same since he was kicked in the head as we'd struggled to herd the half-wild highland cattle abandoned nearby. He'd been unconscious for a long time and afterwards had days when he was confused or simply couldn't get out of bed.

I ran to sit beside him, realising that the steady downhill slide had picked up speed.

'You okay, Dad?' I asked, as cheerfully as I could manage. He gazed at me, then recognised me and reached out a hand to rest on my arm.

'Not so hot, Joel.'

His voice was husky, as though he had a cold coming, but it had been like that for a while. I glanced up at Moth, sitting with Ginny on her knee. She'd accepted that we'd lose him some time ago and a sort of dullness had come over her, except when she bent over him, or he had a good day. Now she looked as though she'd had her feelings disconnected. I wanted to tune her in, like the radio in the kitchen but guessed she could only manage the same white noise crackle.

'Can I get you anything?' I peered into Dad's face. 'Are you hungry?'

'No.' A pause while he struggled with pain, then he said, 'There are things I need to show you.'

I wanted to cry but instead I helped Moth get him up and dressed. We always tried to laugh our way through the awkwardness of dressing a man of six foot three inches, still heavy though he was thin and weak now. It was laugh or cringe with embarrassment for him. So we made a game of it, lifting limbs for Ginny to tug, pull and ease clothes onto. Ginny liked the game but she was only eight and didn't really understand. I often wished I was still eight.

Getting him downstairs was difficult, but we did it, then Moth said she'd make breakfast while Dad and I went outside. I sat him in the sun on a wooden bench in the sparse vegetable garden we were coaxing towards enthusiasm, then sped around to milk the goats and gather eggs. He was still sitting, looking over our field, when I got back and laid his hand on my shoulder as I sat beside him.

'Well done, son. Now, we both know what's happening, so let's not pretend.'

I nodded and he ruffled my hair, trying to make me smile because I was past the hair-ruffling age, and his hand was so bony it hurt my head. I grinned anyway for him, giving him a light nudge with my elbow.

'I know you'll help Moth,' he said, 'and take care of Ginn. Moth's not doing so well, Joel, so you'll maybe have to be in charge now and again. But she'll get better once…well, you know. It's the waiting that's dragged her down, waiting with no hope.'

He was silent then for a bit before he said, 'If the chance comes, Jo – and it must be a good chance, not a wild risk – then get away from here. Find somewhere lower down where the going's easier and there'll be people to help you.'

'You reckon there are people?'

'Of course. We can't be the only ones, can we?' He rubbed at his head and I knew he was suffering. 'You know where the shotgun is – don't get careless with it. Keep it safe – and the cartridges – safe and hidden.' He went on, rambling a little when the pain got bad, explaining to me about mending the leaky roof and managing the imminent lambing of our few sheep, reminding me that the emerging daffodils were poisonous to the goats.

I wondered later if he'd known the horses were coming, because he said, 'There's a few old bridles and stuff in the workshop. I've got them cleaned up and mended.'

Then he fell silent for a long while and I sat with him, covering his hand with my own and noticing for the first time that there wasn't much difference in size anymore. Moth called us for breakfast and he stirred as she came over, reaching out both hands to draw her face down to his. He kissed her on the mouth.

'Not very hungry, Ell,' he said, 'but it's nice here in the sun. Perhaps you could eat out here and I could sit for awhile?'

Moth did what he'd done, cradling his face and kissing him and I wished his lips weren't cracked and peeling. I ran for the salve we'd made out of comfrey leaves, putting a little on his mouth while Moth fetched Ginny and we had a breakfast picnic beside him on the grass.

'Do you remember the caravan,' he asked, nodding towards its shabby hulk, 'before it was a box-room?'

We all knew the 'do-you-remember?' game and joined in.

'Fold away beds,' said Moth and I added, 'Pumping the water.'

3

'And the little cupboard with the telly in,' said Ginny, laughing. She liked cupboards and hiding places.

'We had a lot of fun, didn't we?' Dad said, watching us all, and one big tear slid down his face. 'All those miles, and the songs and collecting car numbers…'

'Stopping for ice-cream,' shouted Ginn and Dad grinned. 'Chocolate ice-cream.'

Ginny clambered onto his knees but when I went to stop her, Dad shook his head and they sang the song they'd made, their foreheads resting against each other.

'Give me a kiss, as sweet as a dream,
Your kisses are sweeter than chocolate ice-cream.'

Moth smiled at me. We all knew it was me and Moth, and Dad and Ginny, but that was all right because it was me and Dad, and Moth and Ginny too.

Dad sent Ginny off to climb to the tree house and wave at him from the top, with me to keep an eye on her. When we looked down, Moth was kneeling between his feet with her arms around his neck and her head on his shoulder. They weren't speaking, just holding each other quietly. We sat quietly too, high above them, Ginny on my knee with her thumb in her mouth and I think that's when she knew. She got a bit tearful but when at last Dad looked up and waved, she jumped up and down, laughing, waving back and I was proud of her.

It was Ginny's turn next, so Moth and I cleared away the breakfast things while she and Dad drew a picture with the last stubs of her crayons. It was a good picture with us all eating our picnic in the sunshine. She and Dad were sharing a big bowl of chocolate ice-cream and all our favourite foods were there – strawberries for Moth and pizza for me. Even the animals had big buckets of carrots and there were birds of all colours lined up along the fence waiting for crumbs.

'It's a great picture, Ginn,' I said. 'But what are these, here, on the skyline?'

I pointed to a line of vague animal shapes looking down on our picnicking family.

'Oh, those are horses,' Ginny said, and shared a secret smile with Dad. 'I like horses.'

Then it was me. Dad said, 'Come on, Jo. Help your old man have a bit of a walk.'

He kissed Moth and Ginny and asked me to bring a blanket. He put his arm around my shoulders, half because he loved me and half because he couldn't walk without help.

'Let's go to the wood,' I suggested, meaning the small huddle of trees down by the barn, because I didn't want to go where I guessed we were headed.

'Let's make this easy, Joel.'

I nodded, trying to hold back the sigh that kept shuddering up in my throat and we headed down beyond the barn to the meadow. We were proud of the meadow. The four of us had worked hard on it that first summer before Dad got kicked, to mend the dry-stone wall so our ragged collection of stock couldn't stray. It was big, about fifteen acres, strong and green with good soil and Dad said the surrounding hills had sheltered it when the clouds blew over, burning the land beyond until all the rain that came after could wash away the poisons. Those hills had protected us too, while we watched the changed world through the windows of the farmhouse. The holiday Dad had always wanted to take in the caravan to the highlands had saved us.

Dad and I walked slowly round the outside, close to the wall we'd mended and Dad kept asking me to pick him a leaf or a flower to hold in his hand.

'Look at that, Jo,' he said suddenly and a great eagle rose lazily from a tall pine. 'Well, I never thought I'd see one of those again. I was afraid they'd all gone forever. Now, that's a good sign.'

Something caught my eye and I ran to where a red-gold feather was floating down. It was long and wide and I fancied it still warm from the bird's body. I offered it to Dad and he stroked it.

'What a beauty, Jo.' He handed it back to me. 'You keep it – keep it and think of me.'

5

I nodded, unable to see him clearly though my blurring eyes, but when I ducked my head, he said, 'It's okay, son, come here.'

I stood for a long time with my head on his chest, hearing the slow thud of his heart and feeling his hands, one stroking my hair and one on my back, holding me safe. At last, he hugged me, then looked down at me with a smile. 'What are you never too old to do?'

I grinned, remembering my grandfather's voice. 'Kiss the people you love,' I said and reached up to kiss his cheek.

'Never forget that,' he said, and he kissed me too, on my forehead twice, holding my head carefully.

'I've had a fine family, Jo.' He looked at me and his eyes were bright. 'And since it's been just us, well, it's been hard, but, you know, it's been good too.'

I nodded. I knew.

We wandered with our arms around each other, through the gate into the meadow and down to the hole I'd dug with Moth. No-one had ever admitted what this long deep trench was for but Dad had insisted on it being made, little by little, over the past few weeks.

'Better this way than when it's needed at once,' he'd said cheerfully.

It was covered over with boards and now he and I sat beside it on the blanket, our backs against the sun-warmed wall alongside.

'I love it here,' he said, looking out over the little world we'd found for ourselves. 'I like to look at that skyline and imagine what might come over it.'

We sat and watched as though we were expecting something, talking now and again and the spring morning passed. It was a quiet sort of day, warm and still. The few birds around gave us something to look out for, while our sheep and cattle grazed peacefully and the three goats on their tethers browsed the hedge that lined the drive. The green of the meadow surrounded by its stone wall looked rich and fertile amongst the scrubby surrounding fields. The hill leading up to the sky was green too, though it petered out half way down the far slope. We couldn't see that, but we could see a few celandines and a ragged robin or two.

'It's all coming back slowly, Jo,' Dad said. 'You'll see a change this summer.'

I nodded, trying to look full of anticipation but I didn't want to think beyond that moment. Dad put his hand over mine and we sat quietly for a bit longer.

Moth and Ginny came out to sit with us after a while and we spent the day just watching the sky and the fields. In a strange way, it was a good day. It was the four of us for the last time. Dad needed to lie down in the early afternoon so we all lay in a line, looking up at the cloud patterns.

'There's a rose for you, Ell,' said Dad and we all clamoured –

'Where?'

'Which one?'

'What, that one?'

'It's more like a piece of cake.'

'There's a horse,' said Ginny, 'with a foal.'

'Where?' asked Moth. 'Oh yes, I see – why yes, it really is.'

I saw it too. 'Good one, Ginn – I think they're galloping. D'you see, Dad?'

He didn't reply and we all fell into a breath-holding sort of silence. I didn't dare look but felt Moth lean over him.

'He's drifting now,' she said softly.

I looked. He seemed asleep but I could tell it was deeper than that. We sat and watched him, holding his hands, and little by little his breathing slowed until he'd quietly gone.

Moth started to sob softly and I felt a dam in my chest burst as tears torrented down my face. But Ginny patted us both on the head then leaned over to kiss Dad.

'He's gone to meet them,' she said. 'Go on, Daddy, show them how to find us.'

Moth looked up, bewildered. 'What do you mean, sweetie?'

Ginny had a glow about her, even though she was crying.

'It's a special secret me and Dad had. You'll see. He said they'd come when he had to go.'

Moth looked at her a moment. 'Go and gather something pretty for Daddy, Ginn. Flowers and leaves, grasses – whatever you can find.'

Ginny touched Dad's forehead then scampered off, scattering the sheep.

We said our goodbyes, then worked quickly, using the blanket to lower him into the grave he'd supervised us making, wrapping it carefully round him. I didn't want to shovel earth onto him and hesitated. Moth laid a hand on my arm. 'I want that big round stone, Jo – the one just inside the gate. Can you lift it?'

By the time I got back, she'd done it. I'd never have believed she could work so fast because she was little and frail-looking. But she was tough too. We put the stone at the head and Ginny laid the few yellow cowslips she'd found close to it in an old jam-jar with water from the stream, then scattered daisies over the rest of the fresh earth.

Then we sat awhile before we walked hand-in-hand back to the house, Moth in the middle. It was a fine, clear evening and the sun was falling behind the skyline.

'What's that noise?' Moth stopped walking at the same moment that I heard it too. We were so used to silence by then that the soft distant drumming seemed loud as thunder.

'They're coming. Oh, they're coming!' Ginny was bouncing up and down with excitement, clapping her hands.

'Who, love? Who's coming?'

'The horses – the horses – oh, look!'

And, as we followed the line of her pointing arm, there they were. A few at first, cresting the hill to gallop along the ridge, then more, until ten or twelve were streaming along the skyline. They shimmered and gleamed as though they'd come straight out of the setting sun, manes and tails flying, hooves pounding, shadows doubling their number as they poured down the long slope into our valley. They were wild with the thrill of running together and I suddenly remembered the days when I had friends to run and climb and bike with. I knew the exhilaration of being carried along by the group and wished I could

8

run with them. I started to cry again and Moth put her arms around me. We lifted Ginny up between us and hugged each other in a tight group.

As though this were a signal, the horses wheeled off the sloping path and hurtled towards us. Ginny began to laugh, her arms around our necks quivering with terrified delight as they careered on either side of us, raising stones and dust. I could hear their panting breath and smell the warm sweat, feeling the heat of their bodies and the shaking of the earth beneath their hooves, as they swept past us and down into the valley. We turned and watched, realising that the meadow gate was open and they were going to charge through.

'I closed the gate,' I said slowly, my voice croaky with tears and dust and Moth replied with the same bewilderment, 'I know you did. I saw you.'

The horses circled the meadow at a gallop, the cattle and sheep gathering to a huddled group in the centre, then paused to breathe, ears pricked and necks outstretched, around Dad's grave. Ginny was running and we sped after her, afraid they'd turn again and she'd be trampled. But she closed the gate, calling out to them, 'You're safe now. We'll take care of you. Daddy sent you here for us.'

They swung their heads to look at her, then settled down, starting to graze and roll, as though they'd reached home.

CHAPTER 2

Watching the horses had lifted us all a little, but when we got back to the house, Dad's absence was so noticeable that we could only sit around crying. At last, Moth persuaded us to eat something then I had to go and see to the animals for the night. One of the good things about the animals was that they had to be taken care of, no matter how bad things were. So their needs hauled me to my feet. I told them they were a pain, but felt better by the time I'd done everything. Once I'd locked the chickens and goats away, I went to watch the horses in the dusk for a while.

They were wandering around, swishing their tails, checking the meadow out. I wondered if they'd been from here in the first place and were making sure it was all the same. One of them was lying down by Dad's grave and I went over to say goodnight to Dad and get a closer look at the horse at the same time.

I already liked him. I'd been watching him earlier, when they were all settling down. He was a dark dappled grey, with a long mane, almost black, and his tail was the same colour. I liked his eyes – they were intelligent and curious. He showed no fear as I wandered over to lean on the wall. After lifting his head to glance at me, he carried on grazing, even though he was lying down. I'd not had much to do with horses before and I'd never seen one do that.

'Supper in bed, is it?' I asked him and he pricked up his ears at the sound of my voice. 'Well, you look like you had a long journey, so I suppose you're tired. That's my Dad, there, keeping you company, you know.'

I had a feeling he already knew and wondered if I was going mad, talking to a horse about my dead father. But it didn't seem mad. I noticed that none of the animals had touched the cowslips on the grave or trampled it, though there was a path round it where the horses had circled to pay their respects. I stayed a while longer before I said aloud, ''Night, Dad. I'll be down in the morning.' Then I headed back to the house, feeling as though I'd abandoned him.

We had a bad night. Ginny got in Moth's bed straight away but she had a nightmare almost as soon as she fell asleep. I went in to see if they were all right and, when Moth said, 'There's room for three in here,' I stayed. It was a long time since I'd slept in my parents' bed but I was beyond the stage when proving I was independent mattered to me. Dad said that when the world you know ends, you have to pick the bits and pieces out of it that matter and build a new world. So, I slept in my parents' bed and felt better.

I didn't sleep much though. I lay awake most of the night looking at the pale-coloured ceiling in the moonlight. Ginny fell asleep, safe between me and Moth, but Moth was awake too. We talked now and again, quietly, about Dad. His love of hiking, corny jokes and wildlife books; his hatred of mobile phones but insistence that Ginn and I carried one everywhere so we could call if we needed backup '... anytime, do you hear? Day or night, I don't care what brainless thing you've done or where you are'. Ideas he and Moth had for us before it all changed – university, travel, a round-the-world ticket for our twenty-first birthdays.

'We never planned that you'd learn how to take care of chickens, though,' Moth said. 'Or make goat's milk cheese.'

'Or fix a sewer pipe,' I reminded her. 'I bet you never planned that one.'

I heard the laughter in her breath in the half-light. 'No. We missed that out. What a bit of luck, eh, Jo, that you got the opportunity anyway?'

'Sure. I've got a great future in sewerage when the world gets going again.'

'Do you think it will, Jo? What are we going to do?'

There was silence as we contemplated the empty future, then I said, 'Dad told me that if a good chance comes to get away, we should take it. Find more people and a place that's not so remote and wild in the winter.'

She was quiet again and I could almost hear her thinking about the horses, as I was.

'We should. He was right,' she said, after a bit. 'It's safe here. But it's a struggle. We'd need to be sure it was right to leave, though, because we've worked hard to make this place somewhere we can survive.'

'And Dad's here,' I said, because I heard it in the silence when she stopped speaking. 'We won't leave Dad unless we're sure.'

She was silent but she reached over Ginny and pressed my arm. 'Your Dad loved you, Joel.'

'I know.'

It was a long night, long and sad, so I was glad when the sun started coming in through the window. But our routines had revolved around taking care of Dad for so long that we seemed to have lost our rhythm. We got up and I went to get dressed, then couldn't think what to do for a minute. I usually fed the animals while Moth made breakfast and then we got Dad and Ginn up later, so that was the same. Me and Moth awake first. But it felt different. I had to make myself go downstairs like a toddler not sure which foot went first. I saw Moth standing by the stove, staring out of the window, the kettle in her hand as though she didn't know what to do with it. I took it off her and checked it was full, then put it on the stove and hugged her round the shoulders.

'We'll be all right, Moth,' I said. 'It's going to be hard for a bit, but we'll be all right.'

She looked at me for a moment, as though I was even more bewildering than a kettle, then she nodded. 'I'll get breakfast,' she said, and we lurched into action again.

Outside, things were better. The chickens started squawking as soon as they heard me coming and emerged in flurries of indignant feathers, telling me off for being too slow in getting the shed door open.

'Shut up,' I told them, 'or it's chicken soup for supper tonight.'

They knew I didn't mean it and started scratching around in the scraps and peelings and bits of crust I'd thrown down for their breakfast. They foraged for themselves all day, but we kept all our food scraps for them. I collected the eggs – there were five, which was good – then ran back to the house with them, because I had a tendency to put them down and forget where I'd left them.

When I'd milked and tethered the goats to stop them getting in the garden, I ran down to the meadow and the horses were still there. I'd half expected them to be gone. I went over to the grave. I felt sick at the thought of Dad there with the soil on top of him and insects starting to crawl – I had to stop myself thinking because I wanted to howl at the top of my voice. The sensation of being watched made me turn round sharply and the horse behind me backed away, throwing his head up because I'd moved quickly.

'I'm sorry, boy,' I said, on instinct squatting down so I wouldn't alarm him. 'Did I scare you? Come on, let's be friends.'

It was the grey one that had been lying by Dad the night before and I realised that though he was cautious, he wasn't scared at all – he'd simply been startled. Now he stretched out his neck to an impossible length to sniff the grass in my outstretched hand and it made me laugh,

'You're not a horse – you're a giraffe. I like your colour. I'm going to call you Gray, after my Dad, if Moth says that's okay.' Had I ever heard her call him 'Graham'? I'd never thought about it before. 'Come on, have a bit of grass.'

Gray sniffed again and I felt his warm breath on my skin. It was slightly damp and sent a shiver down my spine because it tickled and he was big while I felt small, squatting down in front of him. He was beautiful, graceful, with neat ears and a finely shaped head. But he was solid too. He had strong legs and lots of hair round the ankles, if horses had ankles. I wished I had some books about horses so I could learn if they were called ankles. His mane was long. The fringe on his forehead came down well below his eyes and the glossy length along his neck swung down like a dark curtain. He was on the thin side but muscular. I'd seen racehorses on the television, and I didn't think he was one of those. He looked a bit like the Shire horses that pulled the beer-wagons round the city at home. I wondered what had happened to them when the world ended.

Back in the old life, when I was Ginny's age and she was a baby, we'd put her in her buggy and go to watch the huge horses with their wagons setting out to do their rounds. Moth knew about horses from when she rode as a girl and I remember her telling me what they were called. She'd know about their ankles maybe. But Gray was much smaller than a Shire – as though he'd shrunk in the wash.

'That it, lad?' I asked him. 'Did you used to be a really big guy, but you got caught in the rain?'

I thought of the rain in the early days, burning but bitterly cold, and hoped none of it had landed on him. He took the grass, but with an air that said he was only being polite, because there was plenty of it in the meadow.

'He's lovely, Jo,' said Moth's voice, behind me. 'What are you going to call him?'

I hesitated, not wanting to upset her. I watched her walk over to the grave and she knelt down to rest her hand against the earth for a moment before coming closer to me and the horse.

'Do you mind if I call him Gray?'

Her face worked for a moment then she smiled. 'No, you call him that. Hello, Gray – are you Jo's new friend?'

'I sort of think he is,' I said.

Moth slipped an arm around my waist. 'When did you get taller than me?' she asked hugging me. 'My big son. Well, we've got a ranch now, it seems.'

We looked out at the meadow, with the cattle and sheep lost among the small herd of horses. Gray wandered casually off to join them.

'Have horses got ankles?' I asked. 'What's the hairy bit round their legs called?'

'Fetlocks,' Moth replied, 'and the hair is called feather.'

'Few birds, but lots of feathers,' I said. 'What shall we do with them? How do you think Dad and Ginny knew they were coming?'

'I have no idea,' Moth shook her head. 'And as for what to do with them, well, I suppose we'll take care of them and think about riding them. We could travel further looking for food and perhaps find out if there is anyone else around. I wish I remembered a bit more – it's a long time since I rode, but I suppose it will come back to me.'

'Are they old enough to ride?'

Moth surveyed the horses. 'Your friend is, I think, though he looks quite young. And those two over there look mature enough. The big guy, he's older than the others, and that mare with the foal. I'll be able to tell better when they're a bit more used to us – you tell their age by looking at their teeth. Take care with them, Jo, I don't want you to get...' Her voice trailed away before she could say 'kicked'.

'C'mon, breakfast is ready.' We found Ginny in the sitting room. 'I've got all the books out,' she said and I went to have a look. 'Moth! Look at this. Ginn, where did these come from?'

On the table were a dozen books on horses. Some looked quite old, but others were newer. There were ones on feeding, illness and injuries, horse breeds, a couple on riding, one on teaching a horse to pull a cart and some on general care. Moth came in and we stood staring at them and at Ginny.

'Ginny, where did you find the books?'

'In the cupboard under the stairs.'

We kept the cleaning things that we'd found in the house – brushes, dustpan, a sweeper, but not the vacuum, which was no use without power – in the cupboard. We used them every day. If there'd been books in there, we'd have known.

'Don't be silly, Ginny,' said Moth and she sounded almost afraid. 'There have never been books under the stairs.'

'They were in that box,' Ginny nodded towards a cardboard box discarded alongside her. She was too busy looking at pictures to take much interest in the box, but Moth and I examined it carefully. It was an ordinary old box and lying in the bottom was a collection

16

of magazines, also about horses. It had a label on it, marked 'Horse books' and I felt cold. 'Is that Dad's writing?'

Moth gripped my arm so hard I thought it would fall off. 'Joel, wherever did this come from?'

The writing was Dad's, but it was faded, as though it had been written years ago. Yet, when I looked at the books and magazines, some were only dated from two years earlier.

Ginny looked up, frowning at us. 'What're you so worried about? The horses are here and the books are here, because we need them.'

Moth turned away then. 'There're lots of things we need, Ginny, that are not here.' But she turned back and kissed Ginn on the head. 'Come along, my love, breakfast.'

We didn't talk about where the books came from anymore. That was the thing about the horses. Ginny was right. There was no understanding and no point worrying. They were with us, and the books were with us. And when I went to look for the bridles Dad had mentioned, I was hardly surprised at all when I found three, with halters, saddles and square pads that Moth said went underneath them. And there was a harness too, the sort a horse would wear to pull a cart. Finding a cart we'd never noticed before, behind the outhouse, well – we took that in our stride.

Within a few days, the horses were as familiar as Dad being gone was strange. Moth and I were careful around them, especially once we realised that the big one was a stallion. We only approached when they showed an interest in us, offering handfuls of grass and talking quietly to them. They'd obviously not been handled recently and a few of them seemed unused to people so I no longer thought they'd been from here in the first place. When I offered Gray some bread crusts in a bucket, he snorted and did his giraffe impression, and while he'd come right up to me, he wouldn't let me touch his head. None of them made any attempt to kick or bite though. Ginny was fretting to get at them but Moth forbade her to go into the field alone and she had to hold our hands when we were with her. She accepted this at first, but a week later, threw one of her rare tantrums.

We were all upset and edgy, remembering the last day with Dad and torn between being unable to believe it was already a week and somehow wondering if it could really be only that long. Moth looked ill. The dullness had settled into her bones so that every movement seemed an effort to her.

When Ginny said, 'I want to go and talk to Daddy,' Moth replied, 'I'll come with you in a bit, love.'

'I want to go now,' said Ginny and, as I looked up to say I'd go with her, she turned on us both. 'I want to go on my own. I can go and see my Daddy if I want to. How come I can't go down to the meadow anymore? I used to go in there with Big Boss and he kicked Daddy in the head.'

'Boss doesn't move as quickly as the horses,' said Moth. 'And you don't want to go and play with him.'

'Well, he's just a stupid old bull. I want to go and play with the horses because Dad sent them. I want to go and see them and Daddy now and I'm going!'

She flipped her nose in the air and swung her pony-tail at us in defiance then stormed off. I was about to go after her, but Moth crumpled in on herself, starting to sob. I went to her instead because I thought Ginny was perfectly safe with the horses, though I'd kept quiet. I could see why Moth was over-careful with us but Ginny and the horses had something special and I was sure they wouldn't hurt her.

I gave Moth a hug and said, 'Come on. It's bad day today. Let's follow her down and see if she's okay. I think you're going to have to trust her and the horses, Moth.'

'But...but...' She sobbed and snuffled and wiped her eyes on her shirt sleeve, then, with an effort, shook herself straight and said, 'She's so little, Jo.'

'She's not so little as she would have been if we'd still been in the old home,' I pointed out and she patted my cheek.

'That's what's so hard, seeing both of you growing up too quickly and working all day when Ginn should be playing and you should be hanging out with your friends.' She wiped her eyes again. 'And thinking that in some ways it's better. That's the hardest bit of all, Jo.'

I knew what she meant. Was life really better when we'd not seen any other people in nearly two years and Dad was dead and if winter was hard we'd be short of food? But we spent most of the time outside with plenty to keep us busy and the air was clean and I liked growing things. Back in the old world we'd been surrounded by birds and I'd never noticed them. Now we saw only a few and I knew their calls and what type some of them were, and what they mostly chose to eat. I valued them. I liked the noise the chickens made when they were scratching in the yard, and watching the sun set over the skyline where the horses had appeared first. I liked talking and telling stories around the fire in the evening and I knew how to fix things and make soda bread and lots else I'd have laughed at the thought of doing before.

We wandered towards the meadow and when we found Ginny, Moth gave a little cry that she stifled at once. She was sitting near Dad's grave with a book on her knee, and all the horses were with her. The foal lay stretched out close to her and the others were all crowded round so we could only see her through their legs. Gray looked as though he was reading over her shoulder and I couldn't help but laugh.

'Moth, she's fine.'

Moth was struggling and then she suddenly let go. 'Yes,' she said with a sigh that came from the soles of her feet. We went down to join Ginny and, ignoring the horses, we walked through them and went to sit with her. The horses took no notice of us either and we all started sunbathing together.

Ginny kissed Moth's cheek. 'Sorry Moth, but see – they love me.'

'I see. So what are they all called, then?'

Ginny was a great namer of things and, aside from accepting that I'd already named Gray, she'd demanded the right to the rest.

'I've written them down in my book,' she said. 'There's eleven of them, so it's a lot to remember. There's Gray, of course, and the other dark one like him is Momma Horse, then there's Poppa Horse and the little foal is Whiskers.' She reached out to tickle the chin of the sleepy foal who did have a wonderful set of long soft whiskers. 'Then there's Beauty – 'cos she's black – and Flicka, she's chestnut, like Poppa and Whiskers. Beauty and Flicka are Gray's sisters and Momma and Poppa are their parents. Then the two light ones are Smoke and Misty. That leaves Sunset, Moonrise and Daybreak – they're bay – I looked up the colours in the books.'

I was trying not to grin. 'Those are some fancy names the last ones have got,' I said, and Ginny looked at me severely. 'They're a family too. Smoke and Misty are strangers to the rest – they met up on the way here.'

'How do you know all this, sweetie?' Moth asked, holding out her hand to Misty, and Ginny shrugged. 'I just do.' She smiled at us. 'Now we start learning to ride them. Oh and Momma and Poppa can pull a cart, by the way.'

CHAPTER 3

I started riding Gray in the third week. Food was getting, well, not short, because it was spring and all the signs were that the world was getting going again. Things were growing, our vegetable plot was showing signs of life and with eggs, the ultimate sacrifice from a young cockerel now and then and some traps for rabbit, we could manage. Just about. We ate salads of young dandelions and sorrel most days and reminisced a lot about Dad and his nature walks.

'All right, Ray Mears,' Moth used to say in the old days, when he'd trek us all off looking for sweet chestnuts and chicken-of-the-woods. 'Just putting on my home-made sandals.'

'Wove my own back-pack,' I'd chip in, 'out of willow-bark and badger fur.'

'You may mock me now,' Dad would wag his finger at us, and the memory of his grin made me happy and sad at the same time. 'One day you'll thank me.'

Well, now we thanked him every day and I sometimes felt chilled thinking about how right he'd been. But I could still see that once we'd grown and picked and foraged all we could, there probably wouldn't be enough once the summer was over, even if Moth and I could face up to killing a sheep. It made sense to save as much as possible for the winter.

We'd done pretty well so far, because our farm and the hamlet three miles away, with its few houses and tiny shop, had all been well-stocked. We'd come across our valley by accident, completely lost after trying to take a short cut to save our dwindling fuel. The burning rains started soon after we arrived, so we sheltered in our little farm over the first winter till they stopped and we emerged into a silent world with no birds. By then we were sure no-one was coming back, so we'd gone though everything in the hamlet and carefully rationed what we found. We divided it up according to its shelf life and then managed it carefully, eked out with our foraging expeditions. But now, we were getting to the stage where I often wanted more to eat than we had to spare.

So, if I could go further, I could get down to the sea to fish. It was a day's walk each way and Moth didn't want me to go alone, but we couldn't all go because of the animals. I'd been with Dad a couple of times in our first spring a year earlier and it really needed a few nights stay to get a good catch, find seaweed for laver bread and driftwood – all sorts there was on the shore. And there were other places, places we'd never yet explored. On Gray and with another horse as a pack-carrier, I could go further, bring back more.

As I tried to persuade Moth, I heard in my own voice how trapped I'd felt since Dad died. I longed to get away and see what was over the hills. And I wanted to know what it felt like to fly over the grass like the horses did, and feel the wind and Gray's muscles powering beneath me. I wanted all that and to have it I needed to convince Moth I could ride him safely. She was right of course – if anything happened to me or her, the other one and Ginny were completely alone and it was hard work as it was, because though Ginn did her best, she couldn't lift or dig very well.

She was a natural with the horses though and the day I headed out with a halter, I found her reading her book sitting on Poppa Horse's back. I almost fell over. There I was, having read the books and running it all over in my head, thinking carefully about how to approach Gray – and Ginn's already perched up on the big chestnut stallion like he's an oversized cuddly toy.

'Hi, Ginn,' I said, stroking Poppa's neck.

They all let us stroke them by then. I'd found that once I did it the right way – moving calmly, stroking, not patting – they started coming over to be petted. "Make much of your horse," it said in one of the old books. They all liked being made much of and sometimes Gray would scratch my back with his teeth while I scratched his with my nails. Well, although it hurt, I knew from the books that it was a compliment so I gritted my teeth and scratched all the more. Gray had a favourite spot on his withers – I knew all the terms now – and he'd stretch out his neck and curl up his lip in bliss while I scratched it for him.

Poppa liked having his neck rubbed and he nudged at me for more.

'How long have you been getting up on his back?' I asked. 'Does Moth know?'

Ginny nodded. 'She saw me a bit ago. I only did it for the first time yesterday. He looked at me and I knew he said I could. He's done it before so he knows all about it. So I stood on the wall, over he came and I climbed up.' She grinned. 'Poor Moth. She looked and opened her mouth, then she shook her head and went back to hoe the veggies.'

'Remember Ginn, we're all she's got. You mustn't frighten her. She misses Dad really bad.'

'I miss him too. But it's better down here, 'cos Daddy's here with the horses.'

I knew what she meant. The horses were Dad's and Ginny's in some way I never understood. But I had a glimpse of him when I was with them. It was as though he was watching from a distance or he'd gone up to the house and he'd be back soon.

'Go on then, Jo. Ride Gray. He's not been ridden before but he'll be all right.'

I hesitated, wishing I was on my own, because I thought I'd probably fall off. But if I did, well, I'd get back on again. I went up to Gray and let him sniff the halter and his laid-back reaction made us laugh.

I fiddled with it a bit because it seemed all knots and ends but he stood patiently until I had it neatly on his head. Once it was secure, I walked a few steps. Gray threw up his head and started to pull back on the rope so, remembering the book, I stepped towards him to create some slack. Then I tried again, taking care not to go far enough to put pressure on, and he thought about it a moment, then dropped his head and followed me, like a big dog. We practised for ages and he seemed to like it, his ears pricked forward and his eyes full of curiosity. Before long I could get him to follow by walking forward and if I tapped my fingers lightly on his chest he'd go back. Pretty soon, I could stand in front of him, making the tapping gesture and he'd go back on his own. I thought it was the best fun I'd ever had. Watching him watching me and judging how he'd move – we soon had a game going where I'd run and he'd chase me, then I'd chase him and we were dodging and running and Ginny was laughing up on Poppa Horse while the others kept grazing, as though this was normal.

The books said to take it slowly and I reckoned I'd already done far more in one day than was recommended. But I couldn't resist sitting on him for a moment.

'Is that okay, Gray?' I asked him. 'If I sit on you bareback for a minute? You cool with that? Then we could try the saddle tomorrow.'

I led him over to the wall and he stood alongside without any trouble. But when I got up and leaned on his back, his head came up and I got an anxious feeling in my stomach. I'd read that horses pick up our feelings, so I stood there stroking him until we both felt better, then I leaned my weight on him, keeping my feet on the wall. His back muscles felt tight so I stroked him until they softened then I got off him. We tried that a few times then I climbed a higher bit of the wall and got right over him so I was leaning across him from the waist and my feet were hanging.

'Well done, Jo!' Ginny called and Gray's head jerked up at the sound of her voice. I overbalanced a bit and he darted forward. For a second, I thought we were in trouble until he hesitated and I said, 'Whoa, Gray. There's a boy, easy now.'

I don't know who was more surprised when he stopped – me or him. He stood there, quivering, with me like a dead body in a cowboy film hung over his back. I suddenly wished I'd paid more attention to cowboy films. The thought made me smile and Gray relaxed. I smiled and he relaxed. I'd learned something.

Smiling for all I was worth, I said, 'Here we go, lad,' and carefully swung my leg over his back.

'Don't start clapping Ginn,' I warned as I sat up and she shook her head, all wide-eyed and grinning. Gray felt ready to take off and I suddenly thought what a fool I was – no saddle, no bridle, only a rope halter. But it was all right. I smiled and stroked him and, though he walked like a drunk, we wobbled over to Poppa Horse and then I got off. I hugged him over and over and we were both so pleased with ourselves, I reckoned he was grinning too.

After that, we barely looked back. He soon stopped wobbling once he got used to balancing my weight. He didn't mind the saddle and while some of the books said he needed a bit in his mouth, some of the others said he didn't. Whoever sent the books sent lots of different sorts with plenty of ideas, so I had to make my own mind up. Gray was my friend so I decided anything that said tie him down or tell him off was out, so that meant no bit. I fixed the reins of his bridle on the sides of the noseband and that was fine. Maybe it wouldn't have worked with every horse, but it worked a treat with mine. He liked me to be confident and then he'd do anything I asked, so long as I didn't get pushy or impatient with him. I didn't make that mistake often, but the one time I lost my temper and slapped his shoulder to get his attention when he'd lost interest, he looked at me with such disdain that I'd sooner he'd kicked me. Most of the time, if I asked him to co-operate, he did. If I was ever nervous, that was when he got jumpy, then I'd get more nervous, he'd get more jumpy – and then I'd fall off. I only did it a couple of times, but I didn't tell Moth.

We got into the habit of riding in the evenings as they grew lighter with the summer, and soon Moth was riding too. She liked Misty and we found that Poppa, Momma, Misty and Shadow seemed to be old hands at being ridden. We decided to get them all used to it, except Whiskers, of course, and Beauty and Daybreak, because they were only youngsters too. But the more we handled them, the easier handling them became and before long Moth and I had backed all the others. None of them took to it quite as readily as Gray, but we reckoned that was because he and I'd paired up early on.

We started riding round our land last thing before dark, from the hill, through the scrubby woodland and down the old cart-track to the lane where there was a faded sign with our farm's name on it, 'Tir na Croabh'. We knew 'Tir' was 'house' and that the last word was pronounced something like 'croove', but we didn't know what it meant. We'd ride along the lane towards the hamlet and, after a mile or so, take an old footpath to cut back up around the belt of ruined fields to the open hillside then down the long slope back to the hollow that sheltered the house. Or we could turn down into the forest and come back through the pines, where the sound was deadened by the dense bed of needles under-hoof and a wide swathe of the trees stood brown and crisp in the centre. Already we were regularly going further than we had before the horses came, just for pleasure, and maybe that was the best way. In the early days we'd avoided seeing the Spill, as we called it, where the land and trees looked as though something burning had been poured across them. But now we could see green slowly coming back, there were a lot more birds and we saw a fox once.

When we were riding, me on Gray, Moth on Misty and Ginn on Poppa Horse like she'd being riding all her life, it was a good time to forget everything. Forget how we ached and cried for Dad, how we didn't know where the nearest people still alive were. How we didn't know if we'd have enough food to get through the winter or how we were going to feed the animals either. Last year, we'd still had a barn full of hay, and there was lots left which smelt good – Gray had eaten some quite happily. But now we had eleven horses, as well as the cattle, six sheep, since the three lambs came, and three goats. If the winter was bad, how long would the hay last them? We needed some grain and more hay – we'd turned all the animals out on to the hill, now we were sure they knew where home was – and we were growing the meadow for hay. But we had only one scythe and a couple of forks. What we knew about making hay, we could have told you in a minute or so. And we were running out of clothes. Moth and I were wearing Dad's and Ginny wore some of Moth's, but even cobbling together everything we had, they were wearing thin and Ginny and I were growing out of our own.

There were lots of things it was good to forget when we were enjoying the horses. But they all had to be talked about eventually and Moth and I tended to do this talking after Ginny had gone to bed. We'd learned to do all sorts of things we'd have said we couldn't do, and aside from the sheer amount of work involved, making hay was something I thought we could handle. As for the clothes and fishing and other possibilities, all I needed was a way to convince Moth that with Gray and Poppa or Misty, I'd be safe going off for a few days to see what I could find. What I didn't expect was that one evening Moth herself would suggest that I went as soon as possible.

CHAPTER 4

I'd known there was something troubling Moth for a few weeks. At first I thought it was part of her grieving. We were in mourning. We didn't try to pretend we weren't. We never tried to avoid talking about Dad or convince each other that it was getting better. But we were getting used to it. That was hard too and sometimes we'd lose patience with each other and one of us, usually Ginny, would start screaming that we'd forgotten him and we were horrible. In a strange way, we needed those times. We were working hard and, much as we loved the horses, from the moment they appeared they brought extra work with them. When Ginny threw a tantrum it was like our communal steam valve going off and we'd all shout or cry and call each other names until we reached the part where we were sobbing in a huddle together. We'd feel better after that, until being alone and missing Dad and worrying about everything overwhelmed us again.

So when Moth was rather quiet and pale, at first I didn't think it was anything more than usual. The dullness that had settled on her when Dad was dying had changed to an empty bewilderment, as though she was suddenly wondering where we were and how we came to be there. I understood that feeling. But she was tough too and with Dad gone, the sense of waiting had lifted from us. I'd not really realised how it had hovered over us, like a cloud we knew was going to break even though it hung about for weeks. I'd have sooner lived with it and still had Dad, but now it had broken, the downpour flooded out all our waiting. Yet Moth had a distracted, inward sense about her sometimes that made me uneasy. When we were riding she was lighter, brighter, and for a short time she looked like her old self. But then I'd notice a deeper level of worry sink down on her. If there was something she wasn't telling me then it must be bad and I didn't think I could cope with anything else right then. So I hovered between denial that there was anything wrong and mulling over in my mind what it might be. But when it came to light, it took me completely by surprise.

It had been a bad few days. A week of sudden storms lifted the barn roof, tore up some of the vegetables and blew the gate to the goat-paddock half-way down the drive. I'd spent the previous day fixing it. Now the goats had burst it open again and gone trotting off in search of something to destroy, bleating and wagging their feathery tails, which liberally scattered what Ginny called 'goat-berries' everywhere. A goat break-out was always the worst disaster because the damage they could do to the garden in five minutes had to be seen to be believed. For all my worries about having to kill anything larger than a rabbit for food, there were times I could have cheerfully ripped a goat's head off. So I ran after them, swearing and stamping, while they turned their devil's eyes on me curiously, bleating in a way I knew was goatish laughter. I resisted my more violent impulses and got them safely on their tethers with only a row of cabbage seedlings sacrificed. I should have been exceptionally pleased with this outcome, but I was too tired, irritable and sweaty. I'd been chopping wood when I realised they were out. My hands were blistered, my back ached and I'd rubbed sweat, goat-hair and sawdust into a cut on my face. I was gloomily anticipating blood-poisoning as I picked up the axe again when Moth appeared.

'What have you done to your face?'

I dabbed at the cut with my sleeve. 'Chip of wood flew up and hit me. Is it still bleeding? It stings like hell.'

Moth pulled a cloth down from the nearby line of washing and dipped it in the water butt.

'Hold still, let me clean it up.' She dabbed at it. 'It's not as bad as it looks – I thought you'd tried to chop your own head off. Did I see you chasing the goats?'

'Yep. I'm always chasing the goats. It's my idea of a good time.'

'Well, here's something even better – the drains are blocked again – can you rod them?'

Her being so casual about the worst job of all was the last straw and I came out fighting.

'For God's sake!' I turned on her, waving my arms and working myself up into a fury. 'I'm sick of doing all the work around here. Sick of it! And the worst thing is that I do it today and the whole bloody lot wants doing again tomorrow. Until the sodding goats got out, I'd chopped wood all day, but before I even started on that, I'd cleaned out the hen-house and the goat shed.' Even though Moth's expression was ringing a faint warning bell at the back of my mind, I charged on with the sensitivity of a bulldozer-driver working blindfold. 'I don't want to rod the bloody drains. This is my life – shunting shit up and down – and I've had it! We can go and squat in the bushes for all I care, with this crapping herd of animals I have to follow around with a shovel all day every day.'

I went on a lot longer, letting myself be angry, knowing my chin was jutting out like a belligerent toddler's and feeling the tight knot of my fists clenched at my sides, but not caring.

'I want my life back,' I told her, bitter and cruel. 'I want to get up and go out with my friends. I want to see a film and wish Katie Fisher would notice me and pretend to look for a Saturday job. Then I want to come home and get Dad to do my maths homework while I complain about it. I want to lie in bed on Saturday morning until I smell bacon cooking and have Dad trek us all off hiking on Sunday. I want all that stuff back, Moth. I'm sick of this, being stuck here and never seeing a bloody soul.'

Moth looked small and frail, dark circles under her eyes, but she was furious too, quietly furious in a way always worse to me than if she'd shouted back. Her eyes fell to my fists as though she'd caught me carrying a weapon and I dropped them open at once. Then she looked into my face. 'Do you think you're the only one? Do you think we wouldn't all like our lives back? Stop being so bloody sorry for yourself and pull your weight around here.'

31

Red rag to a bull. I was off again,

'Are you saying I don't? You think I don't work hard enough?' I picked up the axe and flung it across the yard. 'Well, sod it all. I'm not doing it anymore. If you want the drains rodding, do it yourself. I don't care.' Suddenly I was yelling right in her face, frightening myself but too far gone to stop. 'Do you hear me? I don't care. I wish I was dead like Dad.'

Her hand shot out to slap my face hard and I saw from her eyes that she'd shocked herself as much as me, but we were both still furious too and Moth squared up to me.

'One way or the other, Jo,' she said, 'it has to be done. You can stamp all you like but you'll still be the tallest and the strongest of us and you don't get out of it no matter how bad a mood you're in.' Her chin came up then too. 'I've never been ashamed of you before but I am today. I'm glad Dad's not here to see you.'

Then she turned on her heel and walked away. I was half inclined to go after her and shout at her again but she wasn't the only one ashamed of me. I'd rod the drains, we both knew I'd rod the drains. I wanted my tantrum and somehow she'd taken the satisfaction out of it. I watched her go in the glum knowledge that if she'd crumbled and cried and said she didn't know how she would manage without me, I'd have been pleased. Small and petty, maybe, but pleased.

I left the woodpile and went looking for Gray but he was cool and uninterested in me and I thought myself very hard done by. So I slunk back to rod the drains, which was as horrible a job as I'd known it would be. The pipes were old and had collapsed before so I knew what the problem was. Solving it involved locating the blockage, digging up and fixing the pipe and then getting the sludge moving again until water would flow freely from the bathroom to the septic tank once more. I got filthy and even angrier at myself and my sorry lot in life, so the job in hand seemed to fit in with my world-view. I wallowed at several levels until I felt eyes on me and looked up to find Ginny watching my sweaty efforts. She was dressed from head to foot in waterproofs and armed with the hosepipe. I couldn't help laughing at her and my anger started to dissipate a little.

'What are you supposed to be?' I asked and she held up the hose.

'I'm a drain-hoser-outer. Are you ready for the water yet? Do you know you've got poo on your face?'

I brushed my hair back from my eyes, smearing something I didn't want to identify all over my head. 'Yes, to both questions. I hope it's only mud but you're probably right. I'm pissed-off, Ginn.'

Her blue eyes regarded me seriously. 'That's no excuse for bad language but I'll give you a kiss when you've had a bath.'

I started to laugh then. 'Well, that should change everything. Will you draw me a picture too?'

'Only if you make up with Moth. You made her cry.'

'Aw, hell, did I? Well, she hit me.'

'You deserved it. You were horrid.'

'I know.'

Under the severity of her eight-year-old's honesty, I had no defences. It turned out that knowing I'd made Moth cry didn't feel good at all. I nodded when Ginny waved the hosepipe again and watched as she carefully directed the water from it into the gurgling drain. We didn't speak much more as we completed the task then Ginny ran upstairs to flush the toilet a few times while I followed the water's progress down to the tank. It wasn't glamorous work, but it was done at last. I carefully re-covered the pipe and put the drain covers back in place before some daft goat could fall down the septic tank, because I knew who'd have to fish it out. Then I stripped to my boxers and hosed myself down, gasping at the bitterly cold water before I plodded, dripping, back to the house, picking up a towel that had been laid out on the doorstep for me.

'There's a hot bath waiting,' Moth said, without looking up from the stove where she was stirring something that smelt good. 'Ginny will put the poultry away.'

'Thanks,' I mumbled and shuffled off upstairs.

We stumbled awkwardly through the early evening, Moth and I barely speaking, until Ginny was ready to go to bed. She got up and turned to us, her hands on her hips and I knew we were in for a talking-to, modelled on Ginn's memories of our grandmother.

'If you two haven't made up by morning, there'll be trouble,' she told us. 'We've got enough problems without you shouting at each other. Daddy didn't send the horses here so they could listen to us fight and we've not been for our ride tonight. No matter how horrid we are to each other, there's no need to miss our ride.' She fixed us with the eye of someone who chose not to remember that the last tantrum had been hers. 'Just think on that, both of you.'

Then she kissed us both goodnight and headed off up the stairs with great dignity.

We were silent for a moment then Moth said, 'Well, that told us.'

I looked up sheepishly to find her trying not to laugh then I started to laugh, but we were both crying a bit too. I was sitting on the floor and when she held out her arms, I crawled over to kneel beside her, hiding my face against her legs. 'I'm a git,' I said. 'Shovelling crap's all I'm good for. You should beat me, starve me, stake me out for the chickens to peck…'

'All right, all right,' she said. 'Don't lay it on too thick, sonny-Jim, or I might do all that.'

I looked up at her and I saw it then, that deep worry that made me feel sick. 'I'm really sorry,' I said. 'Do you still love me?'

She smiled and shook her head. 'Not even a little bit.'

Then we were hugging each other with the wonderful relief that comes when a row is over and as we let each other go, she said,

'Stay there. I need you to be six for a while.'

I settled down beside her with my arms on her knees, more than happy to be six for a while, and she placed her hand on my head.

'I know you work hard, Jo. You really do. This week's got on top of us all.'

'Tell me about it. One disaster after another. Those flaming goats, Moth – just let me kill one of them. We'd all feel better.'

Moth smiled. 'All right then. Which one? Lucy, who sits on our knees like an enormous dog, or Amy, with her sweet little face? Or what about Holly, who helps with everything?'

'Goat help I can do without. Okay, you kill one of them then and I'll cheer.'

'I'm already going to hell for abusing a broccoli plant. Kicked it round the garden yesterday.'

That made me smile. 'What had it done? A bit green, was it? Annoyingly leafy?'

Moth nodded. 'And smug-looking too. I hate smug brassicas. It had mould on its leaves and I was browned off because it was one of the biggest but it was looking like dying. So I ripped it out and booted its sickly backside the length of the veggie plot.'

By now I was doubled up laughing at this image of vegetable cruelty, clearly the dark underbelly of our blameless life. Once we grinned at each other, we were really all right, past both the pain of fighting and of making up. We planned an excavation of the drains to locate any more potential collapses, then talked about dealing with the mouldy broccoli plants before any more went flying down the garden. After that, we fell silent, simply enjoying being at peace again.

I was still sitting on the rug beside Moth, leaning back against her chair, gazing into the fire, and looked round when she tickled me on top of the head.

'Are you and Gray ready to go down to the shore, do you think?'

'Yes, of course we are,' I said, startled. 'I'm fretting to go, Moth. I need to know what's just beyond our easy reach here. There could be people, a town, food...'

'I'm going to have a baby, Jo.'

She stopped me in mid-sentence and her words hung in the air like my mouth hanging open. I stared at her, mouthing questions that I couldn't really shape until at last I said, stupidly, 'Are you sure?'

She nodded. 'I'm certain. I've being trying to convince myself I wasn't since Dad died. But I know. I've done it twice before, I know how it feels.'

I was still gaping, unsure how to go about asking my mother about her sex life with my sick father. But she helped me out, smiling gently at my embarrassment.

'He had his good days, if you remember, Jo.'

I hated myself even more for my outburst.

'God, Moth, I'm so sorry. I knew something was worrying you but I never guessed… I'm such a pillock…it'll be all right, we'll manage – we'll need stuff, I suppose, and you won't be able to work, but Ginn's getting big now and Poppa Horse is so cool with the cart…' I could see relief washing over her face and knew she'd been scared of how I'd take the news. 'One thing though… could you try to make it a boy? Then in ten years or so, I'll have someone to talk to about women.'

Moth opened her arms to me. 'I'll do my very best, I promise you.' She hugged me tight, then brushed my hair back with both hands. 'If you need to talk about women, I know all about them too, you know…'

'I know that. When I find one, I'll ask you how to go about talking to her.' I leaned on her knees again. 'I miss talking to Dad about, you know, that stuff. He was good at that sort of thing.'

She smiled. 'Yes, he was.'

We both stopped, hearing what we'd said, and then we were giggling and sniggering like kids in the playground until an alarming thought stopped me laughing.

'I'll have to deliver it.'

'You've delivered lambs.'

'Hardly the same as my baby brother, is it? I tell you what though, Moth…'

She smiled at me, looking happy for the first time in days.

'What's that, my love?'

'We can't let Ginny name him, or he'll end up called Cuddles or Little Nose or something.'

'That's a thought. If it is a boy, I'd like to call him Christopher.'

'Dad's middle name.'

'Well, I can't call him Gray, now can I?'

I hesitated. 'Did you want to?'

She shook her head. 'And if he's a girl, I thought, maybe Maria, after Gran.'

'We'd better get into planning mode, Moth. If Gray and I are going off hunting, we need to go while you can still cope here alone.'

'That's what I was thinking. I thought perhaps we could get the hay in, then you could go.' She paused. 'Though I don't want you to go at all.'

'We'll be fine. Honest, Moth. Gray's intelligent and what's to be afraid of? There's no-one around. I might find somewhere better that we could move to. Or maybe I'll find other people – hopefully a midwife and her farmer husband with their six strong sons and two or three hot daughters.'

Moth laughed at me. 'One hot daughter would cause you less trouble.'

'I'd be so scared of them now, that'd be best.' I sobered then. 'Do you know what Dad said to me once? He overheard me and some of the guys talking about Lisa – you remember Lisa?' Moth winced a little and I grinned. 'Yeah, that Lisa. We were – well, I'm not telling you what we were saying, but after the others had gone, Dad said to me, "Remember that any girl you look at or think about or date, is like Ginny, then decide how you're going to behave".' I shrugged. 'That was all he said, but I'll never forget it.'

'It was good advice.'

We sat a bit longer, keeping each other company and the night drew in and the sky was full of stars.

Ginny was very excited about the baby and Moth put forward 'Christopher' and 'Maria' just in time as, after a few calculations on her fingers, Ginn was very keen on 'December' or 'Christmas'. I got in trouble for suggesting 'Boxing Day' and 'Plum Pudding', but at least we avoided 'Jesus'. That would have been a lot for a baby to take on. The reality of Moth's pregnancy and coping with a new baby in winter came home once Ginny knew about it, and brought into focus all the things we would have had in the old days. But Moth told me off when I tried to stop her lifting or working.

'In days past, women used to work in the fields, give birth and go back to work the next day,' she kept telling me, so we agreed that if she felt tired, then she'd rest and, after that, I left her to do what she felt able to.

She started looking better at once. Sharing the news she'd been fretting over helped her and the thought of a new baby, while it could fill me with terror, was part of the future that we hadn't dared think about much. We needed a way to get through our first Christmas without Dad, and I couldn't think of a better one.

CHAPTER 5

Moth started making baby clothes from things we'd outgrown, I chopped wood for the store and Ginny dried herbs for all she was worth, so we were promised a lot of mint soup if nothing else. Our winter stocks built up slowly. We sheared the sheep with hand clippers then had a go at trying to dye and spin the wool, ending up with a horrible stew of fleecy sludge. We managed to dye our arms yellow, but the sludge settled on khaki and refused all attempts to brighten it up. Though there was a spinning wheel in the house, we thought it was probably only decorative and had no idea how to use it anyhow. In the end, we pounded the mess we'd made into a felty mush, dried it out and used it to stuff draught excluders, having to admit that we'd wasted the lot.

I started a get-fit programme for myself, Gray and Misty, who were both coming with me on the big foraging expedition. I rode further, making sure I went every day and walked myself at least half the way. We were pretty fit anyhow because I was working outside all day and the horses spent their lives charging up and down the steep hills behind the house because when Whiskers wanted to play, everyone had to play.

I thought of taking Poppa with Gray on our trip at first, because he was very steady pulling the cart. But he was also protective of Ginny so I really wanted him to stay behind in the role of guard-horse. The cart was unwieldy too and might slow me up. So we decided on Misty because she led easily and the basket panniers we'd found in the back bedroom fitted her well. We didn't bother wondering where they'd come from and why we'd not noticed them before.

Getting ready to go meant making sure everything was up to date so I worked like a slave for days before but there was a growing excitement in me. I was going out like an explorer. With Gray, the horse I had trained myself, my trusted companion, I was going to fend for my family. And I was going to have some time away from the daily routines, which, despite my frequent complaining, I mostly coped with well enough. But like anything you have to do without fail, the thought of a few days free of them was sort of a holiday. There was an irony in that though that scared me. I remembered standing with Dad looking over the Spill and him saying,

'The world ended, Jo, and we missed it because we were on holiday.'

I was afraid of holidays now. What if our own small world ended while I was away, escaping the daily routines? When I thought like that, I didn't want to go or tried to work out ways we could go together, trailing horses, cattle, chickens and goats behind us. But it wasn't practical – it had to be just me and Gray and Misty. I wanted to go but as it grew closer, I was scared too. I'd never been on my own, not really. With no parent, no phone, no adult to go to for help if I was in trouble. With no living person for miles and miles. Only me and two horses.

But no matter how I felt about it, our trip had to wait on the hay. While most of my illusions about the slow pace of country life had been sweated out of me by then, I still felt that making hay by hand would have a romantic charm to it. I was wrong. Of all the back-breaking, muscle-tearing, sweaty, prickly, uncomfortable and exhausting jobs there are, making hay by hand shoots confidently to the top of the list.

We'd been watching the meadow grass waving gently in the sun, waiting for it to reach the peak moment our books said we should look for and the day it did seemed perfect. I'd honed the edge of the old scythe from the barn to a sharpness a Samurai warrior would have been proud of and it was a fine, warm day, a light breeze stirring the golden seed heads on their long stems.

So I set off with my scythe and the hat Moth insisted I wear against the sun and the first few sweeps of the blade were wonderful. I got into a rhythm, turning at the waist, keeping my torso straight, a slight bend to my knees and the long grass fell willingly before the natural expertise evident in my every movement. Then, after maybe five minutes, the scythe got heavier, my back started aching and the whole mood went downhill. After that, it was hour upon hour of torment and even though Moth made me take frequent breaks, I was afraid to stop in case I couldn't get going again. It took forever, the sun blazed, I hurt and my hands blistered up even through gloves, but eventually it was done. I'd spent too much time watching the blade, instead of where I was going, so rather than neat rows of hay, we had something that looked as though the goats had gone on the rampage, but at least it was all on the ground.

Then came a few anxious days of watching the sky while we turned the hay to let it dry out then turned it again. Moth and Ginny could help with that and it wasn't so bad, though you could understand all those old photos of cheerful country folk pulling together to get the hay in. The weather was kind to us and gave us warm days and nights with a soft breeze. By the time we hitched Poppa up to the cart to gather the hay in, it smelt wonderful – like childhood summers, Moth said. Poppa thought it smelt like dinner and wanted to eat it where it lay. He was a bit of a role-playing horse – we called him 'Poppa-poser', because he was always standing in some noble posture against the skyline – and threw himself into the proceedings with vigour. He plodded up and down the neat loose stacks we'd made of the hay, pausing when someone shouted, 'Whoa, Poppa' and setting off again as we called, 'Walk on, lad'.

When we eventually found ourselves looking with enormous pride at the great pile of hay filling the barn, he stood between Moth and Ginny, seeming as pleased with the achievement as we were.

'Poppa says, "Well done",' said Ginny. 'He says, "I'll make farmers of you lot yet".'

I pulled a few wisps of hay from his mane. 'Praise from you, Poppa, is praise indeed.'

It was done, the hay was in, and suddenly it was time for me to go with Gray and Misty to see what I could forage in the way of nappies and crayons to get us through the winter. Now the moment was upon us, the only thing to do was joke about it. The list of things I was looking for became more nonsensical every day – a pasta maker, guinea pigs, a map of New Zealand, a large wooden chest filled with custard powder – but we were parting for the first time since Dad died and weren't sure how else to handle it.

I said good-bye to Ginny the night before I left and she gave me a bracelet made out of hair from all the horses.

'It's a special invention for bringing you safe home,' she said and I didn't doubt its value for a moment.

At dawn, with her still asleep, I got up and checked my gear while Moth made me breakfast and packed food for me to take. We ate together, struggling to find things to say, so that I was glad when it was time to go.

We tacked up Gray and Misty and they both seemed part of the mists of the morning, grey ghosts who'd come from nowhere to change our lives. As they stood patiently waiting for me to mount up, I was overwhelmed and suddenly turned to catch Moth up and hug her.

'Tell me I can do this,' I said, burying my face in her neck and wishing I was still the smaller of us, small enough to hide behind her to be taken care of and never need to worry. She wrapped her arms around me, so fierce and strong that I knew I would always be that small to her. But she could be that small to me too, now. I could go and she could let me, even though we were both terrified.

'You can do it, Joel. You go and find what you need for yourself as well as for us.' She got hold of my head and looked up at me. 'I'm so proud of you, Jo, I can't begin to tell you. And so's Dad – I promise you that.'

I couldn't speak so I nodded and kissed her, then tore myself away and swung up into Gray's saddle. I felt better at once.

'I'll be as quick as I can. Tell Ginn that, too.'

Gray moved off, Misty followed and we set out, up the long slope the horses had come pouring down all those weeks earlier, and over the top. The other horses, grazing on the hill behind the house lifted up their heads to call out, but Gray had his eyes on the distance and he didn't look back.

The sun was coming up as we left our own land and I was glad it looked liked being a clear day but not too hot. I didn't expect to have trouble finding water, but although I'd been getting the horses fit, they'd never been on a really long journey under saddle before. I wondered how far they'd travelled to reach us in the first place and where they'd come from. Certainly, Gray was striding out like a horse on a mission without waiting for any directions. I let him choose the path, as he was heading for the sea, and started to feel exhilarated. We were really going at last. For all the fear I felt, the excitement was there too and this was an adventure I needed.

The first morning was steady plodding down the road I'd walked with Dad when we'd been to the sea. While it was familiar, I noticed a lot of change. It was nearly a year since I'd been on it and the grass was working to take over the road. Also, the trees that had been blighted by the Spill were looking better. We startled a small herd of deer once and both the lochs we passed had noisy ducks on them, while I was sure I saw an osprey on a nest high in a pine. Maybe that was wishful thinking, but there was a strong feel that the world was recovering. Dad had always said that no matter what stupid things humans did to each other, nature would come back just when we thought everything was over. That gave me hope, though I couldn't decide if that included hoping to meet some people too. We'd looked over a wide area when we'd first taken refuge on our abandoned farm and found only signs that people had left in a hurry, half-packed suitcases, animals turned loose or starved to death, even front doors open. There were two or three farms within walking distance of ours, as well as the tiny hamlet. Our animals were chosen from those places, animals we needed or ones that needed us to take care of them. We found two hungry old sheepdogs on one farm and took them with us, but they both died. Beyond our isolated valley, we knew there were no villages between us and the sea. But once I reached the sea, if I continued on along the coast and returned home from the south, well, we'd never been that way at all and it had been off the edge of our map. It was unknown, uncharted, like those old maps my Grandad used to tell me about, with empty spaces on, marked, "Here be dragons".

I was glad of the known though, that first day on my own. Gray's warm body was good to have beneath me. His strong steady muscles and bones and the soft thud of his hooves on the ground, the flop of his mane on my hands when he shook his head, the flick of his long tail catching my back when he swatted a fly. Misty too, she was calm and steady, though not quite as bold as Gray, but she had a sweet nature. She was good at noticing if any of us felt sad or lonely and she'd wander over to offer undemanding company. Now, when I turned and scratched between her ears, she rubbed her head on my leg, as though she was saying, 'Don't worry, I'm still here.'

I gave up with the lead rein very soon, and trusted her to follow Gray. It was easier for us all as I kept getting it tangled up, so I looped it round her neck and she jogged along behind at whatever speed Gray set, as though she'd been a pack-horse all her life. We felt like three, not me and them, and that was a good thing. But I wished they could talk. I found myself telling them about my Dad, jabbering away as though they understood. Maybe they did. I told them about places he'd taken me and games we'd played, while the miles passed by and the road stretched towards the sea.

We reached the dunes after riding through a big expanse of sandy heath-land full of wild orchids and thyme plants. It was the place I'd come with Dad and I remembered him explaining to me that it was called 'machair' and that it was fragile, even endangered. Two years with no people had helped it flourish and the horses trod carefully, keeping to the sandy track. I could imagine how pleased Dad would have been to see it thriving.

I wasn't thriving by then though, because I was getting tired. I'd been walking on and off all day because it seemed sensible not to get too stiff and sore. So I'd rested Gray and loosened up my legs and aching backside now and then, but I was still glad to smell the sea and know the day's journey was over. I hoped Moth and Ginny weren't worried about me and began to look for somewhere to camp, hoping to find the place I'd stopped with Dad.

I needed water and grazing for my friends and found it in a little hollow at the edge of the dunes. I wasn't sure if it was the same place, but there was plenty of rough grazing and a small stream quietly working its way down to the sea. I untacked the horses, told them not to eat the orchids, then rubbed them down and they both went for a long drink before heading for the sand to have good roll. I had a moment of panic when Misty trotted off and Gray followed. But when I went after them, I saw that they'd gone to check out our surroundings and they soon ambled back to settle down grazing. I toyed with the idea of tethering them, but then felt ashamed. They'd come when we needed them. They wouldn't leave me.

I had the small tent with me that Ginny and I used to set up outside the caravan back in the old days. It made me smile to think of it because Ginny never made it more than an hour or so before she got bored or scared and started whining. But I always wanted so badly to sleep in the tent that Dad or Moth would come and share with me. Moth fitted inside, but Dad's feet stuck out through the flap, which I'd always found hilarious. I thought that perhaps it would be a bit short for me now. It wasn't cold or raining, so I decided to lay out the groundsheet and sleep in my bivvy bag.

I wandered up and down the shore gathering driftwood, then made a small fire pit with a wall of stones. The blaze started easily, making me aware, as the good smell of wood smoke wafted around me, of how vital the skills learned for fun when Dad was in a hiking mood had become. Then I opened the saddlebag Moth packed for me. Carefully wrapped were hard-boiled eggs and our own special burgers, made from rabbit or chicken and oatmeal. They were pretty good actually, once you got over your expectations of what a burger should taste like. I had a small frying pan with me so I cooked one of the burgers and ate an egg with it, smelling the rest to check it was fresh enough to last another day. Moth had made me a cake too. It was cut into thick fruity slabs, each one wrapped up separately, made from precious supplies.

I had a moment where I wanted to cry then busied myself taking out one piece and putting the rest away, saying out loud, 'Thanks, Moth. Don't worry about me – I'm okay.'

CHAPTER 6

That first night away from home, camped on the shore with the rush of the sea close by, was a strange one. Any fears I had that most of the wild creatures were gone soon disappeared. The night was alive with rustlings and squeakings and things calling to one another. Once I heard a dreadful howling sound and was very glad that I knew it was a vixen, because it was like a baby screaming, or something dying in torment. Dad told me about the sound they made when I was very little and we were away in the caravan for the first time. We were sitting on the steps watching the night and he was telling me about the animals that might be out looking for food while we slept. Hearing it was a shock though and I remember Dad grinning to reassure me when I turned to him, terrified. Even after hearing one a few times since then, it still made the hairs on the back of my neck stand up.

Then an owl hooted right over my head, making me and both horses jump. Another one answered from the distance, a faint response. I liked the sounds but they made me edgy, especially if the horses suddenly threw up their heads as though they'd seen something. Although it alarmed me, once I thought it through I realised they were useful companions. If anything really scared them, their hearing was so good, I'd be able to get out of sight before it came near us. What 'it' could possibly be, I didn't know. We'd visited a wolf project on our holiday before everything changed, with the wolves kept in huge ranges, but enclosed with electrified fencing. It stood to reason they might have escaped by now, if they hadn't died. But how dangerous they'd be if they weren't threatened or hungry was hard to say, and it had been far from where I was now. What else could there be out there?

Well, probably nothing that would hurt any of us. I realised that back in the old days, the biggest fear would have been of other humans. I wanted to see other people very much, but wondered if I also needed to fear them.

As I settled down in my bivvy bag, listening to the horses' swishing tails and steady chomping jaws, I remembered Dad saying,

'The only way forward, Jo, is for us to stop mistrusting each other and the only way to stop that is to start respecting each other. The trouble with humans is, we think that if you have something I need, then I have the right to take it from you. I can do it in the name of survival, or religion or even business, but ultimately, if you go down, so long as I'm all right, then I'm not bound to care.' He'd grinned then. 'That's a bit sweeping – not everyone's like that. But too many are and I think that's why we're in trouble.'

So now the world had ended, would people be more or less concerned for one another's welfare? If I did meet anyone who, say, needed Gray and Misty, would they think they had the right to take them from me if they could? Did they have that right? Or would they, now everything was different, think of asking if I'd let them use my horses? And would I let them, was it my choice even? They'd appeared from nowhere – did they belong to me or only to themselves? We certainly lived on a farm that was someone else's. All our animals, the stores that had kept us alive, they'd all been someone else's. If those people returned, would they demand back what was theirs and would we give it up? I remembered a book I'd read, where some people had the option of starving or attacking their neighbours for their stores of food. And they said, "Better to die like honest men, than live as murderers", or something like that.

Dad had said, 'We spend a lot of time, Jo, trying to sort all our dilemmas into black and white, from the colour of people's skins, down to what's right and wrong. But even black and white come in shades that look different when you lay them along side one another. Who's to say which is the true colour? How can we even know whose eyes see the most clearly?'

I'd listened to Dad think aloud a lot when I was little, not really understanding the things he was interested in. He and Moth were lecturers with lots of books about the environment and friends who'd sit round our kitchen table drinking coffee and wine all night while the conversations got heated and people waved their arms around. I'd grown up hearing discussions on sustainability and the future and the way people behaved towards one another, and was starting to realise how much I'd absorbed. Now what I'd learned might have to be put into practice, but what did I truly believe and what had I simply accepted? Clearly, I wouldn't stand by and let anyone hurt Ginny or Moth. I knew I wouldn't let anyone take the horses either, because we needed them, and, even more because they felt like part of our family. But I wouldn't attack anyone else because we were hungry, and I wouldn't gang up against other people. At least, I didn't think I would.

I fell asleep when I'd worn my brain out by thinking, lying on my back looking up at the stars. It was a clear, still night and while I stirred a few times, disturbed by an owl or one of the horses moving nearby, I woke up surprised that I'd slept so well. It was barely dawn and a suggestion of sunrise was turning the sea a glimmering gold, so bright I could hardly look at it.

It was then that I realised I wasn't alone and knew Dad was there. I didn't see him, but I was aware of him, beyond the corner of my eye. I didn't turn or look because I knew instinctively that I'd lose him then, but I started rolling up my bedding, knowing that he was keeping me company. The horses were browsing along the edges of the hollow and when Gray ambled over, nudging me in the back, I turned to rub his neck and once I'd done that, Dad had gone. But it was all right. I'd fallen asleep thinking about what he'd taught me and he'd come to keep an eye on me while I slept. The world was different now and things that might have seemed strange before had become part of the newness. Once I'd have thought of ghosts but now I knew my Dad was around and I didn't care how. A rush of energy took me and I vaulted up onto Gray's back without any tack.

'Come on, lad,' I said. 'Let's go for a run.'

He swung round at once and set off down to the sand, then with Misty loping behind we cantered along the shoreline, on the edge of the waves with spray flying up all round us, sparkling as the sun rose. I stretched my arms out wide and dropped my head back, sun on my face, salt water on my lips and the wonderful strong body of my horse alive under me. It was what I'd been wanting. Freedom from everything for a while.

We slowed to a walk after a bit and went to see what was round the headland. A path led up from the beach and, although it looked overgrown, I could see that it had been some sort of hard track once, so presumably led somewhere. I decided that we'd go that way after breakfast and see what was in the valley below.

I jumped down from Gray and left the horses to go back along the shore while I scrambled up a steeper rocky rabbit track that cut back round to where I'd camped. Panting and out of breath, I needed to use my hands to get up onto the cliff top and looked down to see that Gray and Misty were running again, play-fighting and chasing each other. They looked beautiful with the rising sun on them and a small party of seagulls scattered, squawking indignation, as the horses thundered through the picnic they'd been making of something on the shore. The birds were coming back, they really were. There were lots of seagulls once I started looking, and other seabirds nesting on the cliff-face.

A sudden panic seized me as I dropped down towards my camping place and all my gear was missing. There was no sign I'd ever been there and I began to run, my heart pounding in fear and a thousand unlikely scenarios rushing through my head in a few seconds. Then, topping the next rise, I started to laugh, feeling ridiculous and wishing I had someone to share my own daftness with – I'd been in the wrong hollow. All my gear was as I'd left it. It was strange, but that was the first time I felt desperately lonely, because I had no-one to laugh when I said, 'Look at me. I'm such a prat.'

It wasn't long before I'd eaten, packed up and started on the way again. We rode back along the shore, slowly this time, and I saw that the gulls had been pecking at a huge dead crab. I wondered if it had many friends, because that would make a good meal. I needed to do a bit of planning, because I both wanted to see what I could find, but also fish and get the catch back home while it was still fresh. So I needed to do that as the last thing before I headed home. I had a map and thought I could make my way down to what had been a largish fishing town I knew was just beyond its edges. Maybe that would be a good place to set up my lines and nets while I had a look round.

The path we'd seen earlier led us in a winding S-shape up the steep cliff. Old way-markers showed that it had been part of a trail for tourists. Reckoning that those usually ended near a teashop, I thought that sticking with it seemed as good as heading back to a road. I pictured a little teashop, waiting there on the path, still open and with the kettle on, wondering why they'd had no custom for the last couple of years. At first the idea made me laugh, then it chilled me and I grew edgy, wondering if there were places like that with perhaps one person stranded in the middle of nowhere, becalmed in a sea of not-knowing. If I'd been all alone, what would I have done? Set off to try and find someone, or stayed put? I didn't know.

To cheer myself up, I started singing, silly songs I'd made up with Moth and Dad when I was little. They used to sing them occasionally to embarrass me as I got older, knowing I secretly liked them and was pleased when Ginny inherited them, because I could sing along, rolling my eyes and pretending I was doing it for her. We were a great family for singing – in the car, while we made tea – and it wasn't until one of my friends nearly fell over when we all started singing the theme song from 'Chitty-chitty Bang, Bang' while we cleared the table, that it occurred to me that maybe everyone didn't behave like that at home. I liked family jokes and the little rituals and traditions. They were our own language. So I sang home-made songs at the top of my voice while Gray and Misty pricked up their ears and the sun glimmered on the sea below. I felt better for it, though I hoped this wouldn't be the moment when I discovered I wasn't the only person around.

The huge emptiness struck me as the track led down to what I suppose had been a visitor centre, complete with teashop no doubt, in the middle of the open heath-land, with its own small forest nestled round it. It looked lost among the trees and the wildness of the countryside. The car park was slowly covering over with weeds and grass, and the wooden building itself was mossy, with creepers escaping from what had once been a garden area to colonise its roof. It made me think of those old pictures, before people realised that ivy crawling all over ruins destroyed them.

'In a few years,' I told Gray, 'the cabin will have blended back into the ground, or become some big feature in a natural garden, where squirrels hang out and birds nest.'

The trees were quietly making a takeover bid too and, once I got down from Gray to walk round the building, I saw that a branch had made its way in through an open window like a long, sinuous arm heading stealthily towards the cash register.

The horses were a little spooked and I was too. There was no sign that anyone was there or had been there. Obviously, it wasn't a house or somewhere people would stay no matter what happened. It hadn't really been abandoned, like our house. One night, after all the tourists had gone home, the owners had locked up and never come back. But there's something uneasy about an empty building so I was glad when Dad was with me again. He was there the way he'd always been when he was alive. I hadn't needed to see him to know that then and I didn't now.

'Okay Dad,' I said aloud. 'I'm a bit creeped out here but I'll see if I can get inside.'

The tree had taken the open window and both a back and front door were still locked with grills and padlocks. This was the world we'd lost – where you had to lock up a little tea-shack in the middle of nowhere. It made me hesitate. While it was still pretty secure, I didn't want to break in. I was part of the new world – I didn't mind taking what I needed when no-one else appeared to want it, but I didn't want to damage anything or leave the building so that it was less useful to anyone who came after me because I'd let the weather get in. I was getting hungry so I turned back to Gray, who was watching me as though locked doors were highly interesting, and rooted around in his saddle bags for Moth's cake.

While I ate it, I leaned on him, scratching his withers.

'What's so interesting, sausage-brain?' I asked him. 'Never seen a door before?'

He still looked as though a bucket of carrots was hanging on it so once I'd eaten my cake, I ambled back over. The padlock was undone, swinging gently on its curved hasp with a soft rusty wheezing noise. I'd grown used to odd things happening since the horses arrived but I still gaped like a goldfish as I stood staring at it. I glanced round at Gray – I swear that horse was smiling and Dad was somewhere at the corner of my eye laughing.

'All right, all right, you two,' I said. 'You're in this together, I know.'

I gave Gray a hug and Misty too, so she didn't feel left out, then I thought about letting them loose for a bit but decided I'd wait to see how I felt once I'd had a look inside the cabin. I might want to leave in a hurry.

I unhooked the padlock and carried it in with me, not wanting the door to suddenly lock behind me, then pulled the grill open and tried the door. It was swollen where the rain had got in but no real problem once I put my shoulder against it. With a sudden soft sound it burst inwards and I found myself standing inside the abandoned visitor centre in a semi-shuttered light.

I peered through the shadows for a moment then went to open the wooden shutters that covered the windows at the front. Sunlight came pouring in like water rippling over the wooden surfaces, illuminating a reception area, small café section and doors to the offices and toilets. It was bright and quite cheerful in an abandoned, dusty sort of way and, after a quick look round the other rooms, I went and let the horses loose to graze before going back inside.

I found big catering tins of coffee and tea, dried milk and biscuits in a tin, though they were soft and pretty unpleasant. I didn't even look in the freezer because the green slime crawling out from under the lid was warning enough. While the rest of the place was thick with dust and home to a million spiders and mice, overall it was in reasonable condition. The shutters had kept the sun out and most of the fleeces and outdoor clothes in the tiny shop were untouched. A few near the ground had become home to mouse families, but there were plenty of good things I knew we'd be glad of. I began to wish I'd brought Poppa Horse with the cart.

I chose carefully, knowing I could return but still wanting to take back what we needed most. There was good waterproof gear – boots, jackets, hats – I packed a selection into the sort of backpack I'd have drooled over as an expensive impossibility in the old days. Now I brushed cobwebs off it and shoved my finds in. I also took three Swiss army knives, waterproofing spray, sweets and chocolate – which I had to test, of course, and they tasted fantastic – a cuddly deer for Ginn and a couple of paperbacks from a rack for Moth. Then I saw a baby's bobble hat with antlers on it and folded that in too. Into another backpack I loaded as much dried and tinned food as I could from the storeroom, as well as toilet rolls, soap and cleaning things. Best of all I found a big stock of Kendal Mint Cake that smelt and tasted fine – even better than the chocolate – only slightly past its use-by date. I took the lot, feeling guilty because I couldn't really argue that we needed it. But then, we didn't need the sweets either. I felt like Father Christmas surveying all the lavish goodies. Much of the stock felt a bit damp but it wasn't mouldy or damaged. I disturbed a few mice and jumped when I walked into the branch that was groping its way in through a back window. After a bit of thought, I carefully wrestled it back out and closed the window. There was still plenty there that we – or someone else – could benefit from as long as it stayed dryish.

I toyed with the idea of a night there but there was plenty of daylight so I closed all the shutters, on a whim helped myself to a fleece car rug and another bar of chocolate, then packed up the horses, unsurprised to find that the padlock was neatly done up by the time I was ready to go.

'Thanks, Dad,' I said aloud. 'Or Gray, or both of you.'

We pressed on till dusk and spent the night in a tiny cottage that had been abandoned long before the world ended. I didn't like it there and had a bad night, jumpy, chilly and agitated, glad of the extra warmth of the fleece rug. Dad turned up when I couldn't settle and I sat for a long while, staring into my fitful fire with him at the corner of my eye. I told him everything. All the things I'd never said while he was alive, partly because they would have worried him and partly because it never occurred to me that they needed saying. I talked about the things I missed, TV, films, music, food. Then I talked about the way I didn't miss them as much as I'd thought I would and how that worried me, as though I was losing my past. I asked if he'd seen our grandparents – we'd long ago guessed they must all be dead – or any of my friends, his own, Moth's, Ginny's.

'Sometimes,' I told him, 'I lie awake at night going through all the people we knew, from our friends to the postman and neighbours we only bumped into occasionally. I think about people we saw every Christmas and people we saw every day, seeing if I can remember them all, counting them on my fingers. I get scared sometimes because I can't see their faces anymore. They're all dead, all of them, Dad, it's like there's only me and Moth and Ginny to hold the sky up and keep the world going. Then I think, maybe the world never needed people anyway and we shouldn't try and keep it going the way we want it. Maybe we're supposed to fade away quietly.'

I told him all that, I asked him questions and his advice. He didn't say anything but I didn't expect it. He was there to listen and he did. I knew what his advice would have been mostly anyhow. I talked about how I wondered if I'd ever have a girlfriend – ever see a girl aside from Ginny, for that matter.

I grinned without looking in his direction,

'You won't have to worry I might start getting wild now, Dad,' I said, 'or getting drunk, or doing drugs.' I looked across at the bulging backpacks. 'Though I could start snorting ground up Mint Cake for the sugar rush, I suppose. You'd better keep an eye out for that. It tastes so amazing, I tell you, I could get hooked on the stuff no trouble.'

I rambled on all night, hearing words spilling from me as though I was emptying myself out, nonsense most of it, but some important things I never got round to telling him. I grew a bit sorry for myself and started snivelling, but got over it to worry about Moth and Ginn instead.

'I've got a baby to deliver,' I complained, before I dropped off at last. 'You really landed me in it, didn't you?'

When I woke, it was a grey, damp, dawn and my two horses were dozing nearby, looking like swirls of cloud in the hazy air, swirls of cloud that had decided to settle there and join me.

CHAPTER 7

We pressed on harder the next day. I was heading for a port called Corrycreag, small by most standards, but one of the main towns in that area not so long ago. During our holiday, we'd passed through it on our way north and had been heading back in the same direction when we began to realise something had changed. So I'd been there before, only for a day, but I remembered there were small branches of chain clothes shops and chemists. While the outdoor clothes from the visitor centre were a real find, what I was after too was some jeans, hardwearing work gear, underwear, and things like flour, tinned food, toothpaste – essentials we never gave a second thought in the old days. I reckoned that a lot of that sort of thing would be still useable, even after two years, so long as it was airtight or hadn't been exposed to too much damp. We couldn't carry a huge amount, and were already pretty laden, so I knew a second trip with the cart was on the cards, but if Moth had struggled while I was away, or being pregnant was making her ill, well, it might be a while before I could leave again. The other thing I wondered about was fuel – we'd kept the car in running order, turning the engine over once a week.

'We've got half a tank of fuel,' Dad had said. 'It's not enough to take us on a round trip anywhere, so there's no point wasting it. We'll just keep the car running, for now.'

We had no idea then, still had none now, as to why the villages we passed were abandoned, where all the people had gone. We knew that if they hadn't come back, something bad had happened. Then the black clouds came, and the Spill had spread over the land, so we stayed put. Once that passed, we spent time simply living, then as we were starting to think again about using the car to look for more people, Dad got kicked and the world ended a second time. Now, though, if I could find some fuel, it might be enough for Moth to drive us down to the port or the visitor centre. A week's journey with horse and cart, a day by car.

Reaching the town was strange. A deserted town is even more eerie than a deserted house. Even the quietest town had always had someone around, people on the streets, shopping, on their way to work or school, doing everyday things. But when we joined the main road, still cutting a black line through the countryside even though the edges were overgrown and weeds had forced up through the tarmac, the complete emptiness of the town below us was evident from a mile away.

Part of me wondered if we should be moving from the farm to somewhere like this, somewhere people would come back to, if there were any people, and where what was left was easier to get at. But another part of me thought we'd be like ghosts living among the abandoned houses as they fell into disrepair and that if people did come back, what if they weren't people we'd want to know? Our farm was isolated and remote and you'd never find it except by accident, like we did. That made it safe, and this town, even empty, didn't feel safe.

The first thing that caught my eye was a garage. What I didn't know was how I'd get at the fuel, but there was no reason to think there wouldn't be any. If the world ended overnight, as it seemed to have done, then there wouldn't have been any gradual decline in supplies or anything like that. If everyone was evacuated, then maybe all the cars stocking up to leave might mean the fuel tanks were low. But there seemed to be a lot of cars around. How had everyone left? The possibility of Moth riding out and picking up a car with fuel in dawned on me too. The cars here hadn't been maintained like ours had, though. My head was like a mixing bowl, all the different thoughts and ideas churning around until they made no sense. I had to hope they'd come into some sort of shape, given time.

'It's not ready for cooking yet,' I told Gray, as I dismounted outside the garage. 'There's probably going to be a lot more ingredients first.'

The garage wasn't a big one, but there were a few second-hand cars for sale and whoever had owned it had left in a serious hurry – nothing was locked. It didn't take long to find where the car keys were kept. But I didn't know how to drive and while I knew how to keep a car running, I didn't know how to get it going when it had been standing for two years. Moth might though. I had a go at turning the engine over on an old Land Rover, but it could only manage a dry, coughing noise. I put the keys back and decided that for now, my priority was to see what there was to see, then get home. So I left everything as I'd found it, helped myself to some bags of sweets from a rack, and, sucking on some slightly sticky wine gums, rode on down into the port.

Corrycreag had been a pretty little place, with a scooped-out harbour that the town curved round and a wide sea-front. It was a fishing port first, so the front wasn't that touristy. There were gift shops and cafés and so on, but aside from a couple of plain benches and some tubs of flowers, now either dead or running riot, it was a practical sort of place. A few boats were still tied up, but I supposed most had broken their moorings and drifted off over time. Nets and creels were mouldering on the solid stone harbour wall and cats were doing well, no matter if everyone else had gone. Most of them hissed and slunk away when they saw me, but a few remembered the days when humans meant a warm fire, food and curling up on someone's knee. So they came over to me, a bit wary at first, but soon purring and rubbing round my ankles.

'Hi, moggies,' I said, picking up a large black furry one who nestled up to me like her best friend. 'You don't feel too bad, do you, girl? Not too thin. Where's the food around here then?'

I put her down and turned to scan the row of shops behind me. They looked as though I'd happened to call when everyone was out. Aside from being overgrown, with storm and weather damage here and there, everything looked pretty normal. There were a few cars parked along the road – about as many as you'd expect for a mid-week afternoon. An ordinary day in a small town, except for the stillness and the silence. I remembered that the few chain stores that had made it this far north were in the main market street that ran parallel to the harbour, so I headed towards a narrow lane that cut between the quiet shops. That was when I noticed the dust.

I suppose I'd seen it already but there was a lot of debris, wind-blown paper, fallen branches, and it didn't register at first. Then I began to see it was in piles here and there, dry in sheltered spots, damp and slightly sludgy on the streets. But as I peered in shop windows, it was there too. A sick feeling came over me and I began to hurry, though I wasn't sure why.

I tried a door to a shop – it opened and I went inside. It was a baby-clothes shop, very small and crammed with stock that had gone mildewed and mouldy, because water was leaking from above somewhere. I managed to find the sort of baby-carrier Moth had carried Ginny in, which was fine because it was made of nylon, so I took that, but left the rest, because it seemed beyond use. I was turning to go when I saw a pile of dust near the counter. Although it was damp, when I prodded it with my boot, it was like the contents of a hoover bag or the ash-can from under the fire. Then I realised that a baby-buggy by the window I'd taken as stock had a handbag looped over the handlebar and a teddy bear tucked inside the covers. With the dust. There was a very small pile of dust on the frilly pillow that had slithered down under the little sleeping-bag the baby would have been tucked in.

My knees went weak and I had to get outside quickly to sit down on a bench. Gray and Misty came over, pushing at me with their noses, disturbed and uneasy, while the black cat wound itself round my legs,

'It's people,' I told them. 'The dust is people.' Then I was sick.

It took me a while to get going again after this glimpse of what had happened, and I tried not to get the images clear in my head. I was wandering round a graveyard where no-one was actually buried. I was stepping over bodies and once I knew what the small, sludgy dust piles were, they seemed to multiply till I was avoiding them with every footstep. Gray and Misty spooked at each one and the buildings leaning over us bothered them too. They'd probably spent their whole lives in the open until now. That helped. I stopped thinking about the piles of people-dust and paid attention to my horses. I stroked them both then, suddenly remembering that Moth had said horses like mint, I broke a bar of Kendal Mint Cake into pieces and we shared half of it. They liked it so much they made me laugh, eagerly snuffling at the wrapper for more. Misty, whose tongue seemed a good ten feet long, started licking at my hands.

'Yuk!' I said, wiping them on her neck. 'That's gross, you daft horse. Here, lick the wrapper.'

They both licked the wrapper and then Gray shied away as a sudden breeze blew dust around our feet. He sniffed at it then stretched his long neck out and curled his top lip back. I'd seen pictures of stallions doing that in the horse books and I was pretty certain it meant he was trying to get a better smell of the dust by rolling it over his taste buds.

'It's dead people, Gray,' I told him. 'You don't need to smell them. I know what they are.'

That strange sort of sick humour that comes along at the worst moments took hold of me. 'We were taking up too much room,' I explained to Gray. 'So they've been dehydrated for easy storage. We can try pouring water on a couple – they should pop right back into shape, no trouble.'

I went on like that till I reckoned Gray thought I was losing my grip, so I gathered my wits and blamed it on the sugar in the Mint Cake. It was good though, so we shared the rest of the bar, standing half way down the winding side-street, with cats milling about and the buildings leaning over as though they needed our warmth.

Then we carried on and found our way out onto the main street, which was much more open so the horses relaxed a bit. The black cat was clinging to us, with a few more following hopefully, making me feel like the Pied Piper. Then I stopped short. Across the main road where the cars were all parked neatly and dust had long been blown or washed away, the plate glass windows were all broken. There was a Barclays bank, a small Woolworth's, a Marks and Spencer, a few other local shops and a tiny Morrison's at the far end of the street – each one had its main windows smashed in. I turned and saw that the shops behind me were the same. The hair on the back of my neck stood up. Piles of dust and cats, even masses of cats, don't break plate glass windows.

I stood as still as I could and listened, but there was nothing, not a sound. The cats, horses, even the buildings, all held their breath so I could hear the utter silence. Then everything sighed and I heard the creaking and rustling of the town, the swirl of debris as a breeze caught it, the shifting of leather as Gray moved his back, the slow flap of wings overhead as a huge gull flew down to settle on a car nearby. But no sound of people.

I wanted to get into Marks and Spencer first – there would be clothes, tinned food, all sorts of useful supplies. Also, somewhere in this fishing town, there must be a chandler's, a fishing shop too. And a Smith's – was there a Smith's somewhere, with a two-year-old newspaper that might tell me anything about what had happened? But if there'd been any warning, would all these people have been turned to dust while they shopped? It was time to get moving, especially if whoever had smashed the windows was around somewhere. A thought made me shiver. What if they had been here and were now heading randomly towards Moth and Ginny?

I decided to take the horses with me into the cover of M&S so, kicking glass out of the way for them to pick a path, I led them inside through the unlocked doors. The front of the shop was ruined from the weather getting in, as well as having been the food section. The slime of what had once been flowers and fresh stock made a carpet of compost that housed some unusual specimens of mould. Rats were everywhere, startled out of display cabinets, spilling from racks, darting between my feet, and a strong smell of sewage came from the customer toilets near the little café area. I led the horses to a cleaner aisle at the back of the shop, trusting them to stay – I never tied them up after debating with myself that first night. So I promised not to be long and left them standing in the space between the aisles and the checkout, out of sight of the street, just in case. Then I took one of Misty's panniers and headed up the long-dead elevator, two steps at a time. It was only a small branch, so all the clothes were on the first floor. I skipped the old-lady's-jumpers section, reckoning that, as there was a choice, Moth might as well have something that would make her feel good, and headed for the denims and shirts. I didn't bother with the formal wear either – we didn't get out that much – and cast a depressed eye over the menswear. Practical was what mattered and even if I wouldn't have been seen dead wearing clothes from M&S once, now I had to make do.

The clothes were in good enough condition as the windows on the second floor were sound. That had kept the piles of dust neat too, but I ignored them. I chose two pairs of denims each, getting sizes I thought would be a bit big for me and Ginn and remembering, from the days of Christmas and birthday shopping with Dad, that Moth was a size 10. She was only little too, so I went for the shorter lengths at first, then changed my mind, thinking it would be better to chop them shorter if I'd got it wrong. I got us all some joggers, choosing a couple of men's sizes for Moth as I couldn't see any clothes for pregnancy. That was a bit of a relief really. I knew the clothes Moth used to wear – jeans, shirts, 'smart casual', as it used to say outside pubs. At a push, I could probably have made a guess at one of the silk skirts and a top if she'd been going to a party. But what a pregnant woman would like, or even need, was beyond me, except that I knew it would probably have an elastic waist. So joggers it was, and a couple of shirts that would have fitted Dad. I chose half a dozen of those in sizes to fit us all. The pannier was full and after a quick, half-embarrassed turn though ladies' underwear and a few frilly bits and pieces with ribbons on I thought Ginn would like, I found myself some socks and boxers, then headed back to the horses.

I tied the first pannier on tight before heading into the food section to pack the other one up with tinned food. Then, leaving the horses again as they seemed settled, I headed over to Boots, which I'd spotted across the road, and helped myself to a generous supply of simple medicines and toiletries, a bit confused by the choice after such a long time. That filled another backpack. I reminded myself that I was supposed to be fishing too but I badly wanted to get home and I had far more supplies than I'd reckoned on. A mood of urgency was on me and I was speeding here and there, finding a Smith's (pens, pencils, notepads, crayons for Ginn, and a selection of newspapers, half of which I ditched as I was getting too laden) but no chandler's, wondering what the panic was, when I realised two things. First, daylight was fading and secondly, when I stopped running and making a noise myself, I could hear something. Somewhere, a distance away, there was a crashing noise, which at first I'd thought was something metal flapping in the wind, a loose gutter, a shed roof. But it was starting to sound more random than that, and then there was shouting too, someone losing control. Just one voice, I thought, but raging, furious. Most of the cats had disappeared and the last few were slinking for cover, low to the ground with their fur on end. I set off again too and, not looking where I was going, crashed into a car then reeled back across the street into Marks to find the horses.

They'd gone.

CHAPTER 8

After a moment when abandonment flooded through me, my faith in Gray and Misty returned. If they'd gone, it was for a good reason. They'd gone quickly and quietly – there was none of the chaos I'd have expected if they'd crashed through the shop in panic.

So, for now, I was alone with the sounds of destruction and rage getting closer. I hovered, indecisive, then all the choices were made for me as a ferocious man tore along the main road. I ducked behind a rack near the main door and kept my head down, peering through the space between two rusting tins of biscuits to watch him pass. He was long. Long legs, long body, a long wild beard hanging down his chest. His gangling arms were high over his head, with a chunk of wood in them, long too, like part of a door-frame, and he was howling in some terrifying mix of pain, despair and fury. In a headlong charge, he hurtled down the empty street and I crept forward open-mouthed to watch him disappear into Smith's at the far end, but I could still hear him demolishing the place.

I sunk down on to the floor for a minute, my heart hammering away like an engine in my chest. The first person outside my family I'd seen in two years, the first I'd seen at all in four days. I suddenly heard Dad's dry irony in my head, *Perhaps he's lonely.*

'You make friends with him, then, mate,' I told him. 'He's a complete nutter and I'm getting out of here.'

Dad was with me then, watching my back though, as I pointed out to him, the man was in front of me. But he wasn't there to protect me, a pang in my chest then, he couldn't protect me, he was dead. He could give me courage though, keep me on my feet, and he did, while Smith's was loudly dismantled a few shops down.

I needed to get away. Whatever else happened, I had to get back to Moth and Ginny. There was no point to heroics or risk. They needed me more than all the supplies I'd gathered. I needed Gray and Misty but I had to trust that they'd find me. On a day-to-day basis they and their companions back home may have been ordinary horses, but when it mattered they were something else entirely. I had to believe that they'd turn up at the right moment.

Smith's was taking a severe hammering so I decided to see if M&S had a back door, winding my way between the aisles and out into the staff area at the back of the shop. There were stores there too, neatly packed with tinned goods and clothes in plastic wrappers. This town was too good a find to abandon because a lunatic had taken it over. But I couldn't do anything then, so I packed the knowledge into the general chaos in my head. I got lost in the maze of tiny corridors, surprising in a shop that hadn't seemed very big from the front, but then saw a sign for the fire exit. I ran towards it and threw myself at the door, all my weight on the metal handle. Three things happened at once then – the door burst into the street – I realised it might be alarmed – the alarm went off.

The unbelievable racket left me dazed and bewildered and, in the still street I fell into, it sounded like the only noise in the whole world. Shrill, clanging, metallic, every cat, bird, house and car jumped skywards and my heart bounced off the inside of my skull before plummeting into my boots somewhere. The row in Smith's stopped and, beneath the hysterical wailing of the alarm, I could hear the sound of a maniac listening. Almost wetting myself, I sped off down the small street I'd exploded into, away from Smith's or so I thought, but I'd got disorientated and crashed straight into the chest of the man with wild eyes, who was standing staring at me, his arms raised over his head for a better swing of the cricket bat he'd found on his rampage.

I shrieked like an alarm myself and the sound that came from my mouth was so alien it scared me as much as the madman did. He took a breath that pulled all the buildings in towards him and released it in a roar that sent them staggering back, fetid stale-liquor breath billowing over my face. The cricket bat swung downwards but I was too close to him and as he tried to step back I shoved him hard in the chest, setting him off-balance, then ducked out under his arm and vaulted over a bench, distantly impressed with my own athleticism. Then I was out of there, like shit-off-a-shovel, as Grandad used to say to make Gran scowl. That homely thought seemed to steady me as I ran but I recognised hysteria in my urge to start laughing. I ducked into a side-street, over a wall into a little garden, through a gate into an alley then stopped, leaning against the side-wall of a cottage, knowing I needed to take hold of my panic.

There was no sound of immediate pursuit and the alarm had cut off abruptly in the middle of my flight. Once my heart had stopped hammering and the blood thumping in my ears had settled down, I listened hard and there was nothing. That unnerved me, because I had no idea where the madman was. The thought that he was looking over the wall at me brought me close to wetting myself again, but when I carefully raised my head, then peered out like one of the half-wild cats round the corner of the building, there was no sign of him. I forced myself to breathe deeply then Dad told me to go inside the building. His voice in my head was calm as a summer sea. I could see the gentle swell of it like one of those soft days when the waves barely break, and I kept that image in my mind.

The back door of the cottage was open and I went into a neat kitchen, then a largish room that had obviously once been two but knocked through to make a tearoom. It had half a dozen tables and chairs, all with dusty tablecloths, cobwebby now, but it still gave off an air of old-fashioned charm. In the old days, I'd have thought it very fuddy-duddy but now it seemed like a wonderful haven. I remembered the home of my great-grandmother, who'd died when I was knee-high to my Dad. She had a real old-fashioned living-room with big ugly vases and a clock I could hear ticking even when I'd fallen asleep on someone's knee. This took me back there, like a time-warp.

The tables and chairs were dark wood and spindle-legs, the cloths all lacy, with little glass sugar-bowls and salt-and-pepper sets. The sugar was still dry and, although the room was getting gloomy as the daylight faded, I began to see that some of the tables were clean. Only the ones at the edges of the room were covered in cobwebs and dust. The three nearest the window had fresh flowers, and the tablecloths looked fresh too, with neat settings, placemats, tea-plates, china cups and saucers. I reminded myself that Dad had prompted me to enter and this didn't look like a madman's sitting room.

Still, when I turned at a sound behind me, the little girl standing in the kitchen doorway with an oil-lamp made me jump and shout. She stared at me with cool composure, while I had to work hard on avoiding a pant-wetting situation for the third time that afternoon. Then she said something in a language I recognised but was too overwhelmed by then to identify. When I didn't respond, she drew a breath that suggested she was a bit disappointed in me, then came over and put the lighted lamp down on the table nearest the window.

She wasn't a ghost. I could feel the warmth of her body as she moved past me and realised she was dressed up. She was wearing jeans and a worn old jumper, but over that she had on a waitress outfit, right up to a little doily head-dress on her dark hair. I'd wandered into a game of tea parties. Or I'd gone mad, too. It was hard to tell by that point. She pointed to a chair by the table she'd made ready for me, but I was agitated about the lunatic outside.

'There's someone out there,' I said. 'He's dangerous – you shouldn't have a light by the window.'

She stared at me without comprehension and spoke again, clearly dismissing whatever fears I had with a wave of her hand. I began to think it was probably French, in which I knew only a few simple phrases.

'Bonjour?' I ventured. *'Parlez vous Anglaise?'*

She made a little gesture with her mouth and a shrug that was so French somehow that I knew I'd got that much right, but I guessed too that it meant she didn't speak English at all. She said something I didn't understand, but I picked up *'une tasse de thé'* at the end and gathered that I was being offered a cup of tea. I gave up then and went along with whatever strange thing was happening to me.

I sat at the table in the little tearoom while she disappeared into the kitchen. Then I smelt gas, a match strike, water running and gathered that she was putting the kettle on. Well, that was still how to make tea, so why was I so confused? I sat, trying hard to use the moments of waiting politely to work out what the hell was going on. Where were my horses and where was the lunatic? These things were my main concern, aside from the thought that I'd now come across a little girl, not much older than Ginny, who I could hardly leave here with a maniac on the loose. And not only her. There was the small boy, sitting watching me through the banisters of the stairs in the centre of the room, his arm around an equally small dog. I nodded to him and waited for my tea.

Both children joined me at the table, the girl removing her waitress outfit, and I guessed that this was one of those games where everyone plays more than one part because numbers are a bit thin on the ground. The dog, a small mongrelly Jack Russell-Labrador-a-bit-of-Collie type, sat bolt upright looking at the boy with the sort of appeal that only a cute dog can muster. He made me grin and once I did both the kids relaxed and started to chatter away to each other, too polite to discuss me – we were in the middle of tea, after all – but I got the idea they were discussing the weather. I suddenly realised that they were playing at being English – afternoon tea, polite conversation – the way Ginny might play at being a French onion-seller on a bike. Well, there were worse clichés of national behavior, so I went along with it.

I found myself touched by their resilience. Here alone in the middle of the dusty dead, with a madman tearing the place apart and a strange boy bursting into their refuge, they were calmly keeping life going by playing at still being on holiday. That was it. A sudden flash of intuition told me that, like us, they'd been on holiday here when the world ended. But had they survived alone ever since? The little boy couldn't have been more than five or six and the girl was maybe eleven at the most. They were both very clean and neat, although their clothes were pretty much worn out. But the girl had new trainers on, pink ones, with sparkly laces, and the dog had a new collar. I guessed that, like me, they'd foraged in the town for supplies and set up home here, perhaps some time ago. The boy went running upstairs and came back with a colouring book, so it looked that way. I admired the book and tried hard to make some sort of conversation.

We got as far as names – they were Sophie and Laurent. The dog was Souris, which made me smile, because I remembered Moth teaching us *'Madame Souris est dans le jardin'*, recalled from her French lessons at School – Mrs. Mouse is in the garden. It was Moth who'd suggested we all learn a little French conversation to prepare for our holiday the year before the world ended. We'd bought a couple of teach-yourself CDs and played them during every car journey for months before the trip. Remembering that time started bringing it back to me.

'Bonjour, Souris,' I said. *'Bonjour, Sophie et Laurent. Ça va? Je m'appelle Joel.'*

After tea – I drank two cups, it was so good – with biscuits which weren't bad either, it seemed it was Laurent's bed-time. Sophie was playing mothers now so she bustled around and I followed, slightly bemused, to watch her shoo him round the small upstairs, where there were two bedrooms and a bathroom. They'd obviously been there some time. The place was as much a home as our farm. Laurent cleaned his teeth, got into pajamas that were too big for him, then into a neatly made bed, with Souris curled up on the foot. He stuck his thumb in his mouth, Sophie kissed him goodnight, indicated that I should too, which I took as a sign that she'd decided to trust me, then she led the way back downstairs.

She was fascinating. Once her brother was safely tucked up, she underwent another transformation into some sort of stealth raider. She put on a black coat and hat, found a black hat for me, which was a bit small, so I guessed it was Laurent's, and we went out into the dark streets. There was no moon, but Sophie had a couple of torches – something I needed too. When I tried to explain this to her, she nodded and headed off at a low run. She knew about the madman obviously, and while we'd been safe to have lights on in the house, we had to keep our heads down on the street. I was struggling to make sense of this, but she was so confident that I trusted her.

She made her way expertly through the streets to the edge of the town and into the garage of what seemed to be quite a large house, closing the doors behind us. Sophie rooted around in the darkness for a few moments then emerged with three oil lamps. She lit them all, placing them carefully so we could get a good view of the four-wheel-drive pick-up, all shiny black and new that stood proudly in the centre of the garage. Sophie indicated to me with the combination of a mimed turning on of the engine, a thumbs-up and a finger to her lips that the car would go but she wasn't going to demonstrate now.

She then pulled back the canvas cover of the pick-up and showed me the car's long flat-bed interior. It was laden with blankets, tinned food, dried stuff – flour and pulses and fruit – batteries, candles, clothing, books – if I'd ever thought of it, it was there. Nothing that needed power aside from the batteries, all really useful supplies. Then she stood and looked at me, her hands on her hips, as though waiting for my reaction.

'Were you leaving?' I asked. *'Venez? Vous et Laurent?'* I made gestures of getting out, going far away. 'Do you want to come with me? *Ma mère et ma soeur et* ....over there somewhere.' I had a brainwave, wishing I had my own gear with me, but remembering the books I'd seen in the pick-up. Sure enough, after a moment of rooting around carefully, so as not to disturb Sophie's neat packing, I found a map. I spread it out over the bonnet and showed her, pointing to the town where we were – *'Ici…'* – then to our isolated farm, a tiny square – *'Ma maison – où Maman et ma soeur – Ginny – et mes chevaux et les vaches et poulet.'* I was on a roll by then and managed a string of farm-words.

She nodded some sort of understanding, then gestured to herself. *'Sophie, Laurent, Souris – nous allons avec Joel.'*

I nodded, then had to admit. 'I can't drive.'

71

She was one amazing little girl. She gestured to the car, mimed driving and pointed at her own chest. I never doubted that if she said she could drive, then she could, though I wasn't sure how she'd see over the dash.

Of course, when we went outside Gray and Misty were grazing on the large front lawn as though we'd never been parted. I hugged them both and got a bit blurry-eyed, lacking their cool acceptance of the reunion. I unloaded all their gear, packing it in the garage and taking what I needed for the night, then left them there to fill up on the good grass and followed Sophie back to the cottage. I had a bath, missing the hot water we could heat at home, and slept in the spare bedroom in a big old-fashioned double-bed about three foot off the floor. It was wonderful luxury after my nights on the ground. Dad lay on the bed next to me and if I kept very still I could feel his shoulder against mine. I mulled everything over quietly while he listened and advised me silently on what to do next. Then I went to sleep, hearing Souris snoring in the next room, while Laurent talked French rapidly in his sleep.

CHAPTER 9

That I'd ever wondered what I should do with Sophie and Laurent became a bit ironic. Sophie, I soon realised, had been waiting for someone to come along to help them. So from the moment she laid eyes on me, she was planning that they'd come with me. The afternoon tea was a test, which I seemed to have passed, so it was settled before I ever understood what was going on. Any vision I had of myself as the hero on horseback, turning up to rescue them in their hour of need, soon faded. Sophie was in charge from the moment I met her and that was the way it was. I did as I was told.

She was as self-possessed a little girl as I'd ever seen, but it was a long time before I saw her being Sophie. She was always playing someone else – feisty single mom, urban tracker, overland trail guide. They were usually tough roles then she'd suddenly dig out her waitress costume and want to play tea-parties. Laurent was quite different. He seemed very young for his age and I wondered if he was in shock. He sucked his thumb a lot and, probably because I was physically bigger than Sophie, liked to curl up on my knee. I guessed he really needed an adult and I was the nearest thing he'd seen in a long while, not counting the crazy man with the big hunks of wood. I didn't fancy asking him for a cuddle myself so I couldn't blame Laurent for overlooking him.

He liked Misty, who was always ready for a bit of cuddling, so that first morning while Sophie and I played street raiders, Misty and Gray baby-sat with Souris in the garden of the big house. Every time we returned with more supplies, Laurent was standing with his arms round Misty's neck as she lowered her head down to him, his little face buried in her mane, or asleep somewhere with all three animals keeping watch over him. He barely spoke at all but watched everything with wide dark eyes, his mop of equally dark hair flopping over his face.

Sophie was dark in colouring too and they were so obviously brother and sister that only the age-difference stopped them from looking like twins. Sophie and I spent that morning packing, making stealth raids through the shops and houses, the sounds of crashing helping us keep our distance from the only other person around. When he went quiet, having no idea of his whereabouts was far worse than his destructive racket.

I couldn't understand how Sophie knew the things she did. She'd siphoned diesel out of the storage tanks at an old-fashioned fuel station near the edge of town into several big cans. The four-wheel-drive was already full of fuel – we'd turned the engine over briefly first thing, when the man was at the far end of town piling up all his bits of wood. Wood seemed important to him. He appeared to be going through the town gathering enough for an impressive bonfire. I wondered if he was trying to signal but he didn't really seem sane enough for that.

I guessed that Sophie had learned her survival skills from an adult but couldn't converse with her enough to understand who that had been or where they were now. I gathered that they'd travelled by car a long way, changing vehicles as they went, stocking up on fuel when the opportunity arose. But at some point there'd been a tragedy and they'd ended up alone. I couldn't work out if she knew where the fire-starter came from either or how long he'd been there.

I made a brief return to Smith's, which was badly wrecked after the big party our noisy friend had there the previous night. After a trawl through the debris, I found English to French and French to English dictionaries. I also found some GSCE study guides on French, and a few other coursework aids. That was the great thing about remote highland towns – they were small but they had everything. I'd remarked on it while we were on our long-ago caravan holiday and Dad had said it was for both for the tourists and the local people. They were real centres, lifelines. Or had been, anyhow.

I found the chandler's too and picked up plenty of useful gear. I was torn between not wanting to starve the wild man out and feeling reluctant to have him destroy good things other survivors like us could use. But we couldn't take everything so I kept to my 'what-we-need' policy. There was still plenty of food left for him – it was a whole town and we couldn't have fitted in all there was if we'd tried. But I did replenish our supplies of tools, nails, fishing gear, kitchen utensils, pans – it was like Christmas and birthdays all rolled into one. Everything would be easier now. And seeds – I found seeds and, to my great surprise, a small flat-packed poly-tunnel in the overstocked garden shop. Growing food was the most important thing so that was probably the best find of all, along with the new clothes, because as Grandad liked to say, 'So long as your arse is covered, you can get by.' I thought of Grandad the whole time I was in the gardening shop. He was a keen gardener and I remembered a lot I hadn't realised he'd taught me. Thinking about his delight in saying scandalous things that would make us shriek with laughter, while Gran scowled and hit him with a tea-cloth, kept me smiling and smiling helped more than anything.

Sophie didn't smile much. She was too busy being in charge but I was glad of her company, and Laurent's, who was a cute kid. He made me really miss Ginn, who was still little enough to like curling up on my knee too. I thought of the new baby that was coming. He'd have lots of knees to curl up on now. Suddenly we were heading towards being a group of six. There were other people. We weren't the only ones. Finding Sophie, Laurent and even the fire-starter proved that.

Once the four-wheel-drive was overflowing, I covered everything with the canvas sheet we'd found on the back seat, lacing it down tightly. It was a bit of a snug fit because we'd packed so much in, but I managed it. I'd loaded all Gray and Misty's gear into the back seats, except my saddle and bridle.

Obviously, the car could go faster than the horses, but the roads were quite bad now, pitted by weather and overgrown, and Sophie wasn't very tall. Driving wasn't going to be easy for her. I reckoned that we'd go in fits and starts, me waiting for her when the going was rough, her waiting for me when she got ahead.

We checked our maps and marked the route on each one to be sure we both knew exactly where we were going, so I could take short cuts across country. It occurred to me that if I went in the car, the horses would follow, but somehow I didn't want to leave them, so I chose to ride. I thought of the first night and the wild gallop along the beach. Those few moments of freedom were over and I was now more tied to other people even than when I was at home. But that was all right. I'd had my time alone, talked to Dad in the darkness. I was settled again.

We waited until the man was back in Smith's. It seemed there was something about Smith's. Then we made our way to the car, taking the last of Sophie and Laurent's belongings from the cottage. On a whim, I quickly packed up the tea-set Sophie liked and, while she sniffed at me for this indulgence, there was a tear in her eye and I realised she'd really wanted to bring it. I stored the knowledge away, feeling that getting her home to Moth soon was important. She needed an adult as much as Laurent did.

Once Laurent was safely strapped in the passenger seat with Souris on his knee, Sophie confidently started the car and eased it out of the garage. She was sitting on a booster seat for toddlers we'd found in the back and could just reach the pedals. Her serious dark face frowned out, barely visible over the dashboard. She certainly knew how to drive. Despite the difficulties it posed her, she handled the car expertly and I guessed she'd learned in a much smaller vehicle. She also must have got this one going and kept it in running order for however long they'd been waiting for someone to turn up.

I closed the garage door, got up on Gray, and followed her slow but steady progress down the road. She turned out of town at the earliest opportunity, as we'd agreed. While going through the centre offered the main road, it also meant that the man could leap out at us and would know we'd left. So she took the side streets and the back roads, leaving the town on little more than a cart-track which cut into the main road through a farm-yard a little further on. As she negotiated tight corners and narrow lanes in the big vehicle, I felt proud of her, as though we were family. Gray and I, with Misty following, cantered on ahead as she came to the gate onto the road and I jumped down to let her through. She drove onto the tarmac and kept going till she reached the top of the long sloping hill that led out into the countryside. It took a while for me to catch up and when I did, she and Laurent were standing by the side of the car, hand in hand, looking down at the town. They were both in tears and I dismounted again to go over to them.

For the first time I saw Sophie as small and alone, trying to convince Laurent and herself that she could manage. I wondered if it was the sadness of leaving the cosy house that had been their shelter or going into the unknown with me, a stranger, that was upsetting them. Then, as I placed a hand on Laurent's head and he lifted his arms up for me to carry him, I saw that they were watching the small figure of the madman. The only movement in the distance, he was clearly visible, a long dark figure on the outskirts of the grey and white town, tearing up and down by his huge smoking bonfire. As the wind shifted a little, the smell of it reached us and I could hear him shouting. Laurent buried his face in my neck and sobbed but Sophie wiped her eyes on her sleeve and turned away.

'*Mon Papa,*' she said, and got back in the car.

She barely waited for me to get Laurent strapped in again before she drove off, her dark eyes fierce, face stern as granite. I was torn between wishing I could comfort her and relief that I had the time following on horseback to assimilate the information. I didn't speak much French but I knew what "*Mon Papa*" meant. Was the mad fire-starter really their father? Or did she mean something more obscure that I'd missed? Could it possibly be that they'd been in the town avoiding him for so long that he felt like a father, being the only adult on hand? No, he was their father. Now I thought about those few moments he spent looking over me, he'd had the same dark eyes, even though his wild hair was greying.

Sophie didn't speak again all day and I didn't try to make her. We travelled with a sort of grim resolve, the horses and I took short cuts whenever possible, Laurent slept most of the day, so we made very few stops. I reckoned that, now the horses were unladen and the speed of the car kept us pressing on, we'd be back home by the next evening.

Sophie and Laurent slept in the car that night and I slept in the tent. Half way through the night, Laurent came in and wriggled up beside me then went back to sleep again. I was a bit worried about Sophie waking to find him gone, but Souris was on guard at the mouth of the tent. She'd soon realise where he was. He had that slightly-damp-pants and runny-nose smell small children have when they need a bath and I felt sorry that we'd arrive back with him like that, because Sophie took really good care of him. He'd been scrubbed three or four times in the hours I spent with them before we left, as though Sophie could clean off his slightly dazed distress. Now he'd sunk deeper into it and I felt concerned about him. He snuffled away behind me in the darkness, developing a cold or perhaps he'd cried a lot that day. Poor little kid, I thought, finding it no wonder now that he was dazed. The thought of them losing their father even though he was still there brought the day Dad died back to me. I couldn't sleep then, and lay awake until the first hints of daylight made the pale walls of the tent glow. Quietly, I slipped out into a damp dawn and sent Souris inside so Laurent wouldn't wake up alone.

Gray and Misty had gone again but this no longer bothered me. I knew they'd turn up when they were needed and guessed it meant I was to ride in the car so I loaded Gray's tack in the back seat. This meant a bit of reorganisation, but by the time Laurent woke, Sophie and I had it all sorted out. She fed him, still a bit grim-faced but brighter than the day before, and then she turned to me. 'La voiture,' she said, pointing with a stern finger at the vehicle, then at me while she mimed driving. I started to say I didn't know how, then I thought about the times I'd played at driving with Dad. I could probably give it a go.

So we set off again along the potholed road, which seemed particularly bad as we crossed over a purple expanse of open moorland, startling peewits and curlews, then dropped down towards the sea again. I had us lurching and stalling a bit, while Sophie told me off and gave me instructions I didn't understand. But, as Grandad used to say, necessity is the mother of all kicks up the backside. He'd adapted that one a bit from the original, but I agreed with him now. I was learning to drive because I needed to. On a straight road, I could take the car faster than Sophie, because I could see easily over the dash. I still took it slowly though, because every now and then I got flustered, trying to remember what to do to change gear, but we trundled along, with the murky coloured sea getting closer all the time and Sophie's instructor voice rattling around my confused brain.

We stopped a couple of times and there was no sign of the horses, but then, as we headed down a long hill, I saw a real problem and wondered if this was why they'd found their own way. The road dipped into a deep hollow then ran right alongside the rocky beach but the shifts and changes of the past two years had altered the shore line. Now the road disappeared into the sea and emerged half a mile away. There was no way round as it cut through the roughest bit of boggy, tussocked moorland I'd ever seen. Even a four-wheel-drive wouldn't cross it, I was sure, and I could see that at the lowest tide, the road would be far behind the waterline.

I stopped the pick-up, sending us all lurching forward and then rocking back and hearing the light thud of Laurent's head on the pillow behind him.

'Sorry,' I said, and Sophie rolled her eyes, getting out of the car with Laurent trotting along holding her hand. I followed her down to the water's edge then ran back, dug out some wellies from the pick-up and waded into the water. It went almost over the tops in just a few feet.

'I know *la voiture* will *passer la mer*… or…maybe… *passer l'eau,*' I told Sophie, flipping through the dictionary I'd started carrying in my pocket. *'Mais, je ne connais pas quelle est le profonde* – oh shit – deep? how deep *il sont.'*

She nodded understanding, and like me, now speaking a sort of Franglais, said, *'Nous traverson… nous allons à… across… la route.'*

She waved her arms to indicate the road. *'Nous ne…'* she struggled a minute, peering at the book, 'cannot… go back.'

She was right. Turning back meant a detour of half a day and probably spending the night on the open moors. The damp mists of the late afternoon were settling in like a clammy blanket that promised a cold, chill night. The soggy surface of the moor was impossible to pitch the tent on anyway, and, to top it all, we couldn't turn the car round – there simply wasn't room.

As we stood, weighing up what to do next, Souris barked and I heard Gray's voice. I looked up to find him and Misty standing at the top of the hill on the far side of the flooded road. For a moment, I forgot we were in trouble. Both horses stood framed against the late afternoon sky as though they were carved from its cloudy greyness, the gilding of the fading sun lighting up the edges of their bodies. They looked as beautiful as anything I'd ever imagined, like the day we'd first seen them. Hope came back to me – they were there to help.

Gray knew he was cool so he stood a moment silhouetted against the skyline, like a movie star posing for the camera. Then he called out again and hurtled down the hill towards the flood. Misty rippled down behind him, a sleek cloud pouring over the landscape. Laurent started to laugh delightedly at their careering passage over the boggy hillside, leaping and swerving over and around the rocks. Gray was tossing his head and Misty was bucking and I was sure they were doing it to brighten us all up. Souris started yapping, I was laughing and Sophie, after a moment's hesitation, threw her head back and cheered them on. It was the first time I'd seen her laugh.

Once they reached the water, after snorting and spooking, fooling about a bit, Gray pawed at the lapping tideline, while Misty waded in a little way. I suddenly panicked, realising they were going to cross. 'No,' I shouted over to them, starting to wade in myself, '– go back, you pillocks, you'll get hurt.'

But Sophie grabbed my arm and gabbled away at me, waving at the horses, and I staggered out, knowing there was nothing I could do if they got in trouble. She made me look again and, having no option,

I watched. I began to reckon then that my role in life was to be open-mouthed with amazement and I was developing a real talent for it. My jaw dropped so far I was conscious of the hinges swinging like a cat-flap as I watched my friends turn into action-horses.

They waded in, side-by-side, and I swear they were working as a team. They both angled outwards as they moved forward until each one found the edge of the road. Then they started to move across, testing as they went where the safest crossing was. More than once one of them stopped to place, replace, a hoof then snort and move in a bit, away from danger, where the road had collapsed, I guessed. Soon they were over their knees, then over their shoulders, ploughing steadily though. Once, Misty missed her footing but instead of plunging under the water, she went staggering up the higher ground that had once been the moorland edge of the road. She floundered a bit, bogged down, then with a grunt and a huge lurching effort, she found the road and pushed onwards, silt muddying the water around her. Gray's long mane was floating out around him as he stretched his neck out, working against the pull of the tide, but he never quite needed to swim. I looked at the four-wheel-drive, measuring it against the height of Gray's shoulder.

'They're showing us we can get across,' I told Sophie, flipping through my dictionary and showing it to her. '*Ils sont* pointing out *le rue*… or something like that.'

She nodded and Laurent, who had climbed up on the car, was cheering. '*Viens ici, Graay. Viens ici, Mistee !*' he shouted. '*Les chevaux ont bien fait! Bravo!*'

He was waving his arms about, his short stocky figure bouncing with enthusiasm, pulling his t-shirt out from his shorts to show a little chubby belly. I'd never seen him so comical or excited before and he made Sophie and me start laughing and urging the horses on too. By the time they lurched out, water streaming off them, their flanks were heaving and they stood with their heads down to get their breath back. I found the sweat-scraper in my saddle-bags and went over them both with it, sweeping the water off them. They looked wonderful, sleekly shining wet, but then they went to roll in the damp moorland and when they stood up, shaking and snorting, they were covered from head to foot in thick wet peat.

'Look at the state of you two,' I shook my head at them, and gave them Kendal Mint Cake. 'What a pair of scruffs!'

Sophie and I were already tying down the canvas cover on the pickup as tight as we could, checking all the windows and doors were tight shut, then we debated over who should drive – she was better at it, but I found it easier.

'You,' I said. 'If I stall it in the middle, we've had it.' I mimed the car shuddering to a halt and us going under the water and she nodded, rolling her eyes, a characteristic gesture reserved for commenting on my uselessness. She was grinning though, so I didn't mind. I was concerned about the rear end of the huge vehicle getting washed off the road, so I climbed on the back, though I doubted my additional weight would help much. But there wasn't much else I could do, so I rode on the tailgate, poised to jump in the water, like a gnat ready to help an elephant.

As we were about to move off, Gray and Misty, who'd been refuelling on the tough wiry grass, suddenly stormed up, all tossing heads and rolling eyes.

'Don't you start,' I told them. 'It's bad enough when she does it. What have I done now?'

Then I realised what their plan was – did horses have plans? It seemed they did. They trotted past the car and each took position on the widest part of the road, starting to wade back.

'*Ils nous*…. show the way…' Sophie shouted. '*Allons-y!*' She started the car, closed her window tight, and sitting up as high as she could on her booster cushion, drove after them. I felt her push the car into low ratio and slowly, but without pause, she moved into the water.

If we stall, we're dead, I thought, we'll lose everything. But Sophie didn't stall. She kept the revs up enough to push through the waves, almost up to my feet in the first few yards along the drowned road. The horses showed where the edges were, their manes floating like seaweed on top of the water, and she steered the car like a ship between them, taking care not to get too close. I heard Laurent shout as water started to seep under the doors, but Sophie shouted something back at him and kept going. Souris started barking and she shouted at him to shut-up. The car was coughing and spluttering and for a moment I thought it would die on us, but it took heart again. Then we were past the half-way point and it was a little shallower. Things were looking good until a wave rolled up from nowhere and knocked Gray off the path. He staggered and lurched and then he was swimming.

'Keep going!' I yelled, seeing Sophie disorientated by the loss of a marker. Misty called in distress but pushed on and Sophie returned her attention to her task. I turned to look for Gray and my heart lurched as, swimming strongly back towards the road, he was caught up sharp and disappeared under the water. He emerged spluttering and snorting, but was caught and dragged under again. I was in the water in a moment, wading as I landed on the road, up to my waist, then swimming. It was so cold my breath caught with shock and I felt the wellies filling until they were sucked from my feet. Gray repeatedly surfaced and went under, causing huge waves, and I realised he was reaching the end of something that was hauling him back down again. I got to him with difficulty because he was creating so much chaos. He whickered softly to me, struggling to be calm.

'Well done, lad,' I told him, holding on to the mane at his withers to keep myself steady. If he stayed still, he could keep his head above water, but when he tried to swim out of the tangle, he got hauled under. I found my Swiss Army knife, and, able to see that his front legs were clear, I made my way down his back, following the line of his leg as far as I could. But he had to keep thrashing it around to stop from going under and I couldn't get a grip. The waves were more active as the wind got up and the light was failing. I could hear Laurent shouting and registered that the others had reached the shore safely. I took a deep breath and plunged under the water, holding Gray's thrusting leg as tightly as I could.

Before his swimming action flung me off and back to the surface, I felt that a piece of fencing from the edge of the road was tangled around his hoof. I could feel blood, a warm stream in the cold water, flowing from his leg, and the biting thinness of the wire tightening with every movement.

As I surfaced, I grabbed hold of his head. 'You've got to keep still,' I told him. 'You'll go under, for a moment, then I'll get you free.'

I didn't think Gray understood English. But I'd come to know that when it mattered, we understood each other in a way that defied explanation. Right then, it saved us. He looked at me with his long-lashed eyes, rubbed his head on me and stopped swimming. His heavy body sank slowly under the water and the memory of him disappearing woke me in a cold sweat long after. I took another huge breath and dived down. I didn't try to open my eyes – the water was murky with his thrashing about – so I relied on feel, going hand over hand down his leg, completely still now, until I reached the hoof. He felt like a dead creature, his other legs on the ground, but his tail floating around my face and his body swaying, listing towards me as the tide moved him. I tried not to panic, putting the knife in my pocket and holding his foot steady in one hand as I started to unwind the wire. My hands were numb with cold, bleeding too, and my lungs bursting. It seemed I was getting nowhere, but then the wire moved a little. As I loosened the loops that had tightened around his foot, blood streamed out, viscous in the water, then he was free. I shoved him hard as a signal and pushed myself off him, so he wouldn't catch me as he thrust upwards. Then everything went black.

CHAPTER 10

I came round with Souris licking my face, feeling as though Gray had been tap-dancing on my head. Sophie's elaborate mime suggested that he had, and I gathered that he'd knocked me out as he kicked himself free. But then he'd come back for me and I'd wrapped myself around his body as he hauled us both out of the water. I never did remember that part. It seemed I'd been unconscious for a while and it was dark when I woke, feeling sick and dizzy. Sophie had tended to Gray's leg and got quite cross when I wanted to check it. She'd done a good job of cleaning and bandaging my hands, so I apologised and went over to my horse. He was lying down, grazing in bed, and whinnied as I dropped onto the grass beside him. I put my arms round him and hugged him.

'Both safe now, lad,' I told him, unnecessarily, but he knew it was for lack of something more profound to say and rubbed his head on me.

I'd started shaking by then but Sophie had a fire burning and she went into action, hustling me over to get warm, making me change my clothes and dry my hair. She'd towelled the horses down then thrown a blanket over Gray and given them both Kendal Mint Cake. I began to wonder if horses got tooth-decay but reckoned that it was the nearest thing to sweet, hot tea that we could offer them. I gladly let Sophie take charge of me while I concentrated on the pounding in my head. I thought, in a distant sort of way without concern, that I might be concussed and sat in a daze all evening, while she fed me and fussed me. Then I was sick three times and she told me off as though I'd done it to be difficult. I didn't care though. She was scared but I

85

was all dreamy and content. It was the strangest feeling. I knew she was worried and really wanted to reassure her, but I couldn't speak. I lay there feeling so happy and comfortable that I thought I might float away. Words were something other people had and Dad was keeping in me company, so what was there to worry about?

I dozed on and off, vaguely aware that Sophie was bullying me into moving, then realised I was in the back seat of the car lying down and we were driving again. I watched the night passing through the window. The evening mist had cleared to a dark blue sky I wanted to gaze at forever. Dad and I were talking about going hiking across Canada the next summer and there were some French people talking in the background, perhaps on the TV. I wondered where I was, but it didn't really matter because Dad said I needed some rest. So I drifted along contentedly, asking him if I could have one of those new backpacks before we went to Canada and if he thought we'd see bears…

'Joel! Jo, wake up, love.'

A familiar voice cut into my dreaming, and I struggled to surface. I waved my arms irritably and said, 'Go away, it's Saturday.'

'Jo, love, it's Moth. Wake up.'

'There's no school,' I protested. 'Switch the telly off, Moth, why's it in French?'

'Can you help me, Sophie? Here, Ginny, love, take his feet.'

I was manhandled out of the car and tumbled onto the ground with my arms and legs all tangled. Struggling to work out where Moth and Ginny had come from, I started to cry. Then Ginny was climbing on me, Moth was kissing me and I realised we were home. I don't quite remember how I made it up to my own bed, but I had a couple of days then – I think it was a couple – of more drifting, being sick and knowing only the galloping of hooves through my skull while Dad rambled on happily about grizzly bears in the background.

When I eventually surfaced, a lump like a hillock on the side of my head, I found Moth sitting by my bed. She was knitting and I watched for a bit before she looked up and said,

'Hello, sleepy-head. You're back, are you?'

I stretched and yawned. 'Looks like it. What happened? How did we get home?'

'Sophie and the horses brought you home. She realised you were badly hurt and so did Gray, I think. They drove all through the night, with Gray leading the way and Sophie following the map if she got confused or he tried to take her across country and you all arrived back here around dawn.'

She came over to hug me tight and give me a kiss that resounded round my brain. 'I nearly died when I saw you, love. But, Jo, that's a feisty little girl.'

'I know that well enough. Is Laurent all right?'

'Oh, he's fine. He's a dear.'

We looked at each other for a long moment, measuring all that had happened since we saw each other last. The knowledge that, like Dad, I'd been kicked in the head was too frightening to address.

Then she said, 'Well done, Jo. I'm proud of you.'

'I didn't get any fish,' I said.

She smiled. 'I think we'll manage for a bit without the fish.'

So I was home again and a new sort of normal was established around me being ill. Ginny had to move in with Moth so Sophie and Laurent could have the second bedroom and I still had my little box-room. I think that, because Sophie and Laurent arrived with me only half-conscious in the back seat of the pick-up, Moth and Ginny never really had time to assimilate the fact that I'd brought strangers and a car-load of supplies back until they'd already moved in and the car was unpacked.

When I was up and about again, I found that Sophie had inventoried everything we brought back with Moth, while Ginny and Laurent had divided all the clothes between us. The food and tools had been stored away and the first job I took on was putting up the poly-tunnel. Before that, while I was still a bit sore and headachey, I spent a couple of days wandering around, getting my bearings. It felt strange being back, as though I'd been gone a long time. So I walked the boundaries slowly, letting the sun seep through to warm my bones and trailing Souris and Laurent for a while, then Gray, then a couple of the sheep. They took it in turns to keep an eye on me then discreetly drifted off, letting me visit Dad's grave alone. The horses were loafing on the mountain with the sheep and cattle so the field was empty, resting for winter, growing long and full of wild flowers. I sat by Dad, feeling his loss like a great gaping hole in my chest.

I'd been to say 'Hello' to the horses one-by-one on my walk round and I could pick them all out now, different coloured shapes on the hillside. Coming back to them felt as much family as coming back to Moth and Ginny. I'd come home but how could there be any home without Dad? I talked aloud to him, as I'd done on my nights alone, asking him what would happen to us. Was this it now? We'd make a better garden, improve the fields, tend the animals for food and wool and the pleasure of having them. We'd read till we knew all our books by heart. We'd make a smoke-house, maybe dig an ice-pit in the winter. I'd make fishing trips down to the coast from time to time, the others would come with me as they got older. Moth would be like the old woman who lived in the shoe as we all grew around her. We could manage, we could live here indefinitely. But was that it? And if it was, did it matter?

It was all a question of perspective. In the world we'd come from, I'd have gone to university and maybe travelled then Ginny would have done the same. I'd have probably ended up living at least some distance from my family, working as – what? I'd fancied something to do with marine biology but I'd never really decided – well, something useful anyhow. I'd been brought up to think that we should try to make a contribution to the world. I'd have had foreign holidays and met my friends for a drink or the cinema, had a few girlfriends. Most likely, I'd have met 'the One' pretty young, like Moth and Dad and settled down quickly. That would have been fine. She'd have been tallish, with a quick smile and she'd have liked hiking and travelling and swimming, as I did, and she'd have liked things I'd never much thought about – theatre, dancing – and I'd have come to like them too.

She'd have laughed at my collection of glasses from the Hard Rock Cafés I'd been to on travels with my family, but she'd have gone out of her way to make sure I added to it wherever we went. I'd have complained when she wanted to go to the ballet, but I'd still have gone with her. We'd have seen the world together, sent postcards and emails home, moved a few times perhaps, so we could improve our careers. Then we'd have made Moth and Dad grandparents and they'd have groaned and said they were getting old but been delighted.

The lost future rolled away across the meadow leaving me behind. I was here for good, unless the world started up again and became something we could understand. I would never part from Moth and Ginny without some surety that they were safe. But there was no growth here. There was only living from day to day. I'd grown up in a world that said you had to develop a life – learn, work, earn, settle, improve, move on, generate and regenerate. In the end though, did it all boil down to the same thing? Did it make any difference if I travelled the world in a plane, or trekked the countryside on Gray? Did it matter if I went to university and studied marine biology or wandered along the beach and learned how it worked by observation? Was that growth too? I didn't know. And there wasn't much choice anyhow. I thought of the dust – which I hadn't yet mentioned to Moth – and knew that whatever we had here, we were alive, while thousands, millions, of people were dead. Suddenly, getting the poly-tunnel up and planting some seeds seemed as worthwhile as getting a degree and a finding a good job. And I thought a lot about the horses. Were they really special or was this the way horse-human relations were supposed to be and it was us who'd changed? I'd never have had the chance to consider that in the old world.

We'd settled into a new pattern before I told Moth about the dust. The others had gone to bed, after an evening of French conversation. We spoke English all morning, French all afternoon and in the evenings we played Scrabble or one of Sophie's being-someone-else games. We were all learning well and rattled away to each other in Franglais much of the time. That evening we'd all been pupils in school while

Sophie was the teacher. We were a rebellious class, though she kept us in line, and there'd been as much laughing as learning, so as Laurent, then Ginny and at last Sophie trailed off to bed, Moth and I were left feeling comfortable and contented.

Then, as we sat there quietly together, the mood shifted and she said, 'Tell me what you saw, Jo. What's out there?'

So I told her – the visitor centre, the abandoned emptiness of the landscape. The town with its cars and piles of dust. The madman – Sophie and Laurent's father – she knew he existed already, but I told her now about the destruction and the fires. I didn't tell her about the baby-dust in the buggy, because she'd developed a bulge below her waist and got into the habit of stroking it when she was thoughtful. My little brother or sister was becoming a part of our lives and I couldn't bear drawing the connection between him or her and the pile of dust with its teddy patiently waiting. But I told her everything else.

She listened without interrupting or asking any questions, then sat quietly for a long while when I'd finished. She reached out for my hand and held it between both hers, then she smiled and said, 'Our little friend is on the move. Do you want to feel him?'

I nodded and she put my hand over the swell of her waist and I felt a soft fluttering sensation, like a signal tapped out from under a blanket and thought of a small foot or hand trying to get my attention.

'What's it like?' I asked. 'Knowing you've got another person in there?'

Moth smiled. 'A little scary,' she said. 'I'm hoping that midwife turns up before he wants to come out. But it's good too, Jo. We have to find a future for ourselves and for him. He'll make our lives harder but babies bring a lot of love with them and he'll help us plan.'

I nodded, understanding. 'I can't help wondering what we do next, Moth. Do we just go on, living here, forever? Or are we waiting for something to happen that will get life back to normal again?'

Moth stroked my hair back, the way she did when she needed to remind us both that even though I was growing up, I'd always be her first baby. 'I don't know, love. I'm not sure the life we lost will ever get going again. There must be people out there and what about the rest of the world? Is it all piles of dust? If it's not, someone will turn up and I don't know whether we'll like that. If it is, then it'll be a long time before the people who are left can start rebuilding. But Jo, I thought about this a lot while you were away, what we're doing here isn't really that different from before. We work to have enough to eat and time to enjoy each other's company in the evenings. There are fewer companions to choose from and no television or radio, we can't go on a foreign holiday and we're limited in what we have to read or what work we do. But when you boil it all down, it was always about working hard enough to take up the leisure we chose.'

Hearing her echoing the thoughts I'd had myself meant I could share them.

'I miss my friends,' I said. 'Having people of my own age to talk to would be good. But most of the other stuff was about keeping in touch with them really – knowing what's cool to wear, or to see at the cinema, who's drooling over who, who's in trouble at school, what's hot in music. I miss that far less than I would have thought.' I suddenly realised something – 'When Sophie showed us the batteries and the Discmans she'd brought, I thought we'd all go mad for them, but I keep forgetting to play mine. It's been by my bed ever since she gave it to me. I got my CDs out of the caravan and listened to them all on the first night. Then I've not touched it since. Have you?'

Moth smiled. 'I gave mine to Ginny.'

We looked at each other a minute then I said, 'My CDs seemed sort of dated – like watching an old film, but not really old – like, do you remember how if you saw a film that was maybe made ten or fifteen years ago, it looked more odd than an old black and white one? It was like that.'

'If nothing had changed, you'd have moved on in taste a long time ago, Jo.'

'Does that mean that if someone came along tomorrow and said, "Just press this button, and you can go back, like all this never happened", that we'd be disappointed when we got home?'

Moth was silent for a while. 'Aside from having the people we loved back – and we'd do it for that reason alone – I think within weeks we'd be thinking life was all routine again, and bad news in the papers, and worrying about having enough money, and feeling pressurised. And we were happy, Jo, we had a good life. Dad and I had decent jobs and a nice house, smallish mortgage – but what did we talk about, once you and Ginny had gone through uni?'

'Selling up and moving to a house in the country so you and Dad could work part-time and have a slower life.'

We both sat silently for a moment, realising, perhaps for the first time, that in the way of irony, we now had exactly what they had planned for the future. Except that Dad was dead, Moth was pregnant, and the world had ended. Aside from that, it was the same.

CHAPTER 11

We'd been back for nearly a month when everything changed again. It amazed us all how quickly having Sophie and Laurent living with us became the way it had always been. The real Sophie showed up more often and Laurent started coming out of himself as he developed a fascination with the poultry. Collecting eggs was his idea of a good time and his delight that they appeared like magic in the nesting boxes never faltered. Daybreak and Moonrise, two of the horses I'd got to know least, adopted the newcomers at once. Daybreak was only a youngster, so she followed Laurent around like a second dog, and he learned to ride on Sophie's Moonrise. Sophie already knew how to ride, so set about showing me how it should be done. Of course, there were enough saddles and bridles when we came to need them. Gray and I liked to lounge around heckling when Sophie and Moon trotted past like ballet dancers, just to show we were happy with our own casual style. I got beaten up quite a lot for that and when Moonrise set about Gray, I guessed he was getting his own come-uppance for sniggering.

We worked hard too, growing, gathering and garnering as though farming was all we'd ever done. Sophie and Laurent added far more than just two extra people to our group. We all agreed that we felt a lot less alone. I found a contentment of sorts coming over me as I stopped being bewildered by Dad's absence, though that made me sad too. I didn't want to get used to being without him, but there was no choice and we all felt him around from time to time. It wasn't the same as having him there alive, but we still liked it and someone saying, 'Dad thinks we could try such-and-such', happened quite often. He'd become like the horses – inexplicable but very welcome, and both Sophie and Laurent accepted his strange presence without any signs of surprise.

Gray and I went on another exploratory ride, only for a long day this time, and came back with some fish from a loch in the next glen but one to ours, so small and tucked away that we hadn't known it was there. That was a good find. We salted the fish and built a smoke house too, which took a lot of coughing and spluttering to get right. The warm damp environment of the poly-tunnel started coming into its own and the garden was flourishing. The leaves turned gold, fluttering around for the goats to chase and the evenings were getting chilly so I started covering up the seedlings for late winter crops. Moth got bigger and we all spoke French and English interchangeably. Ginny and Laurent had birthdays in the same week. We gave Laurent the clutch of chicks that turned up on the day with the hen we thought had gone missing, and Ginny the shiny new bridle I found in the workshop for Poppa Horse. We didn't ask questions. We simply lived.

Then one morning, Sophie came in from collecting the eggs with Laurent, looking pale and flustered.

'Our father is here,' she said.

'Is he,' I hesitated, 'you know – wild?'

She looked at me as Moth got to her feet. 'I don't know.'

Moth placed a hand on Sophie's shoulder.

'We'll all go,' she said. 'Ginny, you keep an eye on Laurent and stay near the house. Sophie, Joel, come with me.'

We went out to meet him like the townsfolk of Hicksville facing up to a gunslinger, knowing he was too much for us, even all together, if he went crazy, but hoping for strength in numbers. I asked Moth quietly if I should carry some sort of weapon, thinking of but not wanting to mention the gun. She shook her head.

'The world's changed, Jo. If we go out armed, we're thinking it's the same. And he's their father.'

So we went out empty-handed, a child, a half-grown boy and a pregnant woman, to meet the man who'd rampaged through Corrycreag like a hurricane.

All his rage seemed to have gone as he stood hesitating by our gate and I noticed that the horses had come down from the hill. They were some distance away watching him, Poppa Horse in front, standing very alert with his head up, on guard.

Moth had put on a big coat of Dad's and didn't look so obviously pregnant, which I guessed made her feel stronger. Sophie surprised me by taking my hand as we followed and her fingers felt as small and vulnerable as Ginny's. I squeezed them and said,

'It's okay.'

She nodded, but she was so tense her head hardly moved.

We all stood for a long moment, a short length of path between us. Moth, with me alongside her and Sophie behind holding my hand, the two little ones on the step and the man behind the gate, with his big, long-fingered hands clenching and unclenching on it nervously. Although he was quiet and uneasy, he looked as wild as I remembered and I wouldn't have wanted to meet him without warning. His hair was long and as untamed as a lion's mane, greying like his eyebrows and great matted beard. He stank. Even from half-way down the path, I could smell the rank odour of stale liquor, an unwashed body and filthy clothes. But he'd tried to tidy himself up, I could see that too. Though his hair was chaotic, he'd tried to smooth it down and his face and hands were clean enough to show how filthy his neck and wrists were. His clothes were rags, he looked half-starved and his dark eyes, which were like his children's, were red-rimmed. But he didn't look dangerous. Wild and alarming, but not dangerous.

'Hello,' said Moth, and it sounded a ridiculous greeting but I couldn't have come up with anything better. 'I'm Ellen Anthony.'

The man bowed his head, a strangely old-fashioned gesture, and his every movement was full of anxiety. I realised he was afraid of her or perhaps of facing his children.

'*Bonjour,*' he said. 'I am Pierre Dupont, the father of Sophie and Laurent.'

Then Sophie gave a sobbing little cry and ran to fling open the gate, launching herself at him. Laurent wasn't far behind and all three clung together crying. But once the first rush of emotion was over, the children backed away from him.

'I am sorry,' he said, half to them and half to Moth. 'I've taught you all to fear me. I will go if you wish, but I needed to see that my children were safe.'

'They are safe,' said Moth. 'There's no need for you to go. But I need to know that all these children in my care – and I include Sophie and Laurent – will be safe if you stay.'

He was shaking really badly by now and I thought he might pass out, but he nodded. 'I've never harmed anyone,' he said, and Sophie, who'd retreated back behind Moth, said, 'It's true, Moth, he never hurt us. We were scared because he went like a madman, but he never hurt us.'

She'd never called Moth 'Moth' before, and I saw that, although she loved her father, in doing it she aligned herself with us. We offered the security this wild man couldn't and I felt for her. I couldn't imagine what it would have been like to feel that Dad was unreliable, maybe dangerous. I'd been about to say, 'This nutter swung a cricket bat at me', but I kept quiet, put my arm around Sophie and gave her a quick hug.

Moth was weighing things up. 'Come in,' she said. 'You need food, a bath, clean clothes.'

He nodded, humble and grateful, following behind her like a penitent, his head lowered. As I stood back to let him go into the house in front of me, I noticed a small incident among the horses. Sunrise, Daybreak and Moonrise's sister, was agitating to cross the yard but Poppa Horse had his ears back and wouldn't let her go. He stamped his hoof and she swung her head a few times, frustrated, but then accepted his leadership and backed down. She didn't go though, and when the others drifted back to grazing, she hung around on the edge of the yard.

I watched a moment, then went inside to find Pierre seated at the table while everyone watched him eat. I could see that his impulse was to throw himself on the food, because he was starving. But he made a big effort to be quiet and controlled about it, eating slowly and saying nothing. Laurent's eyes were very bright and he was yearning towards his dad so badly it was almost visible, a cloud of longing that reached out to envelop the ragged figure. Pierre looked up and then leaned forward with hesitation, glancing at Moth and then Sophie to see if it was all right. He reached out hands like the claws on a digger, cradled Laurent's head and kissed him with real gentleness on his forehead. I could see Moth getting a bit misty and felt much the same myself.

'I have missed my children,' Pierre said, as though the gesture needed explanation.

Moth nodded. 'I see that.'

She galvanised us all into action then. Ginny was sent to make sure there were towels and soap, while I added fuel to the stove to get the water hot enough for a bath. Sophie had to find nail and hair scissors while Moth went upstairs and came down with some of Dad's clothes. That stopped Ginn and me in our tracks and a huge surge of resentment welled up inside me. Ginn opened her mouth to protest then saw Moth's face at the moment I did – she was in so much pain that we both clamped our distress down and carried on with what we'd been asked to do.

While her dad was in the bath, Sophie, for the first time, started to talk about him.

'We were like you,' she began, 'all alone on the far islands. We were on holiday but Papa was working – he can make anything and he was working on a wind-farm – an…' She sought a word for a moment, flicking through the dictionary in her hands. '…engineer. Papa is an engineer. He was called here all the way from home because he is the very best.' She hesitated a moment. 'Maman threw him out because he…' – another hesitation – 'had a habit.' We all floundered with this a moment, until Moth said gently, 'A drinking habit?' and Sophie nodded.

'So, when he came here to work,' she went on, 'he didn't come back. Laurent and I came to holiday with him. It was far away from anyone else, just the three of us for two weeks, but then we needed to buy food. So we drove across the island to the little town and found that everyone had gone and left us behind. We were stranded. Papa got very drunk, for weeks, and we had to take care of him. Then we managed to pour away all the drink that was left and he came round. He was very angry at first but then I… bullied him, into getting us off the island. We rowed – it was dangerous. He showed me how to start and run a car and I knew much already, because he'd lived in a sort of camp on the island. It was very,' she struggled again, 'primitive – very primitive – to keep himself away from the alcohol. He taught us to survive on what there was around.' She reflected a moment. 'Then we took cars and went from place to place, fuelling them from abandoned garages, changing them for better as we went. So we survived and I tried to keep him away from places with liquor. He'd been sober for some time before that.'

Moth nodded. 'It's hard once the sobriety is broken, I think.'

Sophie looked at her. 'Yes. He taught me all he knew but he did it so he could drink again. I was angry with him because I wanted him to take care of me and Laurent. But he got drunk every time we found a town – even the small villages had a *tabac* or a liquor shop. When we reached the port and realised there was no-one there either, he went wild, like Joel saw him. It was too much. I took Laurent and set up home in the little tea-house. We had been there some time – I am unsure how long – when Joel arrived. We liked it there and he left us alone, though he knew where we were. I woke up once and he was watching us sleep. I mapped the town, finding out where all the best things were, then chose the car,' she nodded through the window to where it sat on the yard, 'and started packing. I trusted someone would come – or else we would go alone, Laurent and I.' She smiled at me then, the real Sophie. 'But then my friend Joel arrived.' She always called me Joel, never Jo.

When Pierre came down wearing Dad's clothes, I had to go and wash-up to get away from the sight. I crashed about in the kitchen and no-one shouted at me to keep the racket down, because I guess I was giving out strong signals that they should leave me alone. When I came back, Moth was cutting Pierre's hair, while Sophie stood looking as angry as I felt, her arms folded across her chest like a fierce teacher, ready to give him detention if he moved a toe out-of-line. He'd trimmed his finger-nails and beard while he was upstairs and once Moth had finished tidying him up, he looked raw, all rough edges, like an unruly bush that had been clipped back. He looked odd too, in Dad's clothes. He was about Dad's height but Dad, before he got sick, had been big in a strong-boned, fit-from-lots-of-walking, sort of way. Pierre seemed to have been thrown together from of a load of spare parts and his arms and legs attached with puppet strings. Dad dressed like the outdoors type but in his clothes, Pierre looked like some tortured artist, adrift and confused. And he'd clearly been through any number of mills, his skin stretched over the bones of his face like too little pasty rolled out over a wide dish. If he laughed, it would have ripped right across. But I reckoned it'd been some time since he laughed and it didn't seem likely any day soon either.

Moth was all action and set us to sorting out the caravan, which we used as a store, so he could sleep there. I was in a bad mood all day, full of complicated resentment towards this big ugly drunk who'd turned up. Yet I loved Sophie and Laurent like family by then and they needed him. Sophie wasn't going to forgive her father easily and her dark face was a featureless mask whenever she looked at him. But Laurent was full of all the wordless need for his dad I still felt in losing my own. For their sake, I had to accept that he now lived with us.

Sunset was in an uneasy mood all day too. She kept hesitating on the edge of the yard, while the others hung around keeping her company. We all went over to ask what was wrong but she stayed agitated. Pierre seemed vaguely aware of her but he was so busy following Sophie round like a guilty puppy that had wet the floor, that he didn't really have time to notice anything else.

Towards the end of the day, I went down to visit Dad, and while I was sitting there, complaining bitterly to him about the newcomer, Pierre wobbled down the path towards me. He stood by the gate and, because I was too bad-tempered to look up even though I knew he was there, he coughed twice politely.

'May I join you, Joel?' he asked.

He pronounced my name 'Zho-el' and I liked the sound of it so that softened me up a bit but I shrugged, all moody teenager, thinking, *Just piss off*, as loudly as I could. Then I felt bad so I moved over to make room for him to sit on the seat we'd made out of an old railway sleeper.

'This is a grave,' he said carefully. 'Who lies here?'

Who lies here? The foreign-sounding phrase seemed to echo round my head and it struck me that, underneath the wreckage, there was a very polite man sitting next to me.

'My Dad,' I said. 'He died in the spring.'

'You miss him.'

I looked at the grave. 'Every hour of every day.'

Pierre nodded understanding then there was silence, until he said, 'Thank you, Zhoel. You didn't speak up this morning and say that I lashed out at you, when we – ran into one another, in the town.'

I glanced at him, thinking he looked like hell after a heavy night out. 'It mattered to Sophie that my mother let you stay.'

'I meant you no harm. You frightened me when you crashed into me and I was – not myself.'

'I bet I didn't frighten you half as much as you frightened me,' I said, my hackles rising, and he nodded acceptance. 'I am sorry.'

We sat a bit longer and, as I was thinking about returning to the house, Sunset came careering down the path, calling as though she'd seen one of the others coming back from an outing. But they were all right behind her. I got up to go towards her, my hands spread wide to calm her down, but she swerved round me and went to Pierre, whickering and whinnying as though he was her foal.

'Hello, little girl,' he said then went on in French too fast for me to keep up. He stroked her neck while she rubbed her head on his chest and whatever she'd been waiting all day for him to do, it seemed that he'd done it, so she could – well, welcome him home, maybe. Was it talking to me? Or finding out about Dad? Perhaps he'd needed to redeem himself in some way before Poppa Horse would let his daughter make friends with this big calamity of a man. But now, Sunny had adopted him and I reckoned that between her and Sophie, Pierre was going to get his life in order, whether he liked it or not.

CHAPTER 12

Seeing Pierre start to make a place for himself was the hardest thing for me since Dad died. The baby was part of Dad so he was welcome and Sophie and Laurent I hadn't minded at all. But Pierre, well, that was different. Having him at the meal table, seeing him around the place, occasionally catching sight of Dad's clothes out of the corner of my eye and having my heart leap – that took some getting used to. I tried to be friendly, but I wasn't very good at it and sometimes I was plain surly with him. In some ways, it was worse because he made himself invaluable from the first day.

He worked like a man trying to pay off his debts in sweat. I'd never seen anyone so doggedly able to keep going until whatever task he'd set himself was completed. He mended the ridge tiles, fixed the leaking roof, helped me weather-proof the poly-tunnel for winter. He even dug up and replaced the crumbling terracotta drains with plastic ones he recycled from an abandoned cottage in the hamlet. He repaired the boiler and the septic tank and the goat shed and the sagging fences and fixed up a bike he found for Ginny. Then he disappeared into the workshop for days of hammering, pounding and bolting till the air was metal-tanged. He evaded all queries as to what he was doing until he emerged to mount his secret creation on the roof. We all gathered to watch in bewilderment until I suddenly got it.

'Bloody hell!' I said. 'It's a windmill.'

'Is it just for fun?' Ginny called up and he smiled down at her, a rare sight.

'Just for fun? I make nothing just for fun.'

'You made my bike,' she reminded him and he nodded, climbing down the ladder slowly. 'Aside from your bike, I make nothing just for fun.'

It wasn't just for fun. By supper-time he had it powering a generator and everyone thought he was a hero. Except me. I couldn't have made us a windmill.

'I'm sick of him, Moth,' I complained the next morning. 'He thinks he can take Dad's place here and mine too.'

'Yours? How's he taking yours?' Her tone of voice said I was on dodgy ground.

'Okay, so I know I never wanted to be the only man here, but I didn't want bumping to one side by someone like him, either.'

Moth stirred her tea and the clink of metal on crockery rang like a bell warning me I'd already gone too far. 'He's much more capable than I'd expected,' she said. 'I thought you were impressed with his windmill and how can you mind him taking so much weight off your shoulders?'

'Oh, his windmill's well cool, of course it is, but he's a flamin' disaster too, Moth. Have you noticed how his hands shake when he's not doing something with them?'

'Yes, I have. That's hardly a reason to dislike him.'

'And I hate how Dad's clothes hang off him. Dad was a fitness-freak and he died, and now Pierre, with his criminally abused liver, is wearing his clothes and looking like a mad scarecrow. And he abandoned Sophie and Laurent but now he thinks he can just come back and pick up where he left off.'

'That's nonsense. He's doing penance moment by moment.'

I'd regretted starting this and was wondering how I could get away, but Moth hadn't done.

'You're being unfair. Jo, you really are.'

'He's just worming his way in, Moth. He thinks he'll make himself indispensable, because he knows you've got reservations about him.'

'I had reservations about him, Joel. I don't anymore. He's a good man, troubled and shaky in every way, no doubt. But a good man.

You're just angry today because yesterday you let your guard down and started liking him. Well, I liked you better yesterday, sonny-Jim, I really did.'

She was right. I'd started to like him, in spite of myself. What was there not to like? He was gentle, polite and endlessly patient with the children. Ginny adored him from the moment she told him, 'Your face is prickly as a hedgehog's bottom!' and he replied, 'That is the fashion where I come from.' He was patient with me, even when I knew I'd hurt his feelings. I always felt bad when I did that, but Pierre never retaliated. He gave me his time, tried to make me smile, asked my advice and permission when he didn't have to and I soon had Dad niggling at my conscience. Like Sophie and Laurent, Pierre accepted his presence without question and that made me feel worse. So, though I dragged my feet, I went looking for Pierre and found him painting the living room.

I hung around in the doorway for a bit and he glanced at me. 'Ah, there you are. How does it look?'

I shrugged. 'Better, I guess. I'll give you a hand, if you like.'

'Sure, thanks. The wall behind the door needs scraping – there's a little damp bubbling the plaster in the corner. You could do that if you like.'

I said I would but didn't move because I needed to say my piece. Pierre started rooting through the toolbox for a scraper and I realised he knew and was afraid of hearing it. So I blurted it out. 'Dad says I'm being a git.'

I'd taken him by surprise. He raised his eyebrows, looking up. 'He does?'

'Because I get mad.'

'I understand that. I'm here and he is not.' He had found some paint scrapers and fine sandpaper and pushed them across the work-bench. 'You could tidy those if you like,' he said. 'Just a light sanding to sharpen the edges.'

I set to cleaning up the scrapers, glad of something to do.

'Dad says I should ask you to help me.'

'Of course. What do you need?'

I felt embarrassed then and he was glancing at me all worried again.

'I need a shave,' I said. 'I look a state. Dad showed me how to use a battery shaver but I've never needed it much before and now the batteries are dead.'

Pierre nodded, saying gravely, 'You too have a face like a hedgehog's bottom.'

That made me laugh. 'Hell, it sounds cool when you say it!'

'I am French. A cool accent is my heritage.' He smiled at me then and I said, 'I'm sorry I get mad.'

'Forget it. Shall I teach you to wet shave? Have you a razor?'

'I found one in the little shop down in the hamlet – it looks pretty dangerous, a real old-fashioned cut-throat type. I should have picked up some ordinary ones in Corrycreag.'

'The old type is better, once you have the hang of it. I can show you.'

We worked in silence for a while but then I couldn't stand it and had to get out of there. And that's how it was. Every time we shared a few moments of ease, I felt angry soon afterwards as though he'd tricked me. So, with Pierre alone, I was the sort of teenager I'd always sworn I wouldn't be – sullen, uncommunicative, all shrugs and what-do-I-care, when I did care, I cared about everything. That was the trouble. But he taught me to wet shave and when I was rude, he would regard me with quiet concern, as though I was the one who was hurting. I hated myself for being small and petty and so, by doing nothing, he wore me down. It was a good tactic and I couldn't help developing a grudging respect for him.

After he'd been with us for six weeks, he and Sophie went back to Corrycreag for more fuel and supplies. It was a tense couple of days because we all knew there was drink freely available there, but Sophie was determined they were going alone. Sunny wanted to go too – she watched over Pierre as tenderly as Sophie did severely. But it made sense for them to go in the pick-up even though he'd started riding, after walking alongside her for a while as though he wasn't good enough to get on her back. So Sunny and I stayed behind to fret while they were away. But Moth couldn't cope alone anymore, so we all held our breath for four days. They returned with Pierre in the pick-up and Sophie driving a small smart-car, which they'd brought because it hardly used any fuel and meant we could explore further without worrying too much about wasting it.

Sophie was so proud of her dad and he was so humbly delighted that he'd accomplished his mission without disgracing himself, that I started warming to him a bit more. They'd found a couple of guitars and some other instruments in the town, and it turned out he was a superb musician. I wondered how a man who had so many accomplishments managed to get into such a mess, but he'd certainly pulled himself together now. Evenings became more interesting and he started teaching me to play the guitar, while Sophie tooted along on a recorder and the little ones bashed remorselessly on tambourines and triangles, Moth covering her ears, laughing. They'd also come back with Christmas presents for everyone, which they hid away in the caravan, making secret plans together. Sophie had forgiven him and he was allowed to be her dad again.

We started preparing for Christmas early because Moth was a little vague over when the baby was due and we wanted everything ready in case he took us by surprise. Also, we needed to build up the Christmas mood to carry us through the absence of Dad, who'd always plunged into the seasonal celebrations with enormous enthusiasm. 'Dadding it' was the term Ginny and I used for any above-and-beyond level of commitment, so we Dadded Christmas, going overboard on everything.

Finding decorations became an important mission, so we trekked off on the horses in all directions in search of holly. Ginny and Pierre came back with a big bunch of mistletoe and he rigged it up over the swinging gate to the hay in the barn, so that a bell rang every time a horse went through. Ginny would go rushing out when she heard it and I reckoned our gang had more kisses than any other horses in history. Laurent and Ginny started making paper Santa hats for them all, which Poppa and Daybreak modelled patiently during the design phase. Ginny was worried that this would spoil the surprise of Christmas Day for them and I went out to find them both blindfold but unconcerned, chewing hay while the dynamic duo went about their work.

The mood of excitement built up. We had plenty of food, between the raids on the town and the harvest from the vegetable garden, and Moth even managed to make a Christmas cake. It was a good time, full of anticipation, with the scent of cooking and pine boughs filling the house and when it started to snow a few days before Christmas, Moth looked out of the window and said, 'I've made the cake – now here comes the icing.'

We all gathered around her to watch the flakes drifting softly down to blanket the yard and rest like baubles on Pierre's wild hair as he crossed the yard carrying a huge Yule log, cut to fit perfectly in the grate.

It snowed heavily for three days, making us all gleeful. Not only was it pretty and seasonal but it proved how well-managed everything was. We weren't just coping – we were doing pretty well. The animals were close to the house, we had electric light in the evenings from Pierre's windmill, there was plenty of hay, wood and food and we were as ready as we could be for the baby coming. I did worry sometimes that Moth had gone all through her pregnancy without a doctor to check her over, but she was very relaxed about it.

'I'm fine, Jo,' she said, and she looked it. In fact, she looked lovely. Her hair had grown long and the dullness had left her. She was lit by a poignant sort of happiness that, although Dad was gone, this child was a final gift from him to us all.

'I've been pregnant enough to know when everything's going well,' she told me. 'The baby's moving, I've not swollen up like a balloon, I'm getting plenty of rest.' She patted my cheek. 'I couldn't be more waited on or looked after. This baby's going to pop out like a pea from a pod.'

I preferred not to think about that bit, because I knew who'd have to be there to catch it. Sophie had found some books on birth in the town and Moth talked us through what would happen. Pierre deteriorated into a sort of jelly whenever the imminent event was mentioned, so he clearly wasn't going to be any use at all except that he could mind the kids. It was up to me and Sophie.

Christmas Day dawned to one of those perfect crisp snowy mornings with sunlight sparkling and long icicles everywhere. Before breakfast, Sophie and Pierre revealed their big surprise – brightly coloured Christmas stockings for everyone, stuffed with underwear, toiletries and chocolate, piled beneath the enormous tree we'd put up in the corner and laden with pine cones and decorations from the storeroom of Smith's in Corrycreag. Topping the tree was a star with a picture of a winged Poppa Horse in the centre, part-horse, part-angel, part-fairy, according to Ginny.

I wasn't sure how Poppa would feel about the fairy bit, but he seemed to like his hat. He ate it anyhow. The horses all wore their Santa hats with aplomb while they crunched biscuits shaped like carrots during our heartfelt rendition of 'We Wish you a Merry Christmas' then ate, chewed and trampled them. We stomped off through the snow to present the other animals with gift-wrapped buckets of treats before heading back to the house for breakfast and the rest of our presents. Soon there was the wrapping paper, also courtesy of Smith's, bundled up all over the living room with the wildly excited Souris tearing around worrying it into shreds.

For people living after the end of the world, we had plenty of presents. I doubted there was much left in Marks and Spencer's and everyone had daft wind-up toys as well as something they'd really missed. But the best things were the home-made presents, because we'd all planned and plotted and worked in secret for weeks on them. Carefully knitted scarves from Sophie with matching hats made by Moth, drawings from Ginny neatly mounted and framed by Pierre, hard-boiled eggs dyed pale colours by Laurent with Moth's help. Some had 'Mery Chrostmis' or 'Joyux Nell' laboriously spelt out on them in rather smudgy black felt-tip, while the rest had kisses on because he'd got tired. I made hand-bound journals for everyone with their names on. I'd sent Sophie on a mission in Corrycreag to the craft shop I'd spotted on my own visit there and she'd come back with treasure for me. I'd enjoyed making them but got embarrassed and tongue-tied seeing them unwrapped because everyone seemed delighted.

Pierre had made beautiful presents – wind-chimes that sparkled and jingled for Moth and the girls, a wooden cockerel weather-vane for Laurent to be mounted right outside his bedroom window and for me a tooled leather belt with a neat little pouch for a penknife fitted on it. He'd also made a cradle that was a work of art and brought tears to Moth's eyes. The man's abilities crowded up to be counted but he was even more nervous than I'd been, as though we might be disappointed. He grinned when he saw that we weren't, then the wrapping-paper-fight began, heralding a riot of food, singing and fooling around, crowned with the unveiling of an enormous box of disposable nappies.

Dad was there all day and that helped a lot. Moth moved around like a ship in full sail and Laurent kept telling us that she had a baby up her jumper, but we'd noticed. We sang all the favourite corny old Christmas songs after an enormous lunch then, as the light faded, everyone settled down to listen to Pierre play his guitar and sing French ballads.

When the little ones and Moth fell asleep in front of the fire, Sophie, Pierre and I went out to see to the animals for the night. The horses were restless and we watched them for a while, charging around under a clear sky crammed with stars, so that they were frosted with the snow raised by their own hooves.

Then Pierre, standing between Sophie and me, put a hand on each of our shoulders.

'It's been a good day,' he said and he was right. We'd had a good time. We more than got through it.

CHAPTER 13

We all headed for bed around midnight, partied out, but almost as soon as I'd fallen asleep, Moth woke me.

'Get your act together, sonny-Jim,' she said cheerfully. 'Baby on the way.'

'Oh shit,' I said, and she rolled her eyes.

'That's no way to greet your new brother.'

She seemed elated, talking me through the preparations we'd made once more, then she took to her bed, holding court like a queen, because everyone had woken by then and was milling around her.

We sat with her for a good few hours, timing the contractions and not much seemed to be happening, except when she squeezed my hand and I knew she was in pain. Pierre kept a discreet distance and when the little ones got bored and Moth had had enough of their questions, he took them off to keep them amused. Snow was falling steadily and the night crawled by. Moth regaled me and Sophie with stories of how long I'd taken to be born then she flared into a sudden anger, crying and swearing at Dad for leaving her alone, before abruptly falling asleep for a while.

By then I was in a bemused stupor, afraid that something was going wrong while Sophie was playing nurses. Moth didn't sleep long as the contractions started up again, much closer together. We rigged up a tent of sorts to give her as much privacy as we could but, at the end of the day, she was never going to have a baby with her knickers on. Actually, we'd dealt with that in the early water-breaking stage and once I'd got over my embarrassment, I accepted that the baby was going to come out of parts of my mother I'd never expected to see. I was ready to cope with whatever cleaning up and sorting out was necessary, taking more comfort in the supplies gleaned from the cottage hospital in Corrycreag than I'd ever have thought disinfectant and plastic sheeting could bring me.

Sophie was all cool efficiency, loving the role-playing, while Moth seemed very brave to me. She hardly made a sound and once she got to the pushing, we were too involved in what was happening to feel awkward. We both encouraged her and urged her on and, as the baby's head became visible, Sophie started hugging us both, Moth was crying and so was I. I knew I wasn't cut out to be a doctor because I didn't stay cool at all but we were getting through it. Then everything seemed to stop. Moth went very pale, and the baby's head, which had almost crowned, slipped out of sight again.

'Something's wrong,' she said. 'Jo, Jo, something's wrong.'

'What shall I do?' I gripped her hand, panic making me babble. 'What can I get? What do I do?'

'I don't know.'

She was scrabbling at my arm, as though getting hold of me would help. Then she shrieked in pain, a long wail that made the hairs on the back of my neck stand up. Her cry brought Pierre flying into the room, shocked out of his cautious discretion and I realised he must have been waiting outside the door the whole time. Sophie grabbed him, talking rapidly in French, far too fast for me to understand. He came to Moth, his usual painful shyness with her completely gone and leaned over, stroking the damp strands of hair back from her forehead.

'Try to relax, Ellen,' he said. 'If you can rest for a few moments and relax, perhaps the baby will come.'

Moth was crying, I was crying and he hushed us both gently.

'We have to trust,' he said. 'This baby wants to be born. We may need to help him.' He smiled a little at Moth. 'I delivered a foal once. It had exceptionally long legs. We will cope.'

She managed to smile too and I saw, with huge admiration, that he'd simply helped her to calm down and her breathing was steady again, though nothing had changed. But we'd all got hold of ourselves so we could think.

'The baby's gone very still,' she said, struggling to sit up a bit. 'I think he's exhausted, Pierre. And my back hurts so much. I can't push anymore.'

Between us, we helped her into a better position, then Pierre sat on the bed, holding her hand. 'Yes, you can. Everything's going to be all right. Rest until the contractions start again.'

'What if they don't?'

She'd said what I was thinking and Pierre must have known this because he spoke to Moth but put his hand out to rest on my arm.

'They will.'

I found myself praying for God, Dad, anyone who could help us, to do it pretty damn quick, because while I could see Moth needed the respite, the last contraction seemed to have been a long time ago. Sophie was bathing Moth's head and Pierre drew me away from the bed but I never found out what his plan was because suddenly Ginny was calling him from downstairs, with great urgency.

He started to tell Sophie to go and find out what was wrong, but then, because Sophie had her arms around Moth, who was sobbing, he went himself. We could hear the little ones getting all excited in the living room and Moth started to grow distressed again, afraid one of them had got hurt somehow. As I tried to comfort her, Pierre called Sophie and she ran off too, her receding feet on the stairs leaving me feeling very alone and afraid my mother and brother were both about to die in my care. But she wasn't gone long. The voices downstairs rose in a confusing French/English babble then she came thundering back and burst in, her eyes wide.

'There's a doctor here.'

'*What?*'

Moth and I spoke at the same time then Moth started crying, hiding her face against my shoulder.

'For's God's sake Sophie, this is no time for one of your bloody games,' I started but my voice trailed away as the door opened and

Pierre showed in a young Indian woman. She was dressed in worn hiking gear with snow on her boots, shaking her hands dry as she walked, obviously having washed them as soon as she understood what was going on.

'Don't be afraid,' she told Moth and smiled at me, her teeth very white against her tawny skin. 'I seem to have arrived at a good time.'

'Are you really a doctor?' I asked, stunned, and she smiled again, nodding.

'My name's Nemisha. Let's see what we've got here.'

She took charge with a calm confidence that left me weak with relief. I don't really know what she did. I held Moth's hand and supported her back as the contractions started again then the doctor-who-came-from-the-snow told her to push hard and almost at once, the baby was born. Sophie had the sterilised scissors ready and the clean towels to wrap the little wriggling thing that emerged from my mother's body, yelling and in a fine temper.

The doctor smiled at Moth over the tent of blankets.

'A strong new son,' she said and, wrapping the angry red thing up, placed him on Moth's chest. He was amazingly alien, screaming face, little fists scrunched up and his head white and greasy. Moth wiped it carefully with the towel and kissed him, then she kissed me and the clammy feel of her forehead filled me with the enormity of the long night's happenings. Watching the unfamiliar bundle in her arms, I realised too that all my mental preparation had been for the birth and I'd given little thought to what would actually be born. A tiny person, fractious and hungry, had appeared and I found it hard to relate him to the growing bulge under Moth's clothes over the past months. I tried to steady myself by watching the doctor – I hoped she really was a doctor – check Moth over, taking on all the cleaning up I'd been supposed to do, but I was shaken further by the bloody horror I'd escaped having to cope with. I'd felt less dazed when Gray kicked me in the head. Then someone placed the baby on my knee and as soon as I held him, he was mine, my little brother. I was torn between grinning and crying, while Sophie cooed at him, Moth looked exhausted and Pierre seemed to be having trouble in the hall, holding back the clamouring Ginny and Laurent.

'There, you can come in now.'

As the doctor opened the door, I realised the bed was remade and there was no sign of the alarming aftermath and ruined sheets. Ginny and Laurent spilled in with Pierre behind them, then it was all laughing and crying and a sort of quiet chaos swept us along.

At last, Moth was asleep with Christopher, fed and contented, asleep beside her in his cradle, the kids had gone back to bed and Sophie, Pierre and I were sitting in the kitchen watching the stranger eat. I noticed for the first time that she was short and wiry with strong hands and glossy black hair. It was twisted up at the back of her head and clipped in place with a large metal slide that caught the firelight when she turned her head.

'Is this like one of those old folk tales where you turn up when you're needed, but you're gone in the morning and you leave no footprints?' I asked, and she grinned.

'I don't think so.'

'Stuff like that happens quite a lot round here,' I reassured her. 'We'd take it in our stride.'

The woman put down her fork, then accepted Pierre's offer of more before she said, 'I've been hoping to find other people for weeks – I'd sooner not go off without leaving footprints, if it's all the same to you.'

Aside from the fact, she'd delivered my baby brother and saved me from being responsible for the loss of him and Moth, I'd taken to her anyhow. She had a humorous face, ready to smile, and was obviously as glad to see us as we were to see her, even though we were the ones who'd been in trouble. She was shattered though, we all were, so we agreed we'd share our stories in the morning and she was asleep on the couch almost before the rest of us headed up the stairs.

I settled down in a chair alongside Moth and Christopher, who looked less angry and red now and was awake, quietly waving his arms about and contemplating the world. I watched him for a while as he thought about having another bawling session, then fell asleep as he opened his mouth to yell. I'd taken to him too, and watched him sucking on the small fist he'd stuffed into his mouth to comfort himself while he slept. Then Dad was there and so really there that I very nearly saw him. He bent over his new son and his sleeping wife and then me and his pride wrapped us all like a blanket.

CHAPTER 14

'There's no-one left in the cities,' Nemisha told us that first morning when we gathered to hear her story. 'I was on a dig in Cornwall when the call to go to the centres came. But I didn't go. I was the only one – every else decided to go back to the University – which is what we'd been told to do.'

'University?' Moth asked, propped up in bed with Christopher asleep against her shoulder, and Nemisha nodded.

'When I was at Uni, I got involved with the archaeological society, so I used to go back during my holidays, to catch up, join in if they were doing anything that interested me. A burial site, possibly Bronze Age, had been found on Bodmin Moor, so I went along. We'd been working for three or four days when we heard that a call had gone out to people in outlying areas to go to their nearest centre. I never really understood what was happening – the army was on the move herding people into the towns, but no-one would say what was going on.'

'So, why didn't you go?' I asked and she shrugged.

'Premonition? I felt I shouldn't but I couldn't persuade anyone else. We were staying in a remote cottage and no-one came to check if everyone had gone. There was no phone or mobile reception so I couldn't keep track of what was happening. I kept my head down, until I ran out of food. I suppose it was about three weeks – we'd been equipped for four of us to stay a fortnight, so I managed fine. But even though I thought it was a bad idea to leave, I never really considered that the others wouldn't be back. Time went on, I walked to the nearest farms – which were abandoned – and caught a few news programmes, but there was no real news. Just this urgent gathering of people –

it seemed to be world-wide, so far as I could tell, but the reception wasn't great where we were at the best of times. Then the radio died, and when I trekked off again – it was about fifteen miles over bogs and rough ground – to the nearest farm, there was no television, no phone, no power. I started to get scared then. There was an old land rover still at the farm so I drove back to the dig for my stuff and moved into the farmhouse. I toyed with the idea of driving into the nearest town but that's what everyone else had done and they never came back. So I waited longer, conserved the Land Rover fuel for when I'd really had enough. When I couldn't stand it any longer, I drove into Truro – there was nothing.'

'Dust,' I said and she looked at me.

'Yes. You've seen it too?'

I nodded and Sophie said, 'So have we.'

I carried on. 'In the nearest town to here, Corrycreag – it's some way – there was dust everywhere. It looks like whatever happened, it was an ordinary day – you know, people shopping, stuff like that.'

Nemisha thought about this for a while. 'I was heading for Corrycreag, in a purposeless sort of way. Dust everywhere – I'm glad I didn't get there. In the big towns and cities, they had people in leisure centres, churches, theatres.' She fell silent for a few moments. 'Once I'd realised what the dust was, I didn't look too hard, but it was piled high in places, spilling out of windows and doorways.'

We all sat, contemplating this for a cold moment, listening to the voices of Ginny and Laurent playing with Souris on the yard.

'But there has been no – invasion, air-attack, no foreign force?' Pierre asked. He looked bad that morning, not really able to get by without a solid eight hours sleep to recharge his batteries. I wondered sometimes if his insides were ruined. He had his hands clasped together and I knew it was to stop them shaking.

'There's nothing,' Nemisha said. 'My gut feeling is that we've wiped each other out – all the big powers lost it at once and pushed whatever button they've been working on within moments of each other.' She shrugged. 'It's a guess but the only one I can come up with.

I've been up to London – walked through the Houses of Parliament – only dust.'

'Mutually assured destruction? God help us.' Moth shuddered and cuddled Christopher a bit closer. 'I thought the irony of that was supposed to mean it couldn't happen.'

'Don't they have secret places for the government to hide?' I asked, but Nemisha shrugged.

'If they did, I don't think it worked. Whatever killed everyone went through walls, below streets – I went into the Underground – but harmed nothing that wasn't organic and only attacked the centres. God knows why people were called in to them – they were sitting ducks.'

'We can't be the only ones?' Moth said, sounding afraid.

'No, we're not. There were others like me, who didn't go, or like you, who were travelling, or who had an unusual way of life. I met a young guy who'd lived his whole life in a commune in wildest Wales. They escaped completely unscathed because responding to a call to go into a centre was the last thing they'd have done. But he fell out with his wife a few days before it happened and she'd gone off with both their children and never been heard from again. He was still looking though – refused to accept they were dead. He was in a bad way. I worry about him still.' She fell silent for a moment then said, 'But I don't think there are many survivors. You're the first people I've seen in nearly two months of travelling north.'

'Why did you come up here?'

Nemisha paused for a moment, and I was already wishing she was a few years younger. She was the first woman I'd seen in two years who was neither a child nor a relation. And she was pretty and sharp and I was impressed that she'd travelled all this way on her own. I guessed she was also about ten years older than me. I tried to be more concerned about the welfare of the world, but the gloom of having a pretty woman turn up who would see me as a kid settled on me as I listened.

'I've come across little pockets of people I could have stayed with. Some living alone, some who've banded together. They're all bewildered and lost but they're doing okay. Yet there's a lot of squabbling and I've come across two bodies that weren't dust, but had obviously been murdered. Most of the world seems to have been wiped out and those who are left are still killing each other. I don't want to survive in some desperate hand-to-mouth way, waiting for authority to start up again and tell me what to do. And I don't want to be part of anything that carries on treating other people like shit – sorry.'

The anger that flared up in her died as suddenly. She looked at us all, sitting around Moth's bed – a big shambles of a man, a woman with a newborn baby, a feisty little girl and a gloomy boy. She can't have been especially inspired, but she was smiling, nevertheless.

'I've been drawn here and if you'll have me, I'll stay. All the way north, I felt I was heading somewhere, though I didn't know where. All I ever seemed to do was travel from one crease in the map to the next. The last car died on me about forty miles away but I couldn't stop. I walked all yesterday, right through the night in the snow, because I knew I was getting close. I chose this house on the map, as somewhere to spend the night, then chickened out – I couldn't bear another empty place so I decided I'd press on to Corrycreag. Then, a horse appeared, tearing after me through the snow.' Her eyes were shining. 'I was a bit afraid – I'm not confident around horses, but it came right up to me.' She grinned round at us. 'It was about the most beautiful thing I'd ever seen, with the frost sparkling all over it. It was chestnut brown with a star that radiated out across its forehead and a coat so thick and shiny I could have got lost in it.'

'That's Flicka,' I said. 'All the horses were agitated when we went out to check them last night. They must have known you were nearby.'

Nemisha looked at me. 'Is that true? She led me towards the house. Then a big gang of them turned up and – well, escorted me to the door. – I can't begin to tell you what I felt when I saw that it was a home with smoke drifting from the chimneys, a light – a light in the window – amazing – the yard swept clean of snow. I heard a goat or a sheep bleat in one of the sheds, disturbed by the hooves, maybe and saw a bike propped up by the gate and knew that a child had run inside for tea or to find his gloves just a few hours earlier.' Her eyes were shining. 'And I was planning to bypass it but the horses made sure I didn't.'

'The horses are special,' Moth said. 'They came the day my husband died. They're important in some way we don't understand.'

Nemisha had tears in her eyes. 'I thought I was going mad,' she said. I shrugged. 'Don't worry. If you are, then we all are.'

A huge smile lit her face. 'That's great. Oh, that's really great. Can I stay here?'

'Oh yes,' said Moth, smiling. 'You're home now.'

And so we were eight. Flicka went wild with joy when I took Nemisha out to see her again and the others milled around too. No-one was surprised when little Whiskers chose Christopher a couple of weeks later on his first trip outside, wrapped like an Eskimo baby, to see our small world. We understood that now – we were each chosen by one of the horses – Poppa and Ginny, Gray and me, Misty and Moth, Whiskers and Christopher, Moonrise and Sophie, Daybreak and Laurent, Sunset and Pierre and now Flicka and Nemisha. That left Momma, Beauty and Smoke. Three more people to come, but then what?

We were starting to outgrow the farm. The caravan was too cold to sleep in through the winter so we had people sleeping everywhere, tripping over one another and getting on each other's nerves. Moth and Christopher had moved into my little room. I shared the next size up with Pierre and Laurent – Pierre's snoring took some getting used to – while 'the girls' as they were now known, had the big bedroom. But because none of them was really big enough for the number of people using them – and because of the various complaints about snoring and bed-hogging – most nights at least a couple of us spilled out into the living room or the hall and slept on airbeds from the caravan. We organised a sleep rota, which helped a bit, but we had to admit that we'd outgrown the place. We talked about the cottages in the village a few miles down the road, but they were tiny and it was a pretty but damp little wooded valley with no real place to grow food for us all. Somehow, they didn't seem to be the answer we needed.

Nemisha was resourceful – she'd travelled a long way alone and her understanding of maps and navigation was better than anyone's. That also started to emerge – each of us had some particular skill and that person led the rest when it was needed most, regardless of age. So we all followed Ginny's intuition regarding the horses and let Sophie organise us. Laurent was the Chicken Master. Even Souris was Ratter-in-Chief. It was a good system. So when Nemisha got her maps out and started looking at where we were and what was around, we all gathered and listened to her.

'You see here,' she said, pointing to a village on the coast about forty miles away, on a peninsula that was almost an island. 'Eilean Tianavaig. I went there a few years ago – it's a lovely place. It's quite small, about fifty houses, then there's one of those big old manses, with a few worker's cottages. It was a sort of living history place when I went there. A few people lived in the village all the year round, and people lived in the big house, but most of the cottages were holiday homes. There was a field study centre for school and university groups and a small boat yard, where they made traditional fishing boats and ran trips. It's a lovely spot, very sheltered, a good port, small but well-organised. Boats used to stop to stock up at the little shop that opened in the summer and for fuel and because it was a pretty place. The houses run in two lines down towards the port and they were in perfect condition – all recently renovated about ten years ago, it would be now. But also it's got windmills, a spinning and weaving yard and a forge – it was a museum of Scottish life you see, where people came on working holidays to keep traditional skills alive, but also to look at sustainable living.'

I saw where she was headed. 'So it might be somewhere, we could pick up those skills and settle too?'

She nodded. 'It's both small and large enough for us to live in alone or welcome others if they come and want to join us. But not so large that we could end up with something beyond a small community.' Her idealism, which I'd heard a lot of over the weeks, was in full swing now. 'This is the way forward. Small self-sufficient communities, egalitarian running, working in co-operation with others but interdependent. See, down the coast, about fifteen miles apart, there are other villages. If more people came in time, they could settle there.'

Moth looked at the map.

'The upheaval is a bit daunting.'

Nemisha acknowledged this with a nod but to everyone's surprise, Pierre, a very quiet presence most of the time, spoke up. 'We could hitch the caravan to the pick-up, then we have two cars and the horses and the cart. We could drive the stock – we could have our own trail ride, eh Zho?'

He still got me every time with the way he said my name and I was quite fond of him by now.

'Yeah, sure,' I said. 'Move 'em out, cowboy.'

Ginny had come in and, with a look that said this wasn't up for discussion, she chipped in, 'I'm not leaving my Daddy.'

Then she turned, trailing Laurent by the hand, and disappeared off upstairs. Souris looked at the rest of us, barked twice and trotted after them.

We exchanged glances and Sophie raised her eyebrows at me, gauging my reaction. I shrugged. This was a big problem for me and Moth too. Dad was here. For all he was around us all the time, physically he was here.

Moth found me sitting by his grave later on and tucked in alongside me, using my body to shelter her from the wind.

'It's cold, here, love,' she said, shivering.

'I know, but I like to think here,' I looked at over the meadow, plucking up courage then asked, 'What do you feel about moving?'

She was silent for a minute. 'He said we should, didn't he?'

'Yes, he did. We couldn't have done it before, but we can do it now. Yet, this is home and we'd be leaving him too.'

Moth was quiet again, then she tucked her hand under my elbow. 'Not really, Jo. I feel it too, the reluctance to walk away from this place where his body is. But, let's be brutal now, his body's been underground for almost a year.'

'Don't,' I tried to get up, but she held on to me.

'Jo, please stay. I know it's hard to think about but it's true. When he keeps us company, or one of us comes in with his advice, is it the body in the ground we think of?'

I shook my head. 'No, it's Dad, as he was, before he got kicked.'

'Yes, it is. And I promise you, he'll come with us. He'll be with us as long as we need him, Jo, I'm certain of it. I don't really think we can stay here much longer. We get on pretty well, I think, but we all need more space. Once Christopher, Laurent and Ginny get a bit bigger, we'll really start struggling. How about you go with Pierre and Misha, Sophie too, and reccy this new place?'

'Yes, okay. But we can't all go and leave you with the animals and the kids. Where's Chris now, by the way?'

'Pierre is singing French lullabies to him.'

'He makes me think of a big gentle dog.'

Moth smiled. 'He's lovely with Christopher. It's hard for me to believe that he and the wild man you described from Corrycreag are the same person.'

'It's hard for me to believe and I was there.'

Moth paused a moment, looking at me sidelong. 'I think Misha has her eye on him.'

I tried to sound casual but took a bit too long to reply. 'I hadn't noticed. Isn't he too old for her?'

Moth pointed across the field. 'Look who's on his way over. Hello, Gray.'

My horse ambled up, nosing through our pockets, distracting us from the discussion, but Moth didn't let it go. She got up and warmed her hands under Gray's mane, watching me. Gray was so round and fluffy in his winter coat that he made me think of the Thelwell cartoons I used to look at in two old books of my Gran's. They were the only books in her house I was interested in and I used to go straight to them anytime I was left with her. They were full of little fat ponies with little fat girls on their backs and they made me laugh, even though I didn't understand most of the riding jokes in them. The thought took me back to before the world ended and there wasn't so much loss around us, but there were no real horses, only the cartoons. Horses were as foreign as loss to me then. I tried to divert Moth with something I'd wanted to talk about for a while.

'Maybe we're selfish, Moth. We forget Dad isn't the only person who died. We've all lost people, so far as we know. All our friends, parents, grandparents. There's not one of us here who isn't bereaved.'

She nodded. 'I've noticed that Laurent and Sophie come down here to talk to their mother. Dad has become a sort of 'everyman' I think, for all the people we've lost.' She kept rubbing Gray's neck and he stretched it out in bliss, making us both laugh. 'We need one another the more for it, Jo. And if Pierre and Misha got together, that would make another family. Maybe more babies in time.'

'She's not much older than me,' I said, sullen at the thought of Misha preferring the old wreck that was Pierre over me as a prime specimen of young manhood. Moth was smiling at me, gently, and I started to feel annoyed with her for reading my thoughts.

'Misha is thirty two, Jo.'

'She's not.'

'She is, love, and Pierre's thirty-six, three years younger than me.'

'Ah, hell.' I admitted defeat. 'I reckoned she was in her twenties.'

Moth moved to sit by me again. 'If you put off growing up for a while, the age difference between you and Sophie is about the same.'

'So I get to be a toy-boy or a perv, is that it?'

'I hope not. I know Sophie's like a sister to you now…'

'So's Misha, Moth. She's a laugh and she's seen so much. I like hanging out with her. I'm not – you know, in love with her or anything, but I guess, at times, I've thought that… if she got desperate…'

I'd surprised myself by saying all this aloud and felt a hot blush rising past my hairline.

'I want more for you than that. Sophie will grow into a lovely young woman, and you went through an ordeal together – there are strong bonds between you. But who knows what will happen? We aren't the only people, Jo.'

I grinned at her. 'You reckon there's an all-girls volleyball team, who were on a coach tour of the Outer Hebrides when the world ended, heading our way?'

'I'd put money on it.'

We sat for a bit, watching the birds. There were lots of birds nowadays, and they were swooping around the feeders Laurent had put out for them. The horses loafed around the field and the poultry were clucking on the yard, busy with important hen-stuff, as Laurent told us regularly. It was a crisp afternoon, the frost still sparkling in a day with no thaw and I knew I'd have to go and start carrying water for the animals soon. But it was good sitting there for a while.

'I didn't really think she'd fancy me,' I said, eventually. 'But it sort of felt like, real life, you know, the possibility.'

'You can't measure yourself by the old markers, Jo. Yes, I know that, if we were still in the 'real life', as you call it, by now you'd be fretting if you didn't have a girlfriend. But this is real life now and everything's different. No-one's watching anymore.'

I hadn't thought of it that way before. She was right, of course. No-one was watching any of us now. I grinned at her. 'Girls only ever wanted me for a big brother, anyhow,' I said. 'They used to come and tell me about their problem boyfriends.'

'You should be proud of that, and when Nemisha comes to ask what you think of Pierre, well, take it as a compliment.'

'Sure – I'll mind their kids along with the rest. Born to be a brother, that's me. What do you call a male old maid?'

Moth got to her feet, smiling down at me again. 'I'd better go and find Christopher before Pierre runs out of songs. We'll talk about you and at least some of the others going to have a look at this new place tonight, but you're right, I'll need someone here. And I'll talk to Ginny.'

We both talked to Ginny and there were a few tears and tantrums as it became clear that we had little choice but to move on. Then, one morning when I was first up and doing the breakfast feed-rounds, Ginny appeared alongside me.

'Where's Laurent?' I asked, because they were like Siamese twins. Ginny was all wrapped up so I could only see her blue eyes, nose reddened by the cold and that determined mouth, peeping out from a hood of blue fur, pulled tight round her face.

'He's not up yet. I wanted to talk to you. I never get to talk to you anymore.'

I put my arm around her shoulders. 'It's more crowded now. Let's go and see the horses.'

Ginny nodded, winding an arm round my waist, and we at once fell into the game of 'big-steps and little-steps' she'd loved as a toddler. For the past few years, she played it to humour our inability to realise she was too grown up for it now, so it had become one of those family jokes. Moth and Dad used to play it together and she'd fall about laughing at them. So now I lifted her off the ground with the big steps and she nearly had me falling over with the tottering little ones, so we were laughing and pushing each other by the time we reached the meadow where the grass cracked with frost beneath our feet. She climbed up on the wall for a piggy-back and I had to be Poppa Horse as we went down the field.

The horses liked silliness so they came hurtling over ready to charge around and pretend we were alarming them. They all had frost clinging to their coats and steam pouring from their nostrils. The real Poppa led a 'we're-all-stallions' parade high-stepping and snorting while Gray and the others followed. Ginny was laughing as I pranced too, following him, then threatened to roll in the cold grass when Beauty did.

'No,' she shrieked in delight. 'Go, horses, go.'

Poppa took off down the field with the others tearing after, bucking and skidding and I tore after them, but got left behind very quickly.

'When did you get so heavy?' I was panting as she slid down from my back and she grinned up at me. 'I growed, like Topsy.'

Neither of us knew where that saying came from, but it was one of Grandad's that we all used.

'Come on then, Topsy – race you up to the top of the hill.'

We tore through the field, Ginny light on her feet seeming to run over the surface of the grass while I laboured in my wellies. I let her win, but didn't have to hold back very much – she was pretty fast. We stopped at the top looking down on the farm, with the horses grazing below us where they'd hoofed away the frost, the yard and garden around the house neatly tucked under a snowy blanket. The chickens were pecking, Pierre emerging with Laurent carried upside-down over his shoulder, and Dad's grave in the corner of the meadow, where the sheep and cattle munched on their hay nearby. It was home.

'Daddy's here,' said Ginn, pushing her hood back, and he was. I stayed very still, resisting the temptation to look round, because that always meant losing him. He stood between us. I felt his arm around my shoulders and heard his voice in my head, *Time to go, guys.*

'Time to go, guys,' echoed Ginny, while I stared at her, still a bit slow about the mysteries of Dad's presence. She was grinning now. 'Daddy says, *Hit the road, Jack.*'

She grabbed my hand and we sang our way back down to the farmyard, scattering chickens and causing a commotion. Then, one by one, all the other mad people we lived with came out to join us and we started the day with a conga, the way you should, of course.

CHAPTER 15

After one of our big group discussions, Sophie, Pierre, Misha and Laurent went to find Eilean Tianavaig. There was some hesitation over Laurent, because he was only little, but the decision was made when their horses all gathered during the preparations with Daybreak in their midst.

They took the smart car too, as Nimesha's riding lacked confidence and it meant Laurent could have a lift if he got tired riding with his dad or Sophie. There was no discussion on why all the horses needed to go if the car was along, as that decision had been made without us. Taking the little car also meant the baggage could be spread out and there was at least some room for foraging-finds along the way. Sophie and I rode out on an advance reconnaissance mission and came back reporting that the roads were quite badly damaged, as we'd had a very cold winter and the frost had done its worst. So the car wasn't going to be going very fast at the best of times. The horses may well travel faster. So they went, four people, four horses, and it was just my family again, for the first time in ages.

Initially, we felt a bit bereft. Ginny and Laurent were joined at the hip and I usually worked all day with the others while Moth did most of the housework, as it was still too cold for Christopher to be outside much. It felt odd doing the routine jobs on my own, then getting Ginny to hold a ladder for me while I fixed a piece of loose guttering. But I enjoyed having some time to myself and then with Ginn. We went in to lunch together and Moth said, sounding bewildered,

'Everything's done – there's less washing, less cooking. It's really quiet too.'

We looked at each other and I said, 'When we move, we'll be able to get far enough apart to have some real time alone whenever we want, but still know the others are close by.' I picked Christopher up because he was grizzling, feeling left out because Moth was seeing to lunch. 'Hey, little bro, it's just the four of us, for the first time.'

Having the house to ourselves gave us a holiday feeling – a room each to sleep in was reason enough. After lunch we lounged around for a while, Moth and I reading while Ginny tried to teach Christopher to talk. Then, once she'd accepted he was still on the young side, we went for a ride. Moth was hesitant at first about taking Christopher on Misty with her but I said, 'Misty won't let anything happen to him, Moth. This is the real life now, remember? Is it any more dangerous than a car-seat on a motorway would have been?'

So Christopher came too, in the baby sling on Moth's chest, and Misty went all whickery and careful, walking as though he and Moth were fragile. Gray was being the lead-horse, striding out and surveying the distance, while Poppa ambled behind with Ginny, letting him take responsibility. The others stayed eating hay but as we got to the end of our drive, little Whiskers, all shaggy and half-grown now, came hurtling after us.

'Look at that,' said Moth, reaching out to scratch his ears as he snuffled at Christopher. 'He's having his first outing without Momma Horse.'

'Big day for everyone,' I said and so we set out for a gentle wander down the road, round our land and back through the woods. Whiskers trotted along beside Misty to keep an eye on Chris, who slept through the whole ground-breaking experience.

We knew Sophie and the others would be gone at least a week, maybe two, as it was some distance, so we decided to ride every day. We also sorted the house out and planned how we would lay out a larger vegetable garden to feed our expanded numbers, keeping busy so we wouldn't worry or start imagining accidents and catastrophes. The riding seemed to do Moth good. She looked well but had been spending a lot of time indoors. Now, as the weather was kind to us, she was outside for most of every afternoon and got a bit of colour and sparkle back, which I'd not really seen in her since Dad was hurt. Christopher had given her a bloom but it was inward looking, focussing on his growth. Now he was born and some distance was between her and the sad days watching Dad die, she'd started to really look outward. She talked about the possible move as though it was exciting, rather than a simple necessity, and we all became enthused, finding endless potential in this place we'd never even seen with the unpronounceable name.

The days passed and the others had soon been gone a week. The harsh winter gracefully made way for an early spring and life was getting easier all the time. The joy of not having to thaw the water out and carry it by the gallon for the animals put me in a very good mood. As we started into the second week, calculating that the others should perhaps be on the way back, I planned an outing with Gray.

I made some food to go in my saddle-bags, rushed round doing the early feeding, then left Ginny to gather the eggs and spend a day with Moth and Christopher, which was as much a treat to her as time off was for me. Gray and I set out while it was still early morning, planning to be back late afternoon and I decided we'd go exploring in a new place. So we turned right as we left our land and headed up the long hill and out over the top.

In an hour or so, we were in uncharted territory and Gray, who'd been ho-humming along the familiar trail, now pricked up his head and went into his alert-and-aware routine. He made me laugh and I enjoyed the familiarity of riding him as though I'd been born astride his back rather than having hardly ever been near a horse less than a year ago. We picked up the pace as an open track wound slowly down the hill ahead of us. It looked like an old green-lane, the grass that springy sort that never grows long, rolling out between ancient stone-walls a cart-width apart. I thought of all the people who'd herded cattle to market long ago, or gone hiking there more recently. Now it hadn't had any feet on it aside from the odd rabbit or fox for nearly three years. I wondered if it noticed the difference, flexing its

131

collective muscles, glad not to have the pressure. Or maybe it missed being travelled by people, with their different missions and purposes, foot-steps and ways of moving. I got so involved with the idea of journeys from the path's point of view that I nearly decided not to disturb it, to veer off and go along the inside of the wall. But Gray had other ideas, prancing a little, wanting to take off.

I decided that if he thought it was all right to tread the abandoned path, then it probably was. So I shouted, 'Go, boy, go!' and sat deep in my saddle, urging him forward. He went off like a firework with its tail lit, his back legs thrusting so hard to power his movement that I could feel his hip joints right underneath me. He was a streak of cloud, a hurricane, a bolt of lightning in a clear sky, and he tore across that short, bouncy turf so fast that tears streamed down my face. I lay low on his neck, urging him on and we flew, hurtled the length of the track, simply because we could.

We were panting hard when we stopped but he was still full of energy, bouncing and prancing so that we covered a lot of ground fairly fast, cantering long stretches, jog-trotting the rest. Travelling at such a pace, we went much further than I'd planned on the map and I was riding casually, eating my lunch, when I began to think it was time we looped round to go back. But almost at the same moment, Gray's mood changed. He'd been high-stepping for a while, his nostrils flaring out and his ears pricked forward. I thought it was because he was feeling feisty, but when I wanted to take a turn and head for home, he wouldn't.

I trusted him so when he insisted that we should go on, I followed his lead. But he wasn't having fun now – he was worried. His steps had become stiff and awkward, as though he was torn between going forward and running away. Then there was a loud bang and he leapt high in the air, scattering my lunch everywhere, and landed snorting, his legs splayed wide with me barely in the saddle.

Now, I'd not heard a gun very often, but I recognised the sound at once. I dismounted to gather my dropped saddle-bag, map and water bottle, then remounted my still-frozen horse. He was taut like wire, his ears pricked so tensely I'm sure I could have snapped them clean off. His attention was focussed as though he could see through the hill ahead of us. I wasn't often afraid when I was on Gray's back but I was then, because I had no idea of what he would do next and another huge leap wasn't out of the question. However, if he planned to leave in a hurry, I wanted to make sure I went with him so I stayed on board and tried to remember the smiling technique. There was a small copse covering the hill and I urged Gray towards the trees so we could look into the valley from the top while keeping out of sight ourselves. A deer track led through the copse up the hill and, from being reluctant to move at all, Gray bounded off at a canter through the trees but then slowed down so we emerged cautiously, staying in the shadows at the edge. I'd grown used to strange things happening now, but the sight we looked out on made my jaw drop.

I stepped down to stand by Gray's head, tucked into the trees but looking over a rocky valley with a road running through the middle. Directly below us, in the centre of the valley, was a black pick-up, not unlike ours, but bigger and carrying loaded gun-racks. A woman appeared to be driving it while a man stood in the back, lining his gun sights on the wolves that were pursuing the pick-up. One had gone down already – that must have been what I heard. I was torn in two. We knew there were wolves not far from us. I'd not heard them on my lone trip with Gray, when I'd been worried about the possibility, but afterwards, as time went on, we heard them occasionally. It was clear they were far away, their howling carrying on the stillness of the night air. We didn't mind them. There was plenty of food for them, without any need for them to come near us. The hills were thronging with sheep and cattle now that the people had gone, aside from rabbits and deer. Hearing the lonely calls at night was a reminder that humans were small in relation to nature. I thought that was good.

But this was something different. These wolves were hunting, pursuing the vehicle as though it was an animal too. I tried to imagine what would cause this while, at the same time, trying to decide what I should do. Although the vehicle was far away, I could see that it was full of people and as it picked up speed, bouncing over the weather-worn road, I saw that there was a second man in the pick-up. He was sitting down, amid whatever the pickup was carrying – supplies I guessed – and pointing at a wolf coming up on the gunman's blind side. He swung his gun round, fired, and the wolf leapt into the air yelping, then fell to the ground and lay still. The gunman went into a frenzy then, shooting wildly and killing two more, until the wolves paused, near the end of the valley road. It struck me that they were seeing the car off their territory, as once it had left the valley they slipped away into the heather on the far side and disappeared.

The road the car was travelling curved round my hill before it turned again to head south. I hesitated over what to do next. Firstly, while I didn't like seeing the wolves shot, there were good pelts down there we could use. We'd cured sheep and rabbit skins before and I was a dab hand at it. Four dead wolves meant four large skins. Yet I felt that by taking them, I'd be aligning myself with the shooter and I wasn't ready to do that. The shattering of the familiar silence by gunfire seemed a sacrilege and there was something about the laden gun-rack that bothered me. It seemed more than anyone could need to hunt for food. There was a macho swagger about it I wasn't used to.

Then, there were the occupants of the car. I was hiding from them, because the incident I'd witnessed had troubled me. But I couldn't judge them out of hand. If wolves had been chasing my family, I would have defended them. Maybe the people had done nothing wrong, but were hungry and tired and in need of help. Maybe the shooting man was as frustrated and exhausted as Pierre had been when I first saw him.

'What do you reckon, Gray?' I asked. 'Do you like the look of them or not?'

By way of reply, Gray started off down the hill to meet the car on the road. I ran alongside until I could get back in the saddle and, as he was eager, we cantered down the long slope. He wasn't happy though and my feeling that he was tempted to turn round and head for home fast made me very edgy.

The gunman, still standing in the pick-up, had his back to me and the other man saw me first. Suddenly, I found a double-barrelled shotgun pointed in my direction and my heart lurched into my mouth. The man swung it upwards, as though I'd foolishly wandered into his range, when in fact, he'd turned with it on me.

'We won't hurt you, son,' he called, standing now with the butt against his foot and his hand around the barrel. I could tell he wouldn't harm me, but I instinctively disliked him. He was dressed as though he was going logging in the wilds of Canada, looking out of place against the mossy greens and browns of a Scottish moorland. His loud red-check lumberjack shirt and bright orange baseball cap seemed to cancel out his camouflage fatigues and he was wearing huge army boots. His clothes seemed quite new and again, I had to remind myself that we were none of us leaders of style any more. I was wearing a pair of Dad's jeans, patched with all-sorts of oddments, with a faded old shirt and an oilskin body-warmer, over a couple of long-sleeved t-shirts, courtesy of M&S in Corrycreag. I'd have died to be seen out like that once. But we were careful with our clothes, having plenty now, but knowing we needed to make them last, as there wouldn't be any more. Maybe these people thought the same way. He was wearing what was warm and practical.

The man in the pick-up with him was much older, and I could see an old lady in the car, with two children – girls – and a younger woman driving. She got out and she was wearing jeans and a fleece over a denim shirt. I realised I was being stupid about the man. They were dressed much the same as I was really. But there was the loaded rack and the gun he hadn't put down yet.

'Cat got your tongue?' he said, showing me a set of broad teeth. He seemed different when he smiled and I relaxed a bit. 'On your own are you?'

I shook my head. 'No, I live some miles over that way, with my family, on a farm. Are you all right? What was going on with the wolves?'

'Vicious bastards.' The man spat over the side of the truck. 'Been stalking us for a couple of days. Starving, I suppose. Had their eye on the kids – you're too young to remember the dingo case in Oz but I wasn't going to let a wolf near my kiddies.'

I wanted to say that they couldn't be starving – even though it was the end of a hard winter, there were sheep and deer everywhere. Why would they attack people when they didn't need to? I seemed to remember vaguely that the dingo was cleared. But I kept quiet.

'Trish, we'll stop here for some lunch.' He nodded. 'My wife, Trish, the kids, Paula and Mandy.' As an afterthought, he added, 'And there's Donald and Maureen too. Picked them up on the way.'

The old man touched the peak of his woolly cap. 'How'd ye do, laddie. That's a fine garron you've got there.'

It took a moment to realise he meant Gray.

'A garron?' I repeated, and he nodded, his Scottish accent as thick as honey. 'Aye, a garron, a real strong highland pony. He's a fine fellow.'

I'd guessed from the horse books at home that Gray and his family were highland ponies, but I'd not come across this term before. The car was spilling out its passengers now and the two little girls were staring at me, while the old man had come over to inspect Gray. Gray whinnied softly at him but when the man with the gun reached out a hand to ruffle his ears, my horse put them back and swung his head away.

'Got a mean streak, has he?' the man asked, and I noticed that although his hand fell to his side, it was curled in a fist.

'Not at all,' I replied, knowing I sounded a bit offended. 'He just likes to be handled gently.'

'Got to show 'em who's boss, or they'll walk all over you.'

He turned away and started bossing the women and children around, but the old man winked at me. 'Not much of a horseman,' he said nodding at the retreating back. 'His name's Phil.'

'Are you related?' I asked and he shook his head.

'No, but we were getting low on food on our croft and a bit past the getting of it. He thought we should go along with them.' He shrugged. 'Seemed for the best at the time.'

I could tell he wasn't so sure now but then Trish, who – to my amazement – had put on what my Gran would have called a pinny to make tea on a little gas stove, called me over.

'Now, dear, I'm not sure how old you are. Do you usually eat with the children or the adults?'

I stared at her. 'We usually all eat together.'

She smiled as though I was the charming relic of some primitive tribe. 'Do you? I always like to get the kiddies out of the way before Phil sits down – it's what people of our class used to do, you know, and it's important to keep up standards.'

I shrugged, trying to stop staring. 'I'm a bit old for nursery tea, I suppose.'

She smiled. 'Well, it's lunchtime, but that's what I thought too. Best to check though.'

We acted out the strangest ritual, whereby the adults watched the two little girls eating around a fold-up picnic table on fold-up chairs. Then they were sent to sit quietly in the car, while Trish reset the table so Phil could sit at the head. The rest of us shuffled around like underlings looking for the right place. I remembered doing Macbeth in English – 'You know your own degrees' – and had to duck my head to hide the smile I was struggling with.

All the food started with Phil before it was passed around the table and no-one ate anything before he'd given his approval. When I almost made the faux-pas of drinking before he'd tasted his tea, Trish looked at me wide-eyed and shook her head slightly. As if I wasn't already uncomfortable enough, I became aware that the two girls were still staring at me and Gray, their small faces visible in the rear window of the pick-up. They were whispering to each other behind their hands, although we couldn't hear them through the glass, and they seemed to make Gray uneasy too. I'd untacked him and left him loose to graze but he kept throwing his head up to stare at the children and I was afraid he might suddenly decide he was heading for home without me.

'I must be going back soon,' I said, one eye on my horse's edginess and the other on the fading light. 'The afternoon starts drawing in early still. Where are you headed?'

'Well,' said Phil, sitting back as expansively as was possible in a garden chair. 'We're heading South. We've been over to Corrycreag, took what we could find, but it's a hole – there's nothing there. Made sure no-one could follow us and now we're making our way down to London. Must be some organisation getting going again.' He puffed out his chest. 'Or someone needed to do it.'

I'd picked up on something that bothered me. 'Made sure no-one could follow you? I don't understand.'

Donald made a strange sound and Maureen winced as Phil turned on him. 'Don't you start that again. It was for the best. We don't know who's around here. It's survival of the fittest now – every man for himself.'

This was so obviously not the case that I had to bite my tongue again. It was survival by accident, of the lost, the wandering, the holiday maker and Nemisha's ideals of co-operation and working together made perfect sense to me for those who were left. But I was still confused.

'I'm sorry,' I said, treading with care. 'What happened in Corrycreag?'

Phil's chest expanded to button-popping proportions. 'Torched the place,' he said. 'Covering our backs, making sure no-one else could raid it and come after us. There wasn't much left anyhow. Other bastards already had the best of it.'

I put my cup down and got up. 'I think I'd best be going,' I said. 'My family are the only other people in at least a fifty mile radius, so far as I know. We're the bastards who've raided Corrycreag and there was plenty there still that we'd have been glad of if you didn't need it.'

Phil met my eye. 'You're not too big for a good hiding, boy, if you get mouthy with me. I know what's best and there was dangerous stuff there – guns and fuel. I wasn't going to have some bastard coming up on my family in the night.'

I was in full sympathy with the wolves by now and concentrated on placing my chair neatly under the table to stop myself saying something that would cause real trouble.

'Thank you for the tea,' I told Trish, who'd suddenly grown very cool. I nodded at Maureen, who I'd not heard speak yet, then Donald who gave me a wink again. 'I need to go home now. Good luck on your journey.'

I moved back to where Gray was waiting, still looking torn, but Phil came after me as I started to tack him up again.

'That's your way, is it? Leave two little kiddies to sleep in a car in this weather, when you've got a house to go back to?'

I tightened Gray's girth and looked at the group, quite willing to see them all sleep in the car – or on the ground in deep snow for that matter – rather than take them home with me.

'I'm sure my mother would give you a bed for the night and a hot meal before you carry on,' I said.

Trish simpered at me. 'Oh, I'd like some girl talk.'

Aside from seeming insulting to Maureen, I couldn't see this idea going down well with Moth. However, I knew I'd be in trouble with her if I didn't warm up and be a bit more helpful. So I got my map out, showed Phil how to find us, then got away as quickly as I could. I was going to take the wolf pelts, but couldn't bring myself to do it. I didn't mind hunting for what we needed but blasting away as Phil had done didn't sit well with me. So I pulled the bodies off the road, though I didn't really know why, before Gray and I headed for home.

I couldn't work out Gray's reactions. He clearly mistrusted Phil but liked Donald. A horrible thought struck me that he knew Momma Horse, Smoke and Flicka would take to these people. But there were six of them, and only three horses left. Suddenly, I hoped Nemisha and Pierre were back, and hurried to get home before these newcomers arrived there.

CHAPTER 16

G ray and I were almost home when we spotted Moth and Ginny riding Misty and Poppa with Whiskers playing alongside. They were laughing at him scooting about and I felt guilty because I was about to ruin their day. Gray called his family and we cantered to meet them.

'Hi, Jo!' Ginny waved so hard she nearly fell off. 'It's us.'

'I can see it's you, sausage-brain,' I replied. 'Moth – like they used to say in the movies, "We're not alone".'

Moth frowned. 'People, do you mean?'

'Be better if it was aliens.' I tried to make a joke of it, but Moth's radar was alerted. 'What's wrong with them? Are they dangerous?'

'They're weird. There's an old couple, who seem okay, but there's this swaggering guy with a neck like a bull elephant and a lot of guns and a ditzy woman in a pinny with two kids like little mice. The guy was shooting wolves, Moth.'

'Wolves? We've never had any trouble with wolves. Why would he need to shoot them?'

'Well, it looked like the wolves were seeing them off, even if it meant some of them getting shot. I was going to take the pelts, but I felt bad about it.'

'The wolves were attacking them?'

I pondered this a moment. 'I don't think they actually were. I think the bloke thought they would, or something. I might be wrong – he's probably a lovely guy.'

I grimaced and she regarded me a long moment, rubbing Christopher's back as he lay gurgling to himself in the carrier on her chest. I reached out to tickle his head and he turned, giving me a big grin.

'Do you want to take him?' Moth asked, smiling at his recognition of me. 'Then we'd better get back before they come.'

I took Christopher and his little warm body against my chest made me feel protective. I didn't want a man with a swagger and a gun around my family. So how could I get rid of someone like that without a swagger and a gun of my own? I had a gun – or rather, we had a gun – at the house. Pierre had brought a deer down once with it, but though we were glad of the meat, none of us liked the way it shattered the silence or the inherent violence of it. Pierre came from a hunting family but took no pleasure in it and was quieter than usual for days afterwards. So the gun mostly stayed well-hidden, out of reach on a high shelf. I wasn't likely to get it out to wave at a man who clearly knew how to use it when I didn't, and I couldn't see anyone else doing that either.

We reached home, turned the horses out, and did all the routine feeding and watering as it was getting dark. Moth made a big chicken stew and it was bubbling away on the stove as the lights of a vehicle came up the drive. For a hopeful moment, I thought it might be the rest of our tribe back, but it was Phil and his group.

Phil was driving now, with Donald wrapped up and bouncing around in the back of the pickup and the rest inside. I went to offer the old man a hand down, but he waved me off with a laugh. 'Away with ye, laddie. Thanks but I'm not that old.' He jumped down as easily as I'd have done. 'Well, we're here and I'll make our apologies now, because I'm certain they'll be needed.'

I liked him a lot, he made me think of my grandad, but as Phil got out of the car, I still didn't like him at all.

He winked at me. 'Mum got the kettle on, has she? Who's the man around here?'

'I'm Ellen Anthony.' Moth had come up behind him and, beneath her best attempts at welcome, I knew at once that she was struggling too. 'You and your family are welcome to a meal and beds for the night.'

Trish and the children were still in the car, though Maureen had got out quietly and stood alongside Donald. Phil bent down to look through the open driver's window.

'Okay,' he said and his family scuttled out.

The little girls were now wearing frilly dresses and Trish had changed into a denim skirt and put on make-up. Phil was still dressed like a big hunter who fought grizzlies bare-handed. He wasn't as tall as Dad or Pierre but he was broader than either of them, solid too, with a neck like the trunk of an impressive tree and a belligerent rounding to his shoulders, as though he was ready to get his head down and his fists flying at a moment's notice.

But he offered Moth his hand with what looked like genuine politeness.

'Pleased to meet you,' he said, and I tried to feel I'd misjudged him. 'This is my wife, Trish, and my girls, Paula and Mandy. Say "Hello" girls.'

The two girls chorused a greeting, while Trish hurried forward to enfold Moth in a warm embrace.

'Oh, it's so lovely to see another woman,' she said, gushing over Moth so much I thought we'd have to wash her down later. 'I've had no-one to talk clothes with for the longest time.'

Moth glanced at the old lady. 'You're very welcome. Please come inside.'

She ushered them all in and turned to greet Donald and Maureen. 'I'm sorry,' she said. 'I didn't catch your names – are you related to Phil and his family?'

'No,' said Maureen. 'We joined up with them because it was getting a wee bit hard on our croft, just the two of us old creaky sticks.'

Donald elbowed her. 'Creaky yourself, old woman. I'm a spring lamb when the sun shines.'

Moth and I grinned and I knew now why Gray had been torn. This old couple would become part of our group, but Phil and his family, well, I wasn't sure how they fitted in and maybe Gray wasn't either.

Once inside, there was confusion about who would eat where, as Phil didn't usually eat with children. Moth got round this as Ginny wanted to talk to the girls so she set up a small table for them. But she didn't put them to eat out of adult sight, nor did she offer Phil a seat at the head of the main table. I saw her think about putting me there, but, with a glance, we silently shared the knowledge that I'd then become the young male challenger to him. I nodded to the kids' table but Moth shook her head and indicated that I should sit by Donald. She sat at the head of the big table herself – it was usually Sophie's place, actually, because she could organise our chaotic mealtimes like no-one else.

Phil held forth during the meal, describing his battle against the odds to bring his family out of the wilderness. I wasn't sure where they'd been but it was a lot more hostile and threatening than anywhere we'd come across. Donald fidgeted a lot and winked at me when the story got particularly exciting. Then Phil reached the part about Corrycreag, and really started to enjoy himself.

'It was clear from the moment we arrived that a base had been established there,' he said, sitting back in his chair. 'Not local people, outsiders, chancers, probably trying to set up a power centre, but moved on in search of better pickings.'

'Me and Gray,' I chipped in, 'and a French family. That's all who've been in Corrycreag in two years.'

Phil looked up. 'French?' He sniffed. 'A landing party maybe.'

I snorted with laughter. 'Why would anyone from France sail all the way around to the west coast of Scotland to set up a colony? For God's sake, they were on holiday and got stranded, like you, like us.'

Phil looked as though he'd like to teach me a hard lesson and Moth glanced at me, so I kept quiet with great difficulty and he carried on his story.

'You're only a boy. You see three people and you only see three people. I've been around. I know how things are. Your French family may have been left behind to watch over the place while the others cast a wider net, or they may have been abandoned because they were too young or slow or useless. Just because they were the only ones there when you got there, lad, doesn't mean they were the only ones ever. Corrycreag had been systematically plundered and I wasn't going to take the chance that they were behind us.' His shoulders rose a little, making him look as though he were crouching to attack. 'We siphoned petrol out of the tanks from the garage at the edge of town and filled as many cans as we could find for our pick-up. Then, once the women had sorted out clothes and food for us, Donald and I laid a fuel trail from one end of the main street to the other.'

'That's not entirely true, now, is it?' Donald's face, crinkly with years of laughing in the face of harsh weather took on a craggy look. 'You laid a fuel trail and I tried to stop you.'

Phil shrugged. 'Take more than a man of your age to stop me.' He sniffed and I wondered how long it would be before he spat on the floor or cocked his leg to scent mark the kitchen table.

'There are times when you've got to nail your colours to the mast.' He hammered an imaginary nail into the wood in front of him, making Ginny, already wide-eyed, jump and squeal. He liked that. 'That's right. You can't sit on the fence, you've got to take a stand, draw a line and make sure no one crosses it. Anyone watching from a distance would have seen that place go up – and it did go up, didn't it girls?' Paula and Mandy looked up from playing with their food to nod eagerly, though Mandy looked a little tearful at the memory.

Phil winked at them then grinned with some malice at the rest of us. 'It went up like firework night. Those old houses along the quay were dry as kindling – probably full of wood-worm anyhow – and the garage was close enough to town to spread the fire goodstyle. The flames tore along the trail I laid with cats and vermin scattering in all directions. It was a fine sight, I tell you.'

He paused in anticipation of some sort of applause but Moth had gone very quiet, putting her knife and fork down. Trish's chin came up, ready to defend her man.

'It was probably for the best,' she said. 'Who knows who might be around? There could be all sorts.'

'There could,' said Moth, and if she'd have pointed at Phil she couldn't have been more obvious. 'It seems wasteful though, when goods are scarce, to destroy anything.'

'Took what I needed for my family,' said Phil, shovelling food down his gullet again. 'No business of mine who comes once we've gone.'

'Well, that's debatable,' said Moth and Trish was looking from one to the other, torn perhaps between a conciliatory remark and a defensive one. 'I believe that we have a responsibility to each other now.'

'Every man for himself and his own,' Phil wiped his mouth with a napkin, a surprisingly neat gesture but Moth had him by the eye and he was looking threatened.

'In that case, I shouldn't be sharing the food for my own family with you,' she said. 'We've relied upon the fuel, clothes and whatever else we could forage in Corrycreag. You may plan to move on but we're staying here.'

'No point in that. You'll come with us. We'll all head south, for the centre – London.'

'We're staying here,' Moth said again and he looked at her like a man who never had anyone say 'no' to him.

Trish, clearly used to defusing tense situations, got to her feet. 'Come along, dear,' she said to Moth, 'let's clear the table and have a girly chat while the men talk.'

'Jo and Ginny will clear the table while I feed Christopher,' Moth said. 'You can all help if you like.'

I'd never seen Moth so confrontational but she was quietly furious. Another situation was sidestepped as Phil decided he needed to unload their car and went off while the rest of us cleared the table. The old couple helped but the little girls sat by the fire, Trish saying they were too young to be trusted with crockery. Moth said nothing to this and disappeared upstairs with Christopher, though she usually fed him wherever she happened to be when he got hungry. I felt sorry for her when Trish followed, once she'd wiped down the table. A forcible girly chat was on its way.

It took Phil longer to bring in his family's bags than it took the rest of us to wash-up and we'd just finished when he returned with a whisky bottle and cigars, proceeding to light up.

'I think my mother would prefer you to smoke outside,' I said. 'There's the baby to think of.'

Phil drew on his cigar and blew a long trail of smoke out at me, his chin up. 'You need a new dad, son. Someone to teach you how to behave.'

'Jo knows how to behave,' said Moth from the foot of the stairs, 'and he's right – I'd sooner you didn't smoke in the house.'

'Not much of a way with guests, here.'

Trish re-appeared, stepping in again to swoop down on Phil, gather up his cigars and hand him a glass of whisky all in one movement.

'Now, dear, Ellen's boy's a bit headstrong – that's a sign of character you always say. He's not used to having a man around anymore. You should take him under your wing.'

Phil fixed me with a paternal eye and I decided I'd sooner be taken under the wheels of a bus. 'Come here then, son, and have a drink. Let's all have a drink.'

I knew this would be a hurdle to peaceful co-existence too when we had an alcoholic living with us. But Pierre was away for now and I could see Moth didn't want to fall out with this newcomer completely.

'A very small one,' she said. 'I'm feeding a baby and Jo's a bit young.'

'Nonsense,' said Phil. 'At his age, I was downing six pints a night.'

He poured generous glasses for himself and Trish, giving me a wink. 'Like to get her warmed up for later,' he whispered and I squirmed, not wanting to know about the sex-life of the big white hunter.

He handed me glasses for Donald and Maureen, considerably smaller than his own, then for me and Moth. I nursed mine for a while, sitting beside Moth's chair, listening to Phil hold forth once more about his past life as a salesman, doing the deal, shafting it to them, pulling fast ones and calling his cussies on the moby. It took me a while to work out what this meant, a mobile phone being something I'd almost forgotten about and my experience of customers limited to having been one. Phil's command of clichés was his only redeeming feature, so far as I could see, offering endless possibilities for amusement. I started to enjoy myself, taking a small sip of the whisky, with Moth's warning knee digging into my back. It nearly choked me and went straight to my head, burning though my chest on its way there. However, it softened the edges of an evening with Phil and for that, I was grateful. I focused on counting the number of clichés he could get into one of his long monologues about his skills and business acumen. This seemed to be based mainly around putting one over on people and reporting his rivals to the Inland Revenue, Trading Standards or any other body that would snarl up a few working days for them.

'Phil knows how to use people to his advantage,' said Trish proudly, 'and he can lie his way out of anything.'

'How admirable,' said Moth, 'we'd better remember that, had we?'

Donald grinned into his glass as Phil gave Moth the Evil Eye and Trish started gushing again.

'Oh no, Phil stands by his friends. It's a dog-eat-dog world in business. Friends are different – you keep on the right side of him and he'll do anything for you.'

I suspected that this was true. Alongside the swaggering macho arrogance was loyalty and protectiveness towards people Phil thought smaller than himself. I'd watched him fix a broken toy for Ginny earlier and he was kind and funny with her. His little girls seemed to adore him, constantly jostling for his attention. But it was all dependent upon others needing and looking up to him. We were in trouble if he decided to stay on.

It was back to sharing bedrooms that night. I ended up on an airbed next to Christopher's crib, while Moth and Ginny had the single beds, all of us cramped into the middle bedroom. I'd have slept downstairs but we needed a family conference. So once everyone was quiet, we pushed the two single beds together and sat cross-legged in a huddle to whisper and complain about our guests. Even Christopher was awake, sitting alert on my knee and we struggled to keep our voices down, because we all wanted to scream.

'What are we going to do?' I said. 'Will he try to make us go with him? Or worse, will he decide to stay?'

'I don't know,' said Moth. 'There's not enough room for them to stay – Pierre and the others will be back in a couple of days.'

'But when we move, what if they want to come?' Ginny had whining in a whisper down to a fine art. 'Those girls are really boring – they're scared of horses and chickens and dogs and everything.'

'I'm more worried about the drink,' said Moth. 'I don't know how secure Pierre is if that big tosser starts waving a bottle under his nose – oops, sorry, Ginn.'

Ginny's mouth was a round 'O' of delight,

'You're like Grandad,' she said, scandalised.

Moth grinned, shrugging her shoulders. 'Like father, like daughter,' she said. 'Forget I said that, young lady. It's not a nice word.'

'Made for him though,' I suggested. 'I mean, when all's said and done, at the end of the day, when the shit hits the fan, it's done and dusted and the cussies on the moby...'

A snort of laughter escaped Ginny and Moth slapped my arm, though we were all laughing in a way that was close to hysteria. Our safe home had been invaded and we'd let it happen in the name of politeness.

It turned out that Phil didn't milk goats, collect eggs or cook breakfast, but he did chop wood, this being man's work. We left him to it and, I had to admit, he could chop wood like a wood-chopping demon. The pile built up and, when Donald joined him to start splitting it, I was quite pleased they were there. Maureen liked the chickens and was a dab hand at milking, telling me about her own goats.

'I used to make cheese,' she said, gazing over a broad white back into the memory, 'and butter, though that's easier with cow's milk. And I had a beautiful flock of little Castlemilk Moorit sheep – bonny they were – so I could spin the wool.'

'Moth would like to learn that – we've had a go but we ruined the lot,' I said. 'The wool she found here is nearly all gone now. Spinning would be really useful.'

'I had to leave them all behind though we left all the gates open so there was plenty for them to eat and water in the beck. Shelter too. They had our old barn.'

She had a tear in her eye and I said, 'I'm sure they'll be fine. All our gang were coping very well when we found them.'

'You'll be needing to get your goats in kid if you want them to carry on milking,' she said. 'You're lucky they've gone on this long.'

As I watched her expert handling of the goats, I was thinking of the museum site the others had gone to find at Eilean Tianavaig. This elderly couple had all sorts of traditional skills we needed now. Maureen was very polite and old-fashioned, but not weird or simpering like Trish. She and Donald teased one another the whole time. They fitted in.

Trish spent the morning cleaning the house and Moth told me she'd had a choice. 'I could either be offended, because she implied that it's dirty – "Now, dear" she quoted in simpering voice "You mustn't feel bad, you've got a baby to care for. We all know a woman's work is never done" – or I could let her get on with it. I decided to let her get on with it.'

'Good plan,' I said. 'You wouldn't want her coming outside anyhow – her make-up might get spoiled in this damp weather.'

'At the end of the day, when the shit hits the fan,' Moth muttered, 'I want them to go, now.'

'What about Donald and Maureen?'

'They can stay if they want to. The others get ants in their bed till they leave. Agreed?'

I grinned. 'Agreed.'

Phil and his family showed no signs of leaving and I saw that despite his urge to start a new government of one in London, he was considering our place as somewhere he could rule as an alternative. He strutted round the fields with me telling me what we were doing wrong, though his knowledge of farming seemed limited. Then we came to the horses.

They'd been surprisingly distant all morning, staying out on the hill even though I'd put their hay in the meadow as usual. Now, instead of coming to meet me in an unruly crowd, they looked up as I approached with Phil, then carried on grazing. Gray put himself out enough to whinny to me, but that was it. Then Whiskers darted over, gangly legs all over the place, tail in the air. This was more usual, until he suddenly shot out his neck and put the brakes on, skidding to a halt. He snorted at Phil, his legs rigid and jerky as he spooked, shied sideways and tore back to Momma Horse, hiding behind her to peep round at us. I'd not seen him do that since the day they arrived. It looked funny, now he was so big, but I didn't like it.

'Don't know what's up with them,' I said, though I had an idea. 'Perhaps it's because you're a stranger.'

'It's the way you're training them,' Phil explained. It seemed he was a horse-expert too. He put his arm around my shoulders, saying, with great indulgence, 'Now, I can see you're highly-strung, son, but don't get a strop on. At the end of the day, you've got to show the horse who's boss. It'll set you up for when you get a girl and a job. You should go into sales. There's good money to be made in sales, though it's no job for a wimp, I tell you now. Get these horses eating out of your hand, then when things get going again, you'll have girls falling on their backs and jobs lining up for the taking.'

He shared a few confidential details about his relationship with Trish to demonstrate his point, convincing me that life-long celibacy wouldn't be a bad thing. Then he winked, thumped me on the back and started to wander off but turned to say, 'This French bloke? With your mum, is he?'

'With? No, he's not. My dad's not been dead a year yet.'

He shrugged. 'Sentiment's all very well, but there's a world to re-people.'

I didn't want to know what might be crossing his mind. I wanted him to go and so, it seemed, did Poppa Horse. I'd been watching him get closer out of the corner of my eye and turned to greet him, holding out my hand.

'What's up, Poppa?' I asked and he nudged me, shaking his head in the way they did if something irritated them.

'Who the hell named them?' Phil asked and I was about to reply when Poppa barged me out of the way and charged at Phil with his ears back. He stopped short of touching him, seeming satisfied that Phil backed off with his hands up. He came back with them in fists though and Poppa stood his ground, stamping a hoof and snorting. I'd never seem him behave like that and when I started to go to him, Phil shouted, 'Get out of his way, you bloody stupid boy! He's dangerous – he should be shot.'

I thought of the guns in his pick-up and ran up to Poppa.

'Look, he's not dangerous. He's being protective – he's a stallion and you're a stranger.'

Phil raised his fist at the horse. 'Only room for one stallion here, you bastard,' he said. 'I'll geld you with my bare hands if you make a move again.'

He turned and stalked off down the hill and I found myself close to tears.

'You big pillock,' I told Poppa. 'He'll shoot you without a thought. Stay out of sight for a few days.' I hugged him around the neck. 'Dad, where are you? We need your help.'

He wasn't there though. He only ever turned up unexpectedly and I wandered down the hill feeling he'd abandoned me. But Donald was watching from the meadow and came to meet me.

'I had a wee walk up there with Maureen,' he said. 'Those are fine ponies. The big fellow came to give us a look-over.'

I looked at him. 'Did he go for you?'

'Ach, lad, no. Like a lamb, like a lamb.' He tapped his finger alongside his nose. 'He's a wise one.'

'I don't need him to tell me Phil's a prat,' I said. 'Or that he'd love to shoot something.'

'No, he's not one to get on the wrong side of, that's true. Let's keep him away from your friends.' He glanced back up the hill. 'Me and Maureen took a real fancy to the black filly and the light grey gelding.'

I felt better – of course they did. There was only Momma Horse now, without a human buddy.

'The black is Beauty and the grey's Smoke,' I said and Donald nodded, his eyes still drawn to the hill.

A shout went up, the horses looked round and on the opposite hillside was Sophie on Moonrise. I called Gray and jumped on him without any tack. We hurtled down the slope, pounding hooves driving Phil from my mind. Meeting Sophie, I didn't know what to do. We'd never got to the casual sister-brother hugging stage. We grinned, then she reached over to hit me so I took off my hat and used it to hit her back.

CHAPTER 17

I rode with Sophie to meet the others. Pierre was driving the car with Laurent asleep in the back, while Nemisha was on Flicka with Sunset and Daybreak cavorting alongside, delighted to see Gray. There was so much squealing and snorting that Nemisha and I could only grin at each other over the racket. When we reached the car, which was bumping its slow way over the rutted track, we got down and untacked Flicka and Moonrise, throwing their gear in the pick-up, so they could go tearing off, chasing and play-fighting.

Nemisha hugged me then and I was glad to see her but she looked different, obviously too old for me. My faint hope that I might become the man of her lonely dreams seemed so ridiculous now that I was embarrassed. But she was acting like a big sister, ruffling my hair and shoving me around so I tripped her up and felt better. Souris was barking excitedly which woke Laurent. He clambered out of the car and reached up for me to lift him so he could wrap his short arms round my neck and kiss me noisily. Pierre hung back with his usual shy reserve but when I went over to say 'Hi', his worn face lit up.

'Dear Zho,' he said and reached out his great long arms to enfold me, kissing me on both cheeks and then holding me, as though he'd missed me. It wasn't until then that I realised how much I'd missed him too and I hugged him back. That moment told me something else I hadn't realised. I was never short of hugs. We were a casually affectionate sort of family. But since Dad died, no-one bigger than I was had hugged me and there was something so good about being in a larger person's arms that I felt choked up.

The others were talking at once trying to tell me everything but as Pierre released me, he saw that he'd brought tears to my eyes.

'Is everything okay here, Zho?'

'Not entirely,' I said and they fell as silent as if I'd switched them off. 'Everyone's well – there's no disaster. But some new people have turned up and, well, I want them to go.'

Nemisha said, 'What's wrong with them?'

I hesitated. 'Well … put it like this: if you tell them we're thinking of moving, the guy will expect to be in charge and the woman will start making curtains – ' I looked at them all. 'Are we still thinking of moving?'

That was it. They were off again.

'There are houses and a harbour, and…'

'And the workshops, tell him about the workshops…'

'The fields and the kitchen garden in the old house…'

'Oh, the old house, Joel, it's so great. There's a library and a snooker-table. We could live it in and go weeks without bumping into each other.'

'I want to live in a cottage – I like the cottages best.'

'There are tools, Zho, machinery, and diesel, plenty of diesel for the fishing boats – I can get them going in no time…'

'The tractor – will there be enough fuel for the tractor?'

'For a while, I think, and we could sail to Corrycreag…'

I stopped them then. I didn't want to but I wasn't sure what would happen if Phil started bragging about it.

'I'm not sure how much of Corrycreag is left.'

They faltered into silence, staring at me as I went on. 'This guy, Phil, decided it was better to torch it behind him and his family.'

'Oh, bloody hell,' said Nemisha, then belatedly covered Laurent's ears. 'What sort of a prat is he?'

'I did some damage in Corrycreag myself,' Pierre reminded her, with great shame, but suddenly I felt protective of him.

'You were ill. This guy's just a – ' I glanced at Laurent, who was gazing up waiting for someone else to say a word he wasn't supposed to hear. ' – he's all mouth and trousers, as my Gran used to say.'

Pierre pressed my shoulder.

'We'll be all right, Zho, whoever this man is. Let's go home. Laurent, do you want to drive?'

So Laurent drove the last mile home, sitting on his father's knee behind the wheel of the car singing, 'Bloody hell, bloody hell, bloody hell, bloody hell', while the rest of us followed on foot, rendered helpless by his tuneless but enthusiastic song. Moth and Ginny came running to meet us and there was a lot of hugging and kissing and talking at once in chaotic Franglais. Then everyone became aware of the silent group watching.

Phil had his arms folded and his feet wide apart in a stance which said that anyone who wanted to enter the house had to go through him, while Trish had Christopher in her arms, one hand cradling his head against her shoulder. The little girls were peering out from behind her skirt. Donald and Maureen weren't around and I forgot about them for a moment as Moth made an uneasy round of introductions.

The posture Phil and his family had adopted was so defensive that everyone became awkward. Trish handed Christopher over to Moth with reluctance and seemed concerned by the way he was passed round for his share of homecoming hugs and kisses. He was gurgling and laughing delightedly but Phil and Trish looked as though Moth had handed him over to a group of child-abusers. He ended up with Pierre who sang quietly to him in French, which Chris loved, while the hubbub of news sharing started again.

'Ellen, dear,' said Trish after a while. 'I'll put the kettle on, shall I?'

'Yes, please,' said Moth. 'I'm sure a cup of tea would be welcome.'

Traditional tea was among our treats because, while we had plenty from our foraging trips, it wouldn't last forever – it was past its sell-by date already – and once it was gone we'd have only our home-made herbal variety. So when we went inside and gathered, a large crowd now, perching on the arms of chairs and sitting on the floor, there was quite a sense of occasion between the homecoming and so much tea being made. Donald and Maureen had reappeared from a walk up to see Beauty and Smoke, realising that the people they'd not met yet were home when new horses careered up the hill with Gray.

We had quite a good evening and I kept telling myself I needed to lighten up and give Phil and Trish a chance. The little girls were so mouse-like that most of the time I completely forgot about them, though something about Paula suggested she was less timid than her sister. I knew I should make a bit more of an effort, maybe help them get over their fear of the animals, though I couldn't raise much enthusiasm for the idea.

At first, when we sat down to a crowded supper, there was reluctance in the air, an unwillingness to let these newcomers know our plans. Then I became aware of a quiet consultation between Nemisha and Moth over the washing up. I could have told Misha that Moth would feel we should be honest with them so, once we were gathered round the fire, she told the story of their journey to Eilean Tianavaig, with Sophie chipping in frequently and Pierre now and then.

'It's a long-three-days' journey,' she started, 'maybe four if we're herding stock. But it's worth it. The village is in excellent condition, aside from weather-damage, and the craft workshops have a forge, weaving and spinning gear, a dairy – the traditional pre-industrial workings of a village. Then there's the eco-living stuff – composted toilets, huge vegetable garden with a geodesic dome, a generator, solar panels – Pierre thinks we'll get them and the two windmills running again without much trouble. There are fishing boats, sailing and motorised, that have survived and – it gets better – cattle, sheep, pigs and poultry.'

'*Les canards*,' chipped in Laurent, looking up from the floor where he was sorting out his feather collection. '*Beaucoup de canards*.'

'That's right,' agreed Misha, 'lots and lots of ducks. The fences and garden are a bit chaotic and there's a lot of repairs needed, but it's a real self-contained little place. And there's the old mansion-house and its outbuildings and workers' cottages, as well as the actual village.

We can make a future there – there's room for a whole community, if other people turn up.'

'And there's Janet,' said Sophie and Misha nodded.

'This is probably the best bit: there's a woman, perhaps in her fifties. She's an artist and was one of the craftspeople who worked in the museum part of the village, demonstrating dyeing and pottery, but she was also the caretaker. She's lived there alone, keeping an eye on everything as best she could. She's very ready to welcome us though – she's used to teaching her crafts and she's desperate for company. Pierre is itching to get his hands on the workshop.'

'I'm a farrier. Maureen can run a dairy, and spin and use a loom,' said Donald. 'We'd like to come, if you'll have us.'

Moth looked round our group, silently asking the question I knew would come and I tried to give her the response she was after with some sort of grace.

'Everyone's welcome,' she said, taking in Donald and Maureen, Phil, Trish and their girls. 'This could be a new start for us.'

Phil stared at her. 'A new start?' he said. 'I'm sitting here listening to you getting excited about weaving and making your own butter? Are you mad?'

'It's not the life we want for our children,' chipped in Trish. 'Even if you think it's good enough for yours.'

Moth looked as though she was biting her tongue but Misha was staring in her turn now. 'What other life do you think there is? Everyone's dead. Don't you understand that? I've been to London, I came up through Manchester, Carlisle, Glasgow – all the places where people gathered in any sort of numbers are wiped out. The buildings are fine but the people are piles of dust. You must have seen it – don't you understand what's happened? Human life has been virtually eliminated. The only ones left are like us – people who were in very small groups or alone.' She dropped her eyes to her hands then. 'I've thought a lot about it. Whatever it was must have been drawn by the energy or heat given off by large groups of people. In some places the animals have gone too, but not others and I don't know why that was.

The aftermath, some sort of fallout I suppose, killed a lot of bird and plant life, but that's coming back now. But humans – there'll be small groups like us – maybe running to thousands – around the country, but when you think of the millions there were, just a handful.'

She looked at Trish. 'You won't find the life you had. Spinning and weaving is it now. There's no supermarkets, no department stores, it's make it or do without it for a long, long time – maybe the whole of our lifetimes. If there were other countries unaffected, don't you think we'd know by now? Don't you think the power lines would be back up?'

'How do you know they aren't?' Phil's chin jutted out. 'In this hole, you wouldn't know if everything was back to normal only twenty miles away.'

'You've been to Corrycreag – that was a major town – any sign of life there? Any foreign aid coming in with food supplies or electricians, doctors, anything?' She fixed him with a hard eye. 'If you thought things were getting going again, was torching the place a good idea?'

There was a long silence and Trish, with both the girls, was sobbing quietly. Ginny and Laurent were a bit tearful too and Sophie was holding my hand. The picture Misha had drawn was so grim that I was glad of someone to comfort.

Phil drew a long breath. 'We'll head south,' he said, 'all of us.'

My gang looked at him then at each other.

'You can head south,' said Moth. 'Or you can come with us and set up a new home where others might choose to join us. But we will make our own decisions, thank you.'

Phil got up, a sense of simmering about him and I guessed there was no way he could work with people who didn't think exactly as he did. He couldn't listen, change his mind, re-think. He had to lead and if we let him, he'd be a good leader, strong and courageous. But we had to be weak and helpless to make him feel that way and I was pretty sure we wouldn't go along with it.

'We'll head south,' he repeated. 'All of us.'

Then he turned and stalked outside.

There was a long silence, until Donald said, 'We'll stay on, no matter what.'

'How can you leave us?' asked Trish. 'How can any of you – you a mother, Ellen, and you, Pierre, a father – how can you leave us and our children to go all that way alone?'

'That's your choice,' Moth said, gently. 'You're welcome to stay here, Trish, though we'd all have to live and let live.'

Trish smiled at her with pity. 'That's not the way the world works, Ellen. It's dog-eat-dog, and all we women can do is take care of our children and let the men get on with it.'

'Do you really believe that?' Misha asked her. 'Do you really think that if you put on make-up and follow Phil around obediently that you're doing all you can for yourself or the girls? Or him for that matter?'

It was getting very tense and I wasn't surprised when Pierre suddenly got up and left. He hated any sort of confrontation. I was interested though – I wanted to understand how Phil and Trish worked. They seemed happy enough together, but I wondered how much of it was a huge act and what it covered up.

'I think that a woman's role should be to support her man,' Trish was saying. 'Phil's a good husband and a good father. I trust him to take care of us.'

'But you pander to his ego the whole time,' Misha said and I saw Moth wince a little. 'Why should any of us have roles? Why can't we just be who we are?'

'This is who I am,' Trish said. 'I like my man to take care of me.'

'So you don't need to think,' Misha said and even I thought she'd gone a bit far then.

Trish was clearly offended but Donald stepped in. 'Now, we're all a little overwrought. Why don't we sleep on it? Maureen and me'll do well enough in here.'

'Not at all,' said Moth. 'You two take the back bedroom…'

He'd shifted the attention and everyone started playing bed-juggling, trying to ensure that small children and personal sensitivities were taken care of. It ended up with me, Pierre and Donald being relegated to the caravan with hot water bottles. Phil, of course, had to have a bed, so his family kept the large bedroom and everyone else sorted themselves out as best they could. This is how it would be if they stayed. I had a sudden insight into Trish's life and why it was easier for her to be ditzy and dependent.

I'd stayed sitting by the fire, Laurent asleep on my knee, with Ginny and Sophie close by. We formed a weary sub-group, unused to this sort of unease. For all the problems we'd had, the hard work, worries about Pierre, bickering with each other, times when we'd been hungry or irritated or even scared, there'd never been this sort of tension. If Phil and his family stayed, there'd be a division in the group and there'd never been that before.

CHAPTER 18

We began our preparations to move with Phil and his family like bad news clouding everything we did. They followed us around, commenting on the faults or weaknesses in our plans, shaking their heads, foreseeing death, doom and the disintegration of essential values. They didn't like it when we spoke Franglais, seeing it as an attempt to exclude them, and thought we should insist on the French-speakers learning fluent English, this still being England after all.

'England, is it?' said Donald, raising an eyebrow in a way that Ginny loved. 'You don't even know where you are, man.'

Donald had the ability to keep Phil in check but, even without that, he and Maureen became an immediate asset. They pointed themselves towards the new location like finely balanced compasses, seeing everything from the perspective of the move. This was helpful to the rest of us as despite our determination to go, we were torn by our attachment to Tir na Craobh.

Timing became important because we didn't want to herd the sheep while they were heavy in lamb and we needed a vegetable garden planting in time to give us crops in the new setting. My poly-tunnel, which had taken so long to get up, was now carefully dismantled, while the workshops and outbuildings were gone through, so we could plan what to take and how to transport it. We had our original car, the pick-up, the smart car and the caravan, but only Poppa Horse who didn't need diesel to pull the cart. We had fuel and knew where there was more but we couldn't afford to waste it. Different schemes were mulled over each evening, and occasionally Phil would warm up and start to help, before he remembered he wanted us to go with them and turned sullen again.

Trish spent a lot of time working on Moth, though she more or less ignored Misha and Maureen, targeting the mother-link to get what she wanted. I understood how they felt – heading south alone was more daunting than going in a group, for all the problems of food and transport that would bring. But all their determination that we'd go with them ran up against ours that we wouldn't.

Phil's bottle of whisky hadn't appeared again after the first night and I guessed that Moth had spoken to Trish about it. But Pierre had a haunted look about him and I wondered if he sensed it in some way, or if it was just Phil's manner with him getting him down. He was fatherly or laddish with me, patronising with Donald and downright dismissive with Pierre.

'You can tell there's been no man around this place in a while,' he'd say, casting a critical eye over work he knew Pierre had done – which was always faultless. Or he'd come into a discussion and sit so he obscured Pierre's view, saying something along the lines of 'You need a man's view on this one' or 'This place is all women and kids. No wonder you get nothing done'.

While Pierre wasn't cut out for the sort of leadership Phil admired, he'd never have got away with it anyhow. Anyone who started throwing their weight around during our discussions was slapped down immediately and most of the time, no-one did. I thought a lot about the horses and the people who'd gathered around our initial family group. We had our differences but overall suited one another so well that the people had become as mysterious as the horses themselves. Pierre had obviously given this some thought too, because one night, as we lay in the darkness of the caravan, him and me and Donald, talking over our plans, he said, out of a short silence, 'It's no accident that brings us together.'

That was all. Neither of us replied but we didn't need to because we both knew what he meant. But I didn't know if that made Phil and his family an accident, and if so, whether it was their accident or ours.

Phil's attempts to undermine whatever contribution Pierre made seemed to give him a lot of satisfaction. He advised him on everything as though he were an idiot, sometimes speaking slowly in very basic English to him, adding '*Comprendez-vous?*' on the end. He moved things Pierre put down, even going so far as hiding his guitar and, we were pretty sure, breaking things he'd worked on so it looked as though his workmanship was flawed. Trish was up to the same thing with Moth, constantly cleaning places Moth had already done, advising her on how to make sure Ginny grew up a proper girl and treating Christopher as though he were at risk.

She'd reach out when Moth picked him up, saying in panicky tones 'Support his head', or scoop him up from the couch if Moth left him with one of us to keep an eye on him, tutting 'He could be on the floor before they even noticed'. We all took offence at this, because Christopher was everyone's pet and, unless he was asleep, we were always bickering over who got to take care of him. But matters came to a head when Laurent brought a chicken in to show him.

We told Laurent not to bring chickens in the house but he still turned up with something feathery and clucking tucked under his arm fairly often. Once everyone had admired whichever of his friends he'd brought in, he would trot off to return it to the rest. The chickens had got used to this and came belting over if Laurent appeared, hoping for tit-bits, their long legs comical as they raced across the yard towards him.

Christopher had been introduced to chickens at a very young age. Moth said so long as Laurent didn't put them near his face and whoever was looking after him washed his hands after he'd patted at them, then it did no harm. Chris liked them and it made Laurent happy. No-one knew what the chickens thought of Christopher, but they never complained. So when Laurent came stomping in one morning, Souris trotting at his heels and a large glossy chicken under his arm, I said, 'Christopher's in the living-room with Sophie.'

Trish, who was washing up with me, looked round. 'What's he doing?'

'He's going to show Chris the chicken,' I said. 'He does it all the time.'

Trish shrieked as though I'd said he'd brought Chris a crocodile to play with. She dropped the plate in her hands to shatter on the floor and ran waving her arms around after Laurent's solidly departing shape.

'Stop him, stop him!' she was screaming.

Sophie's mouth dropped open in amazement as behind Laurent carrying a chicken, came a woman behaving like a chicken, squawking and flapping. Souris started yapping, Christopher started screaming, Laurent jumped out of his skin, dropping the chicken who, unused to being treated with such disrespect, squawked louder than Trish and flew with the grace of a winged brick, straight at Sophie and the baby. Paula and Mandy dived behind the couch shrieking as Trish flung Laurent aside, knocking him hard into the dresser. He started bawling too as everyone else rushed in from all directions. In moments the room was full of people shouting, Souris barking, children crying and the chicken tearing around in a flurry of feathers and crap.

Trish scooped Christopher from Sophie's knee and, for some inexplicable reason, jumped up to stand on a chair, Chris clutched to her bosom, his squalling face red and angry and an impressive sound coming from his small lungs. Sophie started screaming at Trish and the expression 'Pardon my French' took on a whole new meaning for me. Laurent was wailing, his head and knee bleeding, while Pierre tried to comfort him and I stood with my mouth open wondering what to do. Ginny kept jumping up and down, shouting, 'What's wrong, what's wrong? Who hurt my baby brother?' The racket brought Moth running down the stairs half-dressed after a bath, to stand staring at the volcanic eruption in her living-room.

Then Phil, who'd come striding in ready to take on an enemy invasion, reached out a meaty arm and grabbed the chicken by the throat. I saw what was coming and yelled, 'No!' and everyone else shouted 'No!' too, except Trish who was shouting, 'Phil, Phil! It attacked the baby!'

Silence fell like a blow as Phil upended the chicken, swinging its feet into his free hand and broke its neck. We watched in horrified silence and it seemed to take forever. The bird's body swung into his open hand, he raised its feet up and its glossy black wings fell open, then, showing his teeth, he yanked down on its neck and we heard each tiny chicken vertebra shatter, each blood vessel rupture and ligament tear. The wild rolling of the dying eye caught mine, making my heart plummet and my gorge rise. Phil looked around and said, 'Sorted.'

He flung the corpse in a graceful arc across the living room, through the kitchen and out of the open door onto the yard. Laurent's wail followed it as everyone started shouting again, calling Phil all kinds of fool, while he hurled abuse back and Trish refused to give Moth the baby.

That did it. Moth picked up a book off the sideboard and slammed it down with a loud thwack that got everyone's attention. She fixed us with the eye I'd dreaded seeing all my life because in someone so rarely angry it meant trouble. Then she raised her hand and pointed around the room. 'Not a sound,' she said. 'Not one sound.'

Even Christopher's wails had faded to a snuffle and Moth turned to Trish, holding out her arms. 'Give me my baby,' she said, 'and you never, ever, refuse to hand him to me again.'

Trish hesitated for a moment then took in Moth's expression and handed him over, getting down from the chair. 'If you were any sort of mother…' she began but Moth hadn't done. She shook her head. 'Not one word.'

Everyone watched her and time slowed again as she assessed the situation. She turned to survey us, Christopher moulded against her shoulder and chest as though he'd grown there, her hands cradling him expertly. A calm came over me at her ability to restore order and I started to breathe again. I stood beside Pierre with the sobbing Laurent clinging to him, waiting for her to tell me what to do next. We all waited, and even as we did, I could sense Phil's resentment that everyone knew Moth was in charge, we needed her to be in charge and that we'd never have accepted him in her place.

'Sophie,' Moth said, 'will you go and catch another chicken, please?'

Sophie scuttled off, then Moth turned to Donald. 'Would you mind dealing with the body, please?' He nodded and headed off too.

It was Ginny's turn next. 'Ginn, will you take Paula and Mandy upstairs to play?'

Slowly she was dispersing us. She nodded at Misha as the three girls went past her up the stairs. 'Can you see how badly Laurent is hurt?'

Pierre sat his little boy on his knee as Misha knelt down to inspect his injuries, rooting in her doctor's bag for cotton wool.

'Phil and Trish,' said Moth, 'please sit down and we'll play this little drama again the way it would have happened without your intervention.'

She handed Chris to me and I sat opposite Pierre with Laurent while Misha finished cleaning him up and applying plasters to his head and knee. Sophie returned with another chicken. Phil and Trish seemed about to protest, but Moth raised that alarming finger again,

'Please sit down. You are guests in my home.'

They obeyed and I saw that the same code that said Phil didn't eat with children ensured that, reminded of their guest status, they played by its rules.

'Give Laurent his chicken, Sophie. Are you all right, darling?' Laurent raised a tearful face to Moth, nodded and got up to take the new bird from his sister. 'Why don't you show her to Christopher?'

With a wary glance at Phil and Trish, Laurent limped the few steps to where Chris was on my knee, looking around now, aware at some infant level of the quiet in the room.

Laurent held the chicken out a little to Chris, too tearful still to chatter away as he usually did, big sobs heaving up from his chest. I smiled at him and helped Chris to stroke the chicken. He gurgled happily then Laurent, full of quiet dignity, gave Phil and Trish a look and said, 'I don't like you,' before he headed outside, Pierre following.

Sophie brought a bowl of soapy water and we washed and dried Christopher's hands, then handed him back to Moth.

'Now,' she said, 'can you explain to me why that didn't happen the first time?'

'The bird was full of germs and it attacked him,' Trish started and Phil said, 'It was going wild.'

'It didn't attack him,' I said. 'It was quiet until Trish panicked it.'

'You could have stood back and let it run outside.' Pierre had come back in and was looking down at Phil without aggression but there was an edge to his voice. 'You killed my son's pet before his eyes. What sort of person does that?'

Phil rose to his feet. 'A man who does what's needed. You wouldn't understand.'

I knew Pierre wouldn't respond, but I prayed that he wouldn't back down and he didn't. He stood his ground, making Phil go round him to leave the house, while Moth, who'd softened a little, said to Trish, 'You don't like us and we don't like you. We've offered you a home with us, even though we know it would be a disaster. If you don't want to go, then staying has to be very different. You don't criticise my children or my care of them. You don't try to impose your ways on us, either of you, and we'll leave you to get on with your own. You can have the caravan while you're still here and we'll live as neighbours, then at the new place, you can choose your own home. Or you can go. It's your choice.'

My job for the rest of the morning – after I'd cleaned up the liberal distribution of chicken manure from the living-room – was to clear out the caravan and move Phil and his family's belongings into it. While I did this, they went out and I could see the four of them sitting in a united huddle on the hill where the horses usually grazed. They'd abandoned it that morning. Even from a distance, it was obvious the family were discussing us. I could see arm gestures and pointing and had a feeling the situation wasn't going to get better any time soon. They couldn't simply leave. They needed enough fuel to get to the next town and food, but we hoped that they'd start making plans.

That night, they ate in the caravan, refusing to come into the house, so we had a chance to talk.

'So what are we going to do?' Misha asked. 'Donald, Maureen, have we put you in a difficult situation?'

Maureen shook her head.

'We've regretted leaving with them from a wee minute or so after losing sight of our croft,' she said.

Ginny started grinning at once, loving her accent. She practised talking like Maureen and Donald and her rendition of an old favourite song of Grandad's – *Donald, where's yer troosers?* – had brought the rest of us to a horrified silence until Donald started laughing. Now they sang it together and both he and Maureen encouraged Ginny, teaching her obscure dialect words and old songs. So when she piped up, 'I want you to stay with us a wee while,' Donald tweaked her ponytail and replied, his accent twice as strong as usual, 'Will ye no' have us a long while, lassie?'

Ginny grinned again. 'Ach, ai surrrre-ly will.'

'Well, of course they're staying with us,' Moth said. 'And we have to get on with the move. We've got to accept that if the others want to come eventually, then we have to live with it. We can't drive them out.'

'They'd drive us into going with them,' I pointed out and Moth raised her eyebrows. 'So if they're bullies, does that excuse us becoming bullies?'

'Of course not,' I felt as though I was six again. 'But surely we don't have to put up with being bullied either.'

'No, if they want to come, they'll have to bully each other, not us.' Moth looked tired suddenly. 'And Trish must stay away from Christopher. I'm afraid that she wants him for herself.'

Everyone stared at her.

'She can't take your baby,' Misha said. 'And we can't accept them unconditionally, for our own sake. We've got something good here, a new beginning, and yes, in principle, they're welcome to be part of it. Like you said, Ellen, "Live and let live". That's fine. But if they want this macho guff where the women have to wear pinnies while the blokes go out killing stuff with their bare hands, then they aren't going to settle with us anyway.'

I felt the mood needed lightening a bit.

'At the end of the day,' I said, 'when the shit hits the fan, it's down to brass tacks, to sort out the men from the boys and girls will be girls, its raining cats and dogs while you don't suffer fools gladly and in a dog-eat-dog world it's every man for himself...'

I had a lot of things thrown at me then, while Laurent shouted, 'Jo said "Shit", Jo said "Shit".'

Unfortunately, amid this chaos, which turned into a cliché competition, Phil came into the house unnoticed and found us making fun of him. We were mean bad people and properly ashamed of ourselves but, sadly, only because he caught us.

When Ginny hissed 'Phil's in the kitchen' we fell into an embarrassed silence. We could hear him crashing about and the fact that he had come in with the plates, not Trish, told us he wanted something. At length, he appeared in the doorway. 'We'll be moving on,' he said, 'if you'll spare us enough diesel to get to the next town.'

'Of course,' said Moth. 'Phil, if you all want to come in by the fire...'

He shook his head. 'And get mocked to our faces? I don't think so.'

He turned on his heel and the set of his shoulders spoke not of humiliation, but anger.

'I'm sorry,' I said, genuinely ashamed now, 'that was my fault. I started it.'

Moth sighed. 'Oh forget it, Jo, there's so much steam to be let off here tonight that something had to give. If I'm honest, I'd sooner they went hating us than stayed here.' She pushed her chair back. 'I'm afraid that this is the real future – we fail to get on, the same as we did before.'

'No lass,' Donald shook his head, 'we get on well enough, don't we now? Knowing when it can't work and walking away is fair enough. Phil's not learned to do that yet, he'll keep pushing and pushing until he gets his way.' He got to his feet. 'He probably will end up leading the new government, of course.'

This depressing thought made us smile. None of us stayed by the fire very long and though Ginny wanted to get the instruments out, no-one was in the mood. She got cross and planted her feet with her hands on her hips to give us a piece of her mind. 'The trouble with you lot,' she began, and I knew we were in for a talking to, 'is that none of you trust the horses enough.'

'What do you mean?' Moth asked and Ginny let rip.

'They came when Daddy died. Because he had Gray, Jo found Sophie and Laurent, and because they came here, Pierre got better. Then Flicka called Misha here when Moth was having Chris and we needed a doctor. And 'cos of Misha, we've got the new place to go to that Dad told us to look for and we've got the stuff we need to make it good. Then Gray found Donald and Maureen and we like them. And all of us have a horse that loves us best. But you don't trust them to sort it out. You think we're stuck with Phil and Trish or it's bad that they're here, but it's not. It's not nice but it's meant. The horses haven't chosen them. That doesn't mean they're bad, it just means they don't belong with us. There's somewhere else they're supposed to be where they'll be happy too, or we'll get to like each other. So, we've got to sit back and wait and the horses will sort it out.'

With her characteristic pony-tail flip, she took the Chicken-master by the hand and headed for the stairs with him. Laurent quickly got the message that he was to be on Ginny's side. He turned at the foot of the stairs to stick his tongue out at us, then flipped his head in such a neat imitation that they were barely out of sight before the rest of us lost it completely.

CHAPTER 19

Regardless of Ginny's pep-talk, we dispersed fairly quickly. Donald and Maureen were real outdoors people and liked a long walk before bed. I guessed also that they were used to being alone a lot and felt crowded. Sophie and I played cards in a half-hearted way for a while then she went to put Laurent to bed and tell him a story.

Pierre had been upset in some way I didn't understand since the chicken drama earlier in the day and went off alone. Misha seemed irritated with him and my suspicion that the slow burn between them had been dampened while they were away was confirmed when I overheard the back end of a conversation between her and Moth.

'He can't help it,' Moth was saying, 'you won't make a talker of him, anymore than Phil will make a pinny-wearer out of you.'

There was silence so I guessed the point had hit home. At some level we all want other people to be what we want them to be, not what they are. I thought about this and Ginny's lecture until my head was doing its familiar impression of a mixer and I had to go outside to see Gray to distract myself from the churning.

He was in the field by Dad's grave, which I knew I'd been avoiding. I hesitated a moment then asked myself, What sort of prat gives the cold shoulder to a dead man? So I set off down to where Grey's shadowy shape was waiting. But I felt hurt and resentful that there'd been no sense of Dad for weeks. It occurred to me that he was weaning us off him and that made me feel sick. I wanted to know he'd be around always. And now, with Phil strutting around like Laurent's favourite cockerel and Pierre isolated in some private misery, I needed Dad. Donald was like a roguish twinkly grandad and I had the feeling he'd be good in a crisis but, as Moth was fond of saying, Dad was my role-model and that was fine with me. Only, he wasn't there.

I sulked a bit by his grave with Gray loafing alongside, searching among the winter grass for any choice summer leftovers he'd missed. Then he came to stand behind me, his head over my shoulder, a big dark shape between me and the sky. It was a still night, cold but soft. The bite of the winter air had a balmy edge, as though it was dreaming of spring. I fell into a bit of a dream myself, listening to Gray breathing in my ear, his breath warm and slightly damp on my face, while I reached one hand up to warm under his mane, stroking his neck and breaking up clods of mud attached to his long winter coat.

'You're a big scruff,' I told him, kissing him in the hollow above his wide nostril. All the horses loved what Ginny called nose-kisses, burying their muzzles into our necks so we could kiss that hollow. It was a measure of trust on both sides, because the soft curve of fine muscle was sensitive and a swing of their hard heads could knock a person out. With Gray standing behind me, I could rest my face against the nose-kissing spot and feel it move gently with his breath, my own falling into rhythm. Ginny was right. The horses had come when we needed them and had never let us down. Even that moment, though Gray had come wandering over casually, he was there when I was feeling low, something good to trust in when, no matter how we tried to make it normal, the world changed daily.

I sat for a long while in the dark, feeling the stillness of the night around me and when I became aware of Dad, I knew he'd been there the whole time. That was the point, I think, to let me know that he was always there, even when I wasn't aware of it and started feeling abandoned. It was like getting in a panic about losing something then finding it had been in my pocket all along.

'Sorry Dad,' I said aloud quietly, remembering times when I was little and convinced myself he'd let me down when he hadn't. He didn't say anything but he rarely did. I usually knew what he was telling me, even without those odd occasions when I heard his voice in my head. Now, as I quietly relished the renewed understanding that he was there, I knew he wanted me to watch out for Pierre and Moth and Christopher. It was a strong feeling with no detail but I knew it was important.

'Okay,' I said. 'Whatever you say.' I felt his hand on my back and sat very still so I wouldn't lose that familiar sense of safety.

I was so still and quiet that I jumped out of my skin when all hell let loose on the yard. There was shouting, gunfire, the sound of things crashing and raised voices, or a voice, a man's voice, raging in drunken French.

I tore back towards the house as the lights came on to reveal Pierre staggering across the yard with one of Phil's guns in his hands. But he wasn't pointing it at anyone, thankfully. He was firing it into the air, loading, firing, reloading. I could hear Trish and the girls wailing from inside the caravan and Moth came running out of the house, with Misha behind her. Donald and Maureen were running back too but he pushed her behind him as they reached the yard, warily assessing this man they barely knew.

Pierre in a drunken rage wasn't something I'd forgotten, nor how destructive he could be, but knowing him now, I didn't think he'd hurt anyone deliberately. What he'd do by accident was something else and every time the gun went off, everyone flinched and cowered, covering their ears and shouting at him to stop. I saw Sophie's shape at the window of her bedroom, Ginny hovering behind her. She turned away and the light went out as the gun blasted to pieces everything Pierre had worked so hard to build with her. Then I noticed Phil. He was the only one who didn't flinch away with each gunshot. He stood leaning against the caravan, a whisky bottle in one hand and a cigar in the other, watching Pierre with a smile on his face.

Moth was trying to get Pierre to put the gun down, though I'd already gathered that what he was doing was getting rid of the ammunition. This didn't make good sense from any perspective, though I could see his logic. He looked wild and frightening but Dad had told me to watch out for him. I remembered too that he'd hugged me and how that had felt. We had a good friendship growing and I decided to put my faith in it.

With Moth shouting at me to get back, I went up to Pierre and, although he looked completely out of control, he swung the gun up so it couldn't accidentally hurt me. I read that as a good sign.

'I'll take it,' I said. 'It's okay, Pierre. Come on, let's go and see Sunset – she's already on her way down to you.'

He stared at me as though he didn't know me and I felt a pang of fear, my heart hammering so hard it sounded like gunfire, but after a long moment he handed me the gun. Then he became aware, for the first time I think, of the ring of cautious people around him and started to rage at us in French, waving an arm towards Phil. He was going too fast for me to keep up and it was pretty much nonsense, I think, anyway – a combination of apology and accusation and all the self-hatred evident in him so much of the time, along with a good dollop of self-pity.

The horses had come to the edge of the yard and Sunset moved forward, whickering to Pierre, the way Momma Horse did to Whiskers. He went to her, starting to weep and put his arms around her neck, sobbing loudly against her mane. Phil drew on his cigar, tipping his chin up to blow a long stream of smoke into the cold air.

'Just offered him a drink,' he said, shrugging his shoulders. 'Just being friendly. I'll take that, son.'

He reached out his hand for the shotgun but I backed away with it and, as I hesitated, Poppa Horse charged out of the darkness, his ears flat back on his head. He skidded to a halt in front of me, his head thrust out and although he didn't touch Phil, it was clear that he wasn't to take the gun.

'Look, you big bastard,' Phil faced up to the large animal and that took some courage because Poppa had turned into something frightening. 'That's my gun and when I get my hands on it, I'm going to use it on you.'

'Now, to tell the truth here,' said Donald, coming towards us, 'it's my gun. All your guns are my guns. I should never have let you have them and I'm thinking it's time I took them back.'

With great relief, I handed him the gun and Poppa Horse was quite happy with that. Donald gave it to Maureen and quietly went to the pick-up, retrieving another gun from behind the seats and handing her that too. Then, while Pierre staggered off into the night with Sunset and I stood with a hand on Poppa's neck, knowing for certain that Dad was with me, Donald headed over to Phil.

Moth and Misha moved in too, until we were behind Donald, loosely in a circle, but I noticed that Maureen had moved deliberately back with the guns, taking them far enough away that Phil couldn't possibly think he was being threatened.

'I need a gun,' he said. 'I'm heading off alone with my family. I'll need to protect them and hunt for food.'

'Well, we'll see about that when you're on your way.' Donald said. 'It's clear that they need putting under lock and key for now. Thought you'd have taken better care with them.'

He insisted with great firmness until Phil handed over the last gun, which was in the caravan.

'Why did you have it in there?' Moth asked, appalled. 'Who here do you need to protect yourself from?'

Phil gave her a look that was mixed shame and resentment and I saw the weakness in his bullying then, guessing that Pierre had been enraged for the same reason Moth was angry now.

Donald and Maureen managed to disappear off into the darkness with the guns and by the time I realised they'd gone, I wasn't sure if they'd slipped into the house or away round the back somewhere. I trusted them to do what was best though and was more concerned now about Pierre.

'He's been sober for half a year,' I said to Phil. 'Why would you do that to him?'

'He's weak,' Phil replied. 'You needed to see it.'

Then he turned and went into the caravan, as Trish pulled the curtains together, shutting us out.

'What now?' I said. 'Misha, shall we go after him?'

To my surprise, she turned away. 'I can't help him,' she said, 'he's beyond anything I can do.'

'I don't mean as a doctor,' I said, glancing at Moth's concerned face. 'I mean as his friend, I thought – I thought, you and he…'

She shook her head, terse and unhappy. 'So did I,' she said, 'for a while.'

Then she went inside and left me alone with Moth.

'What's going on?' I asked. 'How can she turn away from him like that?'

Moth shook her head. 'I'll go and talk to her. Can you cope with Pierre?'

I nodded, 'Sure. Christ, Moth, what a day.' I caught her arm. 'Moth, is it falling apart?'

She got hold of me then and we hugged each other tight there in the cold darkness with distressed people all around us, battening themselves down against a sleepless night. At length, she let me go and looked up at me, taking my face in her hands.

'It's being tested, Joel,' she said. 'Like anything that needs to be strong.'

She kissed me then went back into the house, while Poppa Horse drifted off into the dark and I stood in the night, with Gray and Dad, glad of a few moments to think.

CHAPTER 20

I decided that the situation warranted a pot of our good coffee. It was valued even more highly than tea and kept in conditions worthy of rare historical artefacts for birthdays, Christmas and emergencies. This seemed to qualify so I brewed up, dug out a flask, two cups and a couple of blankets and headed off into the darkness, Gray at my heels like an overlarge dog.

'Find Sunny,' I said and he nodded – or he may as well have done – and steered me towards the hill. I stumbled along beside him, wishing Phil could have decided to blow Pierre's sobriety in daylight. Fortunately, there was a slim moon so it wasn't completely dark and before long I saw two silhouettes on the skyline. One was the forlorn triangle that only a human sitting on the ground hunched over his knees in misery can form. The other was standing over this sorry outline in an attitude of patient companionship.

Gray whinnied softly, discreetly making our presence known to Sunny without disturbing the cause of our united concerns. She raised her head in response then nudged at Pierre, but he didn't look up.

I threw one blanket around his shoulders, coaxing him into sitting on it rather than the damp ground, then wrapped myself up in the second before sitting beside him, pouring a cup of coffee and pushing it in his direction. The rich smell wafted around us and perked him up enough to reach out and take it. We sat in silence for a while sipping the coffee, Gray taking up a sentinel posture to echo Sunny's alongside me. Then he rubbed his nose on my shoulder apologetically, as though he knew he'd broken his rather fine outline again the sky.

'You big poser, Gray,' I told him, scratching the itchy spot for him. 'How's that?'

He raised his big head, taking up his post again, his shaggy mane flopping below his neck and I said, 'Isn't he great? He knocks me out, he really does.'

Pierre twisted round to watch Gray for a moment, then he said, 'You named him after your father, Zho.'

His voice was so cracked and rough that it took a moment to understand what he was saying, but then I nodded. 'Yes. Moth always called him 'Gray', you know – short for Graham. And Gray is grey, so it fitted.'

Pierre nodded, sending alcohol fumes wafting over me.

'Do you know that Laurent named a pet after me? It sort of fits too.'

I trod carefully, guessing where this was headed. 'What pet?'

'What does Laurent love best?' In the faint moonlight the wreckage of his face took on tragic shadows and hollows, a landscape of his life that made my chest hurt for him. 'Zho names a horse after his father, a fine, brave horse. Laurent, he names a chicken 'Pierre' and not even a cockerel, but a hen.' He gave soft half-laugh. 'I have a hen named after me. It is a gift to be proud of, *n'est-ce pas?*'

I smiled a little. 'Well, the first thing I should remind you,' I said, 'is that Gray's a gelding, so Dad might not have a read a compliment into it.'

He almost smiled, but shook his head and hung it as though it was too heavy to raise.

I nudged him gently. 'But you said the thing that matters yourself – "what Laurent loves best". Laurent's as proud of his chickens as I am of Gray. His horse – which is a mare – was already named, but not the chickens.' I nudged him again. 'He doesn't name them after just anyone, you know.'

'It is too apt,' he said. 'I have blown everything.' He wasn't drunk now. He was sober in a bitterly clear way, more than sober, his usual gentleness honed into something sharp-edged and I was afraid he'd dissect himself into pieces with it.

'Phil set you up,' I said. 'It wasn't your fault.'

'I'm not to be trusted. He knew that.'

'What happened with the gun?' I asked, blundering into his wounds then trying to make up for it by adding, 'Were you trying to get rid of the ammo?'

'He knew I was angry with him, with myself, because I couldn't resist the drink. So he offered me the gun to shoot him with, though he knew I'd have never done that. He jeered at me, said I've got no balls, here with two good-looking women I'm not sleeping with, taking orders from my daughter, letting him move in and walk all over me.'

'He's not got enough in him to understand what you've done since you've been here, Pierre,' I said, meaning it. 'You've got practical skills he's never even thought of and you've got yourself together. And as for Moth and Misha, well, he's all mouth and trousers, and neither of them would be impressed by that. You're welcome here and he's not. Doesn't that tell you anything?'

'I'm a mess, Zho. I'm like an old dog that pisses on the floor but he can't help it so everyone makes allowances for him.'

'Now you're just being sorry for yourself. Okay, so you fell off the wagon – well, get back on, Pierre. We're all allowed to make mistakes.'

'Sophie won't forgive me.'

'Sophie gets scared and then she gets mad. She will forgive you – she worships you.'

He fell silent, sipping his coffee and I topped it up.

'I was offended because Phil had a gun in the caravan. He said his family needed protecting and he'd shoot any of us who crossed him. I started to get angry that he could say such a thing…' He shook his shaggy head. 'Then he said before he goes "that bastard horse has had it" and I knew he meant that. While I couldn't shoot him – I've not sunk that low – the same rage that was on me in Corrycreag took hold of me.' He sighed so long and slow that I expected to see his body deflate into an empty sack of skin. 'It made drunkard's sense that if I used up his ammunition, he couldn't harm Ginny's horse, but it didn't occur to me just to take it away.' There was a slight pause then he added, 'I thought I'd show everyone what he's like, but I showed them what I'm like instead.'

I gave him a hug around the shoulders, pulling the blanket up over them a bit higher. 'He's not fit to have a gun, Pierre, and I'm worried about Poppa Horse. Could we get them to leave till Phil's gone, d'you think?'

Pierre shook his head. 'Poppa's on guard over his herd and that includes us.'

I considered his profile for a moment. 'Would you let him hurt any of us?'

He turned to me, his eyes appalled in the moonlight. 'No, of course not. How weak do you think I am?'

I smiled at him. 'I don't think you're weak at all, Pierre. How weak do you think you are?'

'I let him kill Laurent's pet.'

'Only because it happened too quickly for anyone to stop it. You told him what you thought of him.' I hesitated a minute, all that Englishness that makes speaking from the heart difficult tying up my tongue. Then I thought of my family, who'd never had that problem with each other. Pierre was family now.

'Look,' I said, a bit awkward but warming up once I got going, 'you fit in. You and Sophie and Laurent. My family really gets on well – that's always been our strength – and you three have fitted right in without any problem. Ginn and Moth think that too and look how Chris loves you – babies know these things. I know Misha has fitted in and Maureen and Donald will. But you three were first, you're family now. Having you around helped us learn to live without Dad. And,' I grinned at him, 'you're the only one of them who's bigger than I am and I need that sometimes.' He was watching me now. 'So get up,' I said, 'go back to the house and get ready to say you're sorry for frightening everyone then pick up where you left off and carry on. It'll be okay, Pierre. It really will.' I nudged him again. 'You may have to let Sophie boss you around for a bit, but you'll feel better if she does.'

'I deserve it.'

'Fair enough – then take your punishment. But don't slide into a pit, Pierre, because there's too much to do. We've got to move and we need to do it soon. So, get your act together, buddy, and let's get this show on the road.'

He started to laugh a little then let his head sink exhaustedly onto his knees. He stayed like that a moment then raised it again. 'Okay, my friend, I can do this.'

As though this signalled the end of the crisis, Gray and Sunny relaxed their guarding posture and swung away to amble off into the darkness, joining their friends not far away.

'There we go,' I said. 'We're through, it seems.'

I helped him to his feet where he was a bit unsteady as the alcohol in his blood seemed to have settled around his knees somewhere. I put my arm around his waist, draping his across my shoulders.

'Come on, you can lean on me but I'm not carrying you.'

We staggered back to the house and, once moving, he seemed drunk again and most of the journey back was pretty maudlin. I heard a lot about what a fine boy I was and how he hoped Laurent would grow up to be like me. I accepted this drunken praise because I liked flattery as much as anyone, even from a big lush like Pierre. Besides, I knew that even though he was drunk, he meant it.

Sophie was waiting for us with a face like an ice-sculpture but she didn't say anything, just helped me get her father up the stairs and into bed. His arms and legs, way too long for any normal person, seemed to flop all over the place. We bundled them into a blanket and rolled him up like an old carpet, leaving him to sleep his way towards a bad hangover.

When we'd done, Sophie didn't say anything, but gave me a quick hug then disappeared and I heard her light steps going across the hall to the big bedroom.

More footsteps and Moth's face appeared around the door a moment later. 'Still in one piece?' she whispered.

I nodded. 'Aside from the headache, I think he'll be okay.' I crossed to the door, glancing at Laurent, but he was flat out. 'What about Misha?'

'She's a bit shaken. I think she'd built him up into some sort of tragic hero.' She shrugged her shoulders. 'That's a lot for a man to live up to. An idealist can be demanding.'

'I didn't ask him about her.'

'It's between them, love.' She kissed me on the cheek. 'Thanks, Jo. Sleep well.'

I don't think anyone slept particularly well that night. Pierre rambled in his sleep, arguing with someone. Laurent was dreaming about his dead chicken and climbed in with me not longer after I'd settled down, wanting a shoulder to cry on. I could hear voices in Moth's room and Christopher creating. Someone was moving downstairs once when I woke up and I heard Maureen's voice. Even Souris kept hopping from one bed to another, unable to settle. It was a restless night.

We were like a gathering of the undead next morning and if zombies sit down for breakfast together, they probably look like we did. Pierre was sick three times before anyone else got moving and looked like death on long, tottering legs. Misha and Laurent were both subdued, Sophie in a cold mood and Ginny was whiney.

'Well, we're a happy crowd today,' said Maureen brightly, stirring up a huge pan of porridge. 'A good breakfast will put us right.'

She took charge and while she probably deserved a lot more thanks than she got, she successfully chivvied us into eating and clearing the table. We'd sat down again with second cups of tea to discuss a plan of action for moving, when a deputation appeared in the doorway.

'Come in,' said Moth. 'Would you like some tea?'

Phil led his family in, shaking his head.

'We've got a proposition to make,' he said, pointedly ignoring everyone except Moth, Misha and Donald who, it seemed, were the people who mattered.

Moth glanced at us then said, 'Very well.'

'We've been watching you,' Phil said, 'and this place could work a lot better.'

Trish drew a piece of paper out of her pocket. 'Your standards are poor and your attitude to work is too relaxed,' she said. 'The dog and the birds need to be kept out of the house. Scraps of food should be boiled up for the poultry, not thrown on the yard. I've seen Joel help himself to biscuits on three occasions outside meal times. Pierre took a two hour lunch break the day before yesterday to go riding with his children. Ellen, I've logged the hours you spend cleaning. You're sloppy about it and you need to get Ginny in from tomboying around to make your time more efficient.' She was in full swing now, while Phil stood nodding approval. 'Sophie, you're too quick to take charge for a little girl but your dressing up games are very useful – you'll play house with the other girls every afternoon and Ellen will teach domestic skills. Nemisha, we don't know what you do all day. If there's no-one to doctor, how are you spending your time?'

Phil took up the baton of efficiency. 'We're willing to stay on, supervise this move and help you get the new place more businesslike. I'll draw up a rota of duties and anyone not pulling their weight misses a meal. Girls do inside work, the ladies will have to help outside until more men turn up – that can't be helped, but there's no need to lose their femininity. We'll restore some semblance of civilised values for the sake of the children. I'll be in charge outside and Trish inside. She'll supervise bringing up the baby too – he's handed around far too much. Jo, son, you'll start learning my trade then, when we're in the new place, we'll send you out repping to find other communities and sell our surplus produce. We need to get a seller's market up and running as soon as we can, re-establish income brackets depending on productivity. We'll set up a banking system – on paper until we get cash going again. Pierre will be on the lowest income, because he's a waste of fucking space and Donald, for the time being, you'll be on a full man's wage, but that will drop to a pension as soon as younger men join us. We'll set up a welfare system based on a contribution to society. Once we've got something recognisable established, other people will come and they can buy shares in the place. Market forces are like that – they draw commerce and that's what we need.' He nodded, enjoying himself now. 'We'll keep two of the horses, because riding's a nice hobby for kiddies, then sell the rest once we establish new networks. All except that big bastard, because I'm going to shoot him and make a rug.'

We stayed remarkably cool. I saw eyes flare and people resist their feelings at various points during this long speech. It was touch and go when he mentioned Christopher and his plans for Poppa Horse brought him close to being battered to death with the teaspoon in Ginny's hand. But Moth smiled her into the state of dreamlike calm we'd all adopted.

'Well, thank you for that, Phil, Trish,' she said. 'May I speak for us all?' She looked around the table and we nodded as one quietly pissed-off unit. 'We've thought about it but, on balance, we like being dirty, lazy and disorganised, so we'll pass. Let's get some food together to see you on your way, then we'll help you pack.'

She smiled brightly at Phil and I could see that he was genuinely surprised. It wasn't until then that I understood the tight limits of his blinkered vision. Our behaviour didn't simply anger him – it completely bewildered him. He and Trish were so fully defined by the world that had collapsed, that they had no point of reference left at all. If I'd asked him to find me a palmtop organiser, he'd have thought that was a great idea. Ask him to see that the world had changed, making market forces a thing of the past, and he was lost. Now if they could set up a bizarre ideal world, *Stepford Wives* meets *Wall Street*, where we amassed imaginary bank accounts and talked into defunct mobiles, then everything would be all right so long as the women wore make-up. I'd suspected that we were all a little mad from time to time, but I reckoned that Phil and Trish were bungee-ing over the edge in a way that none of us could match.

But Phil had a vindictive streak too and that was what made him dangerous. There was a moment when I thought he might hit Moth as he seemed to grow larger, seething fury making him swell up like one of Laurent's cockerels when Souris crossed the yard. I knew Moth well enough to see that she was afraid of him, though she kept her chin up and her smile bright, if a little rigor-like. But then his rage subsided and he turned on his heel, his family trailing after him, as he stormed out.

We stayed silent, too stunned to speak at first, then Moth let out a long breath and said, 'More tea, anyone?'

They left before lunch. We loaded them with plenty of food, more diesel than we could spare to be sure they got well away before they ran out, one of our tents and loads of other stuff. Maybe we were making up for not liking them – I'm sure we were – but we were so glad to see them go that we didn't care.

Donald and Phil had a wrangle about the guns until Donald gave in and let him take one. The mood had been very cool and slightly hostile as they packed and at the end Moth, with desperate insincerity, said that we'd be glad to have them move to the new place with us if they could let us live the way we chose. We breathed a sigh of relief when Phil ignored her completely and gathered together on the yard to watch them drive away. At the last minute, Trish came back to Moth and said, 'Please may I say goodbye to Christopher. I've grown to love him.'

Moth hesitated a moment before she put him into Trish's outstretched arms. Trish was tearful, hugging and kissing him. 'Poor little mite,' she said then looked at Moth with desperate appeal. 'Oh Ellen, let me save this baby – I'll take him and bring him up well. There's no hope for him here.'

Moth regarded her with a mix of incredulity and anger. 'He'll take his chances with us.'

Trish gave a loud sigh, started to hand him back then turned and ran, clutching Christopher to her. If she hadn't been trying to steal my baby brother, I'd have laughed. She looked ridiculous, panting and weeping as she tottered towards the car, acting out some drama of her own, while we watched her in amazement. Pierre and Nemisha, with the same instinct, simply stepped from either side of the yard into her path, but Moth was on her heels. She grabbed the hood of the jacket Trish was wearing.

'Not so fast,' she said, with remarkable self-restraint. 'Give him back.'

Phil had the gun in his hands and I thought things were going to turn ugly but Donald got hold of it and said, 'Don't be a fool, man.'

187

Phil was many things, but he wasn't a murderer or a child-thief either and he tore the gun out of Donald's hands, turning viciously on Trish. 'Get in the car, you stupid bitch,' he said, throwing the gun into the back. He dragged the cover over their belongings as Moth took Christopher out of Trish's arms, while she reeled in shock at the way he'd spoken to her.

Nemisha took us by surprise, putting an arm around Trish's shoulders. 'You know you can't take someone else's baby. Come on now, go to your family and stop being silly. Or do you want to stay here with us? The girls too, if you like. Let him go.'

Trish pulled back from her and drew herself up, regarding Misha with contempt that made me recoil even though I was standing back watching this play itself out, with Laurent and Ginny holding my hands. She turned on her heel and stalked to the car, got inside and slammed the door. Phil didn't look at us again. He started the pick-up, gunning the engine, and hared off down the drive in a cloud of dust, spraying stones everywhere and frightening the goats. Then we saw that the horses were hurtling down the hill towards the gate with Poppa Horse doing his best big-stallion-flying-mane-and-thundering-hooves routine.

'*Merde!*' Pierre said and started to run, the rest of us on his heels. We were much too far away and Poppa led his herd down to the drive, crossing it behind the car and then up the other side to stop on the rocky outcrop that looked down on the road. He halted on the skyline, imperious and confrontational, as the pick-up shrieked to a halt below. It scattered the other horses in a panic, but Poppa stood snorting as Phil hurled himself out of the car and round to the back, tearing at the cover. Then, with Ginny screaming and the rest of us shouting, Poppa reared up on his hind legs as Phil raised the gun and shot him.

Tears sprung into my eyes in anticipation of spurting blood and the heavy slump of a big chestnut body to the ground. But it didn't happen. Poppa came down on all four feet, as solid and defiant as before, his mane blowing around his neck and his steady gaze fixed on Phil as the echoes of the shot died away. I felt, rather than heard Phil swear, but he was clearly shaken. We were all moving again, though we obeyed as Donald took charge, telling us to get back, to let him take Phil on if need be. But Phil was staring up at the horse then he glanced up the drive, saw us running towards him and flung the gun in the back again. He left the cover flapping, swore at us and up at Poppa, then got back in the pick-up and tore off once more.

We split into two groups – the one that stood watching the pick-up career out of sight and the one that ran up the mound to check on Poppa Horse. I was in the checking group. Pierre and Sophie went to calm the other horses, while Ginny flung herself at Poppa and I went over his body with Misha, looking for injury. Poppa, however, was gazing off into the distance like the hero at the end of a movie, while we fussed and fretted and couldn't find a mark on him.

'He shot him,' Misha kept repeating. 'The bastard shot him.'

Ginny was hysterical in a mix of terror and joy, kissing and hugging Poppa, who dropped his head down to her as though he was saying, 'There, there, dear, I'm fine.'

I waited until everyone had calmed down and Ginny had gone to cover the others in kisses with Sophie, then I showed Misha and Pierre the round mark on Poppa's chest. It was to one side of his throat, precisely where a bullet would have entered if he'd been shot from below, a neat scorch of darker chestnut in the long hair of his winter coat.

None of us said anything, but we led Poppa down the hill to show the burn to Moth, Donald and Maureen. Then we put Ginny up on his back with Christopher gurgling happily in her arms, and called all the horses up to the house. We fed them bread crusts and closed the yard gate then I went down the drive on Gray to close the main gate, which we'd never done before. But we felt better for it and the horses stayed on the yard for the rest of the day, while we hung around, doing very little except grooming them and drinking tea in a bemused daze.

CHAPTER 21

The departure of Phil and his family didn't result in the upsurge of happiness I'd expected. We were subdued and unsettled as we started the preparations for the move in earnest. It was clearly over between Pierre and Nemisha, not that it had ever got going properly, but there'd been potential that had withered in the bud. However, Sophie rallied to her father's need and took him under her wing, coaxing him back into some semblance of self-respect. The night after Phil and family left, Pierre made a short speech of apology – which tore me up more than his silence – and then he threw himself into work at a rate none of us could keep up with.

Before the end of the first week, Donald and Maureen suggested going on ahead to meet Janet and prepare for our arrival. This seemed like a good plan. We were crowded in the house, even with three of us sleeping in the caravan, and they weren't used to living around other people anyhow. They had cabin fever and Maureen, who'd been attached to the almost silent Paula and Mandy, found it hard seeing them leave. She needed something to do. So two days were spent planning what we could manage without so they could start the moving process by taking a considerable amount of our gear with them. We decided that Pierre, Sophie, Laurent and I would go too, as I'd not seen the new place and Pierre could bring the pickup back. I was pretty good at driving now, but given the opportunity, I'd sooner ride Gray. So Sophie and I would herd over the cattle and goats, leaving the sheep to lamb in peace, while Donald drove our old family car, packed to the roof.

This major removal event involved a lot of planning which raised the group motivation once more and everyone started to look brighter. We left at dawn a week and a half after Phil and his family went on their way, planning to try and make the journey in three long days.

The pickup and car were so laden that the people inside were barely visible. Maureen didn't drive or ride, being a bit rheumatic in the hips, though she was pretty active for her age, which I'd recently discovered was seventy-two. She and Donald both had the robust attitude of people who'd lived a tough outdoor life and their age held them back very little.

Their horses, Smoke and Beauty, joined in the herding process with Pierre's Sunset, as though they'd been range ponies all their lives. To see them tear away to head off a straying goat without a word from anyone was a treat. We soon learned that the cattle could be driven but the goats liked to be led. So we concentrated on Big Boss and Millie, with their young son, who we had to keep reminding ourselves was destined for the table, while the three goats followed at their leisure, only needing occasional reminders from one of the horses of the direction they were to follow.

The first day took us through two beautiful glens. Pierre, with Laurent as navigator then Donald and Maureen in motorised convoy, followed the road round and Sophie and I cut the stock through the middle. There was something about the wildness of the area that made Sophie and me ride side by side not speaking, both overwhelmed. The rivers seemed more sparkling and the lochs more darkly deep than any I'd seen before while the tree-lined slopes that rose steeply on either side were rich greens. The birds and other wildlife were not only fully recovered now, but they seemed to be flourishing in a way that made us reluctant to disturb them. Deer were everywhere, and twice we saw wildcats, or at least, wild cats, slinking away into the trees.

When we stopped for the night, Donald and Maureen told us stories about the crofting way of life that would soon be our future. Donald planned to teach us some farriery, then focus on passing on his skills to whichever of us showed the most aptitude. He had a feeling that

Laurent was to be the blacksmith of the operation, which seemed a lot to place on a six-year-old. I'd seen him with a future full of poultry myself. Now I had a vision in my head of a brawny Laurent with a beard like his father's, a roaring forge and a large cockerel perched proudly on his shoulder.

Talk of the future had me torn between enthusiasm and dismay. It certainly wasn't the future I'd mapped out for myself but the world looked new-made and we never heard the roar of an aeroplane or news of a war anymore. The people we'd loved back in the old life were dead, yet we were making a new life with people we'd come to love, or would come to love. From time to time, I'd glance up and see that someone else looked as though planning the future was making them reflect on the past, then there'd be a laugh or a comment on the discussion and it would be time to re-focus and get the mind moving forwards again.

It was an easy enough trip, aside from the perpetual spring rain, which Donald kept assuring us was a good thing, though it made setting up tents and cooking something of a challenge. Aside from that it went well. We left the glens and struck out over a moorland road with eagles wheeling over us as plentiful as sparrows. I began to feel the anticipation of seeing our new home. Sophie had built it up to something wonderful and I was afraid I'd be disappointed.

But after another long day crossing the moor, pressing on into the night because the cattle wouldn't be rushed, we started to move on an old track that wound gradually but with determination towards the sea. On the third day, tired, wet and dirty, I had my first glimpse of our new home. A small gathering of white cottages in two lines led down to a neat harbour, where boats were still riding the swell. Trees surrounded the hollow with the village tucked in on two sides and standing above, on a promontory overlooking the sea, was the small manse, made of grey stone with two turrets, a cluster of worker's cottages and a wide stable yard at its heels.

A few rare breeds of cattle and sheep swung their heads up at our arrival, and Gray jumped as a small pig appeared on its hind legs over the gate of a sty, front trotters balanced on the top, like an old gossip coming out to pick up the latest news from her neighbours. The place was neat and tidy with the animals looking well and I was impressed that one person had kept it in good repair all this time. The buildings showed some weather damage as we got closer, and the track was pot-holed, but overall, Janet had done a fine job of keeping the place in order.

She came out when she heard the car and a strange sight must have met her. There was the pickup first, then the car, both full to bursting, followed by the cattle with me and Sophie on horseback, then the goats dawdling along with Sunny, Smoke and Beauty chivvying them. But she was so delighted to see other people that she came rushing out with her arms wide to greet Sophie, Laurent and Pierre a second time.

'You've come back,' she cried, sweeping them into a grateful embrace. 'I was afraid I'd dreamed you.'

Sophie did the introductions and I soon found myself being hugged too. Janet was a tall, strong woman, in her late fifties maybe, though I tended to think adults were older than they were. She looked like capability in human form, with her sleeves rolled up and long flowing hair tied back. But what surprised me was that she looked arty too. She was wearing wellies and an oilskin body-warmer, but she had a long full skirt on and one dangling earring, while in the other ear were two studs. The sleeves of her worn blue jumper were rolled up and she had gardening gloves on, and perhaps most surprising, a crisp English accent.

I took to her at once and knew without any doubt that this was Momma Horse's friend. Janet was talking to Gray and I said, 'There's a horse for you too. We all got chosen and there's one still waiting.'

Janet smiled at me, startling blue eyes assessing me frankly. 'I've been waiting for her, I think. Is she a grey mare, with her mane in ringlets and a tail that looks as though she has it tended by a hairdresser? Does she have a half-grown chestnut colt?'

I laughed. 'That's Momma Horse and Whiskers. My sister named them, except my Gray.'

She held out her hand for Gray to breathe on. 'And he's named after your father. Yes, I've dreamed them all, but Momma Horse – I thought I called her that because I didn't know her name – she's been keeping me company every night for a long while.' She laid her forehead against Gray's mane for a moment, and I could feel her loneliness. 'She's what's kept me going all this time.'

'She'll be here soon,' I promised. 'You'll love her.'

'I already love you all,' she said. 'I've been keeping this place not for myself, but for the family who were coming. And now you're here.'

There were tears in her eyes and Sophie gave her another hug. 'Will you show my friend Joel around?' she asked.

And so we went on the guided tour, Donald and Maureen too, with Laurent trotting alongside, while Sophie and Pierre started unpacking.

The place got better and better and I knew that this was what Dad had wanted for us. I could feel the buoyancy of his hope in my chest as Janet showed us the stores and the cottages, the weaving sheds and dairy, the old stable block and then the big house. It was small, as big houses went, but it still had ten bedrooms, a library, three big reception rooms and a wonderful old kitchen, with a table big enough to seat everyone around. I knew at once that the extended combined family that was mine and Sophie's would live here, while Nemisha would choose one of the cottages in the village and Donald and Maureen would take the blacksmith's house at the corner of the stable yard. We'd gather in the big house for meals and planning but those who wanted their own space could have it. But my family and Sophie's – there was room in the big house for us to live together and I was surprised at how happy that made me.

Janet had already reached the same conclusions and had been getting the different places ready for newcomers every since the first visit. She didn't say this until later on when Donald and Maureen, after a whispered discussion asked if they could have the blacksmith's cottage.

Janet smiled and looked at me and Sophie. 'Where do you want, Sophie, Joel? Don't be shy, just say.'

We looked at each other and Sophie said carefully, 'If we had the big house, we could fit both our families in.'

She glanced at Pierre and he nodded. 'We have grown into one, I think.'

Janet's smile grew so broad her ears were involved. 'I was right,' she said. 'Oh, this is wonderful. Yes, Donald, Maureen, please take the blacksmith's house – it's ready and so is the big house and the cottage nearest the sea, across the road from mine. I think that will be for Nemisha. There's one a little further up too, that's ready.'

Instinct seemed to be the thing. Dad's that we should move, Misha's as to where to, everyone's that we should trust the horses, Janet's to prepare for us and which homes we'd choose, though I was intrigued that she seemed to have anticipated more of us than there were. But I didn't ask who the last cottage was for.

CHAPTER 22

We stayed one night with Janet, to get Donald and Maureen settled in and put up the poly-tunnel, then Pierre, Sophie and I headed back. Laurent stayed behind until the next visit as the large duck-filled pond had been calling to him since the last one. Pierre had filled up the pick-up with diesel in the harbour and he was quite excited about the boats.

'I will teach you to sail, Zho,' he said. 'I love to sail and there are boats here in very good condition. I will fix them up and soon we will be fishing and sailing the coast to see what we can find.'

There'd been a difficult moment the night before when Janet tried to celebrate our arrival with two bottles of wine. She'd laid the table carefully with cut glass and linen napkins and we were all saying how great it looked when one by one we noticed the wine cooler between large jugs of flowers. A horrible silence fell and Janet must have felt it chilling her back because she turned with the pan of stew ready to ladle out and stared at us all. We'd been laughing and joking all day but now Laurent was close to tears, Sophie looked as though she had an exam to take and Pierre was sitting with his eyes downcast. I didn't know what to do and only Donald and Maureen hadn't lost their grip completely. But their attempts at complimenting the table and the smell of the food were so forced that I reckoned Janet was wondering what she'd let herself in for.

'You must all be very tired,' she began. 'Pass your plate, Jo – I hope you're hungry.'

'Oh, me? I'm always hungry.' I gave my best laddish grin but was afraid it came out as a grimace. 'That's looks great. Here Laurie, let's have your plate.'

We started helping each other as she dished up and everything lightened up but then she reached for the wine.

'Now, who can I tempt to a glass?'

Another group freeze and Laurent burst into tears. Janet stared around the table, clearly bewildered as to what she'd done.

'I think I'd be happy with a glass of water, if you don't mind,' Maureen said.

Up we all piped, 'Yes, water, please.' – 'I'm really thirsty. Must be all that lifting!' – 'Can I have some water?' – 'Och, you've got a good spring here – nothing to beat a glass of water for thirst!'

Glasses of water had never received so much praise and when Janet moved the two bottles of wine, the relief that swept around the table must have given the game away.

I felt sorry for her. She clearly planned a party meal but it wasn't anything like that. The conversation started up and while Pierre and Laurent were completely silent, the rest of us did our best but the mood was spoiled. Janet was struggling with tears by the time Sophie and I offered to wash up. Pierre disappeared as soon as good manners allowed, looking as though the new world was falling down around him, and poor Janet hurried off too, her buoyant mood destroyed.

But I think they must have met up and had some sort of heart-to-heart because they returned together later, looking reassured. Pierre's list of things he planned to do for us in our new home was more than one man could achieve in a lifetime, but work was his way of making up for his weaknesses. Whatever discussion they'd had, he evidently felt the need to prove himself to her.

As we set off again, he seemed at ease and full of enthusiasm for the boats in his quiet way, having a conversation with Donald about welding right until the moment we left. Beauty and Smoke stayed behind with Donald and Maureen, and that felt strange. They belonged in two places now and it was clear that we'd feel torn until we were all settled in the new home. The journey back was quicker without the stock and Sophie and I could choose a more direct route, so on the second day, we agreed a point on the map where we'd meet up, and Pierre set off along the road, leaving us to trail blaze. We had Sunny loose still, along for the outing, but she liked exploring and tended to go off on her own then come tearing after us to catch up. There was mischief in this, we thought, as her high-speed return always made Gray and Moon excited, so there'd be some prancing and leaping about till everyone settled down again.

After a couple of hours, Sophie and I reached a dead-end, where although there was a track on the map, it was so overgrown and steep that we didn't want to risk taking the horses up it. We could either retrace our path or take an alternative nearby which seemed clear. It was a long way around to where we'd meet Pierre, but we reckoned it was quicker than going back, so we set off. It was still quite steep, so Sophie and I dismounted to struggle, panting, alongside Gray and Moon, holding onto a stirrup to pull ourselves up. Unencumbered by humans or saddlebags, Sunny went up the steep slope in huge bounds, making Sophie laugh. 'That's no horse – that's a gazelle.'

I grinned back at her, glad of an excuse for a breather. 'Knew there was something funny about her.'

Sunny was long gone by the time we collapsed in a breathless heap at the top, sharing a bottle of water, while our horses took a rest too and picked at some grass.

'Look at that view,' said Sophie, 'it was worth the climb.'

It was enough to take the breath away without the climb. A glen dropped away beneath us sharply into a long diamond shape loch. Silver birches, pine and larch trees crowded round its edges before they began the climb themselves. The sound of the waterfall that tumbled into the loch after hurtling down the glen not far from where we sat was like a torrent, even though it was a modest little affair. But it was the silence of the place that made every sound huge and full of soft echoes.

We were so peaceful, admiring the view and sharing biscuits Janet had made, that Sunny's noisy return made us jump. Sophie and I scrambled to our feet, Gray bolted a short distance before turning with his nostrils flaring and his ears pricked forward, while Moon spooked about ten feet in the air, scattering the contents of her open saddle bags.

'Bloody hell, Sunny,' I complained, starting to gather up our supplies, 'did you have to do that?'

Sophie's hand on my arm made me stop. 'Look at her, Joel.'

I looked. Sunny wasn't having fun anymore – her eyes were wide and she was snorting.

'What's wrong girl?' I asked.

Sophie was already packing up.

'Maybe Papa is hurt. Quick.'

We shoved our gear back into Moon's saddle bag, tightened the loosened girths and remounted. Sunny, who'd been dancing about in anxiety, whirled round on her haunches and cantered off in the opposite direction to the one we'd planned to take. But we followed without question, Sophie and I having to duck and lie along our horses' necks as the trail was overgrown, switchy branches whipping across our faces and plucking at our hair. Once I glanced up to see a much bigger branch ahead and shouted to Gray and Sophie to watch out. But Gray had already spotted it and took a detour. Moon followed and then we plunged on, down another precipitous slope into the next glen.

We emerged, a bit dishevelled and disorientated, to find that Sunny was already hurtling down the road. Sophie and I called her, not wanting any of them cantering on the hard surface, but her sense of urgency overcame our caution and we let the others go after her. The road was full of frost-holes and ruts but the horses flew over the top of it at high speed, never stumbling or hesitating once. As we reached the point where Sunny was standing like a strung bow, her head an arrow directing our eyes, we saw what she'd found and my heart sank.

At first I thought the pick-up was ours and it was Pierre who'd gone off the road high above, shock mixing with bewilderment as to why he'd be so far off his route. Then I realised that I did recognise the pick-up, but it wasn't ours, it was Phil's.

'Do you think they're in it?' Sophie whispered, her hand clamped on my sleeve as though she might fall off her horse.

'I don't know. I hope not.'

High above us, the black pick-up hung by its rear wheels, caught on something at the edge of the plunging fall into the loch. There was no sound, no cries or voices. I scanned the slope with wincing eyes, afraid I'd see bodies smashed on the rocky slope, or caught in the trees that grew at right-angles to the cliff. There was nothing.

'Come on,' I said, 'we need to find your dad and see where Phil and his gang are.' I paused a moment. 'Of all the bloody people…'

'I know,' said Sophie, 'but now there are no bloody people, are there?'

I urged Gray on and we headed to the end of the valley at a brisk trot then sent Sunny to find Pierre, who should only be a few miles away. She shook herself then went off as though she'd been catapulted, her shedding winter coat leaving a horse-shaped cloud of bay hair in the air behind her.

The road out of the glen took us in a serpentine climbing roughly parallel to the slope over which the pick-up was hanging. At first there was no sign of any people, then as we were half-way up, Sophie shouted, 'Joel, stop – look.'

I followed the line of her arm, pointing through the branches of the trees growing at the roadside, and caught a glimpse of something pink. I thought of Paula and Mandy's frilly dresses and dismounted. I couldn't take Gray along the rabbit track through the trees. It was barely wide enough for me to walk along and fell away to a plummet over the loch.

'I'll go on foot,' I told Sophie, and though she started to say 'No' she stopped with the word half-formed, because there was nothing else I could do.

I had to walk with my feet almost on the sides and guessed that rabbits there were particularly small. The covering of soil was fine and scrabbled away from under me with each step. The trees' roots clung on by will alone, grimly wound around the rocks. I hung on to their branches, hoping they had a good grip, swinging myself along hand over hand to second-guess the uneasy footing. The track went under a dense growth of determined holly bushes and even though I dropped to hands and knees there, I still crawled out with my face bleeding. But I could see the pink fabric more clearly now and realised I'd come too low. I tracked upwards though the undergrowth, leaving the rabbit track and focussed on the strange alien colour of the unnatural pink against the slate grey, green and brown of the landscape.

I heard Sophie call out, but couldn't catch what she said, then I saw a movement. Using my hands as the shale and rock got steeper, I headed towards it and after forcing my way through another dense bush, almost fell over one of the little girls. She was huddled against the base of a tree, her feet making a pedalling movement in the soil that was slipping away beneath them, threatening to disappear and send her down the slope into the water far below. She shrieked when she saw me, and I recognised her then.

'Paula,' I said, holding out my hand. 'Come on, I'll get you.'

She hesitated then launched herself at me so violently that she nearly took us both into the water. I wrapped one arm around a tree and the other around her and she wound skinny little legs round my waist and her arms around my neck tight enough to choke me. She smelt of scented soap, sweat and pee and, with great shame, she said, 'I wet myself.'

'Don't worry,' I said. 'I may wet myself too in a minute. Where's your sister? Your mum and dad?'

Big tears came into her blue eyes and she shook blonde hair all over my face. 'I don't know.'

'Let's get you sorted first. Can you get on my back?'

She was like a monkey, scrambling onto my back so quickly that the memory of her and her sister being kept clean playing jigsaw puzzles and board-games in our living room jarred. But then I recalled the watchful look in her eye and realised there was more to Paula than we'd seen so far.

She clung on tight as I made my way back and though, by the time Sophie peeled her off me, she was bruised and bleeding from me falling and trees whipping her, she'd never made a sound. I collapsed in a heap beside her, my legs trembling with the effort of walking the sheer path bent almost double.

Sophie wrapped a blanket round her and I registered fully that she was wearing a frilly pink dress, with white ankle socks, as though she was going to a party. She was wet through and her thin legs were blue with cold. Sophie at once dug out her spare trousers and bundled Paula into them. We got some food and drink down her then I asked again, 'Where are the rest, Paula? Help us find them. Do you remember what happened?'

'We were having a picnic,' she said. 'It was a nice day and it's Mandy's birthday so Mummy said we should do something special and Daddy found a picnic place on the map. We turned off the road yesterday to come here so we could wake up overlooking the water as a treat for Mandy.'

So instead of heading directly to the nearest town to top up their fuel, Phil and Trish had decided to have a little holiday, going thirty or forty miles out of their way in a vehicle with a monstrous appetite. Their determination to carry on living in the world that ended nearly three years ago was either impressive or terrifying. I wasn't sure which.

'Okay, so what happened next?'

Paula was warming up a bit now, speaking more than I'd heard in three weeks of living with us. 'So we woke up here, got dressed in our best clothes, and sang *Happy Birthday* then gave her presents. I made her…'

'Tell us that later,' said Sophie. 'We need to find them now.'

Paula pouted a little and I wondered if she'd had a knock on the head or if she was slightly mad like her parents. 'Then we had a special breakfast.' She started to tell us about it, saw our faces and went on, 'but Mummy and Daddy had a fight and he got in the car in a mood. He switched it on and instead of going backwards, it went forward, over the edge.' She was crying now. 'I had the door open because I'd dropped my teddy out of the window – he was shouting at me to close it and not really looking, then we went over and I fell out. I went roly-poly down the hill.'

'Poor Paula,' Sophie gave her a hug. 'Roly-poly should be fun, shouldn't it?'

Paula nodded, clearly in shock, and a troubling thought at the back of my head kept asking why a drama queen like Trish wasn't having noisy hysterics somewhere close by.

'Paula,' I made her look at me, 'when did this happen?'

She had to think a bit. 'There was a night,' she said. 'So maybe it wasn't today, after all.'

Sophie and I exchanged a look – they'd been up there or wherever they'd fallen, all night, a bitterly cold, wet night, in party clothes, aside from any injuries they might have. We heard an engine.

'Papa,' Sophie said, and our pick-up came down the long slope with Sunny trotting along behind. Sophie ran to meet her father, talking rapidly to him in French, and Pierre immediately scooped Paula up, putting her in the back seat of the pick-up covered in the blankets. Then he got back in the car.

'I'll go up to the picnic point where they went over,' he said, and drove off, with us following on the horses.

Paula was asleep by the time Pierre, Sophie and I were standing alongside the hanging vehicle, which was good, because things looked pretty bad. There was no sign of her family outside the car, and we couldn't see the inside because it was so precarious. We spent a few moments assessing the situation then Pierre said, 'I will go in.'

Before Sophie and I could stop him, he'd launched himself at the open rear passenger door of the pick-up, which hung over the drop, swung his legs up and leapt inside. The car creaked and rocked, hanging not by the back wheels as I'd thought, but where it had bottomed out on the concrete edge of the car park as it went over. It was balancing and with Pierre's weight, made a gentle see-saw motion. Sophie and I jumped for the back of it, throwing our combined weight onto the rear sill, like two gnats trying to stop a tree falling.

'Zho!' Pierre shouted from inside, and I ran to the edge of the drop where he half threw Mandy out to me, followed by their luggage. Then he leapt back to solid ground to land in a heap at my feet before vaulting up at once into the flat-bed of the pick-up, which was swaying over our heads. I'd never seen him move like that – our gentle reflective Pierre had turned into an action hero. Sophie and I held Mandy between us, stunned by the risks he was taking and watching him throw the gear out of the dangerously rocking vehicle. At first I wondered why he was bothering, then I remembered that these clothes and toys were all the family had. I went to help, pulling down the tail-gate, and we'd got almost everything out before Pierre had to leap clear as the car tipped severely and the concrete edge supporting it collapsed, sending it plummeting down the slope. It arced through the air and I believed a car could fly for those few moments as we watched its graceful descent before it nose-dived into the loch with an impressive upsurge of water. It reappeared once, bobbing to the surface, then slowly slid under, like some monster coming up for air before returning to its watery home.

Pierre and I stood watching till it was only ripples on the surface, his hand holding my shoulder as though he thought I might leap in after it.

I turned to him, horrified. 'Were they inside?'

He shook his head. 'Only the child.'

Reaction took me then, as I realised how close he'd come to going over with the car so that he could rescue the family's belongings. I threw myself at him as Sophie started sobbing in the same terror and after he'd hugged me, he went to her, where she sat on the ground with Mandy in a huddle on her knees.

'I'm all right, guys,' he said, his quiet self again, stroking his daughter's hair. 'Let's have a look at this little one.'

Mandy seemed to be in shock, like her sister, but she wasn't hurt. She was barely conscious though and it took a long time to bring her round.

'To have her family disappear and then hang there over the cliff all night…' Pierre said, shaking his head. 'Poor little girl. All she could see was the lake far below.'

We got Mandy to eat something then settled her down with her sister, but where were Phil and Trish?

CHAPTER 23

Pierre and I took Sunny and Gray, leaving Sophie with the girls and Moonrise standing over them on guard. We rode back down the road towards the place where I'd crawled along the edge of the cliff to get Paula. Half way down, I spotted a better track, more for sheep or deer than rabbits.

I called to Pierre. 'How about along here? There's a bit more underfoot.'

The difficulty with looking for Phil and Trish along the cliff face was that we couldn't get a good view, so we sent the horses back down into the glen, trusting them to understand and alert us if they saw anything. Then we set off along the narrow track, Pierre almost bent double by the scrubby branches along the way. As the slope got steeper, they petered out, but the track did too and soon we were climbing as much as walking, as I'd done earlier, holding onto tough tree roots and then scrabbling along with our hands.

Gray and Sunny were trotting purposefully along the road far below us and as I paused to get my bearings I saw them swing into a little peninsula that stuck out into the loch. As usual, I was staggered by their ability to choose a vantage point and understand what we needed of them. I would have liked to find a safe seat and watch them, contemplating the mysteries of their behaviour and wondering if it was the change in the world, or the change in us, or the strange sense of Dad around that seemed to link Gray and me. However, it was hardly the time and I recognised a Trish-like longing to ignore what was going on and focus on something less dangerous.

I'll make some curtains when this is over, I told myself, and plan my sales career. At the end of the day, when all's said and done, I'll take that on board.

I felt Dad smile and tell me not to be so nasty, which made me grin and despite the fear of what we were going to find, the pain in my crooked back, raw fingers and grit in my boots, I was okay.

Pierre was pushing on ahead so that I lost sight of him then, after brushing my way through a bush, I crashed into him, where he'd stopped on the other side.

'Sorry,' I said, and he grabbed me as the impact set me rocking backwards.

'Look, Zho, look at Sunny and Gray.'

I peered through the branches to locate my horse again and soon spotted him. He was standing alongside Sunny and they'd reached the point of the small peninsula. They were on the shale beach, up to their front knees in the loch and doing the pointer impression that Sunny had done earlier, both heads and two sets of ears homing in on a point somewhere below and to the left of us.

'Well done, my friends,' Pierre said softly, but Sunny lowered her head briefly at once, and I knew she'd heard him.

'What do you think they are?' I asked him, as stunned by the horses as by the situation. He smiled at me, his haggard face and wild beard making him look like a prophet from one of the old films my Gran loved. 'Zho,' he said, a rare gleam in his eyes, 'some things we must simply accept and be thankful for.' I nodded and he smiled at me a moment more. 'Come on – this way.'

As we went lower, the slope started to angle sharply and we were struggling but couldn't see any other way of reaching the point the horses had aimed their attention towards. Our feet were in the water before long, and we walked with our hands above us, feeling for the overhang of rock above us to protect our heads and have something to hold on to.

'There they are,' Pierre said, his voice heavy with the dread of what we'd find. 'I can see Phil's red fleece.'

We found them together right at the foot of the slope. Phil was a misshapen collection of limbs, like a broken doll badly put back together, and it didn't look good. Trish was sitting upright, his head in her lap, even though I could tell from a distance that this was twisting him even more. She had her fingers interlinked as she gazed out over the loch and if I thought she was mad before, it was nothing compared to now.

She glanced up as we struggled our way towards them.

'Why, Joel, Pierre,' she said, as though we'd met up on our way to church, 'how lovely to see you. Will you have some tea?'

'Not now, thank you, Trish,' Pierre said with great gentleness. 'Shall I have a look at Phil? I think he's hurt.'

He knelt down and I took the blanket I'd tied around my body, throwing it over Trish's shoulders. She looked up at me with eyes full of tears.

'I think the girls are playing outside. I'm worried they'll get dirty.'

I felt sorry for her then, wondering how she would ever live in the new world. 'They're with Sophie,' I said. 'They're fine.'

'Oh good. My leg does hurt, you know, dear. Could you help me?'

Pierre was gently unravelling Phil's body so it looked whole again and I was afraid he going say he was dead. I helped Trish move, once Pierre had balanced Phil's head and put a folded fleece under it. She had a twisted ankle with grazes and bruises all over her face and hands, but aside from that she seemed unharmed. Pierre glanced in my direction raising his eyebrows and I nodded.

'She's okay,' I said, adding quietly, 'Nuts, but okay.'

Pierre looked at her for a moment then returned his attention to Phil. 'He has a broken leg,' he said, 'and his head is bleeding. But he's breathing strongly.'

Trish had tears rolling down her cheeks now and I could almost feel her fighting between the reality of what was happening and what she wanted.

'He tried to right the car,' she said, 'then he fell. I told the girls to play where they were, while I went to find him. It was a long way down and I couldn't lift him. It'll be too late for tea soon.'

I put my arm around her. 'Don't you worry. Sophie will make you some tea and we'll put our best clothes on. You'll be all right.'

She nodded at me, her eyes bright because tea would solve everything, then I looked at Pierre.

'How the hell do we get out of here? There's no way we're going back up with them, is there?'

He shook his head. 'We'll have to swim.'

Trish smiled brightly. 'I can't swim. It's not very ladylike, is it?'

I suppressed the urge to just throw her in and watch her sink.

'You'll be all right,' I said again. 'I'll tow you.'

'The water will be bitter,' Pierre said, thinking aloud, 'and I need to splint this leg somehow.' I kept silent, letting him work it out, then he got to his feet. 'Right, Zho. You're going back up the hill to Sophie – bring the car down to where the horses are and get a fire going. I'll stay here and take care of them, then I will swim them across to you one at a time.'

'I can swim,' I said, but he placed a hand on my shoulder.

'You let me do this, Zhoel.'

I guessed he was weighing up the risk of letting me swim against having to tell Moth he'd lost me. But I swam well and didn't want anything to happen to him either. Then Dad was at my back and Pierre was saying, 'You won't be leaving me alone. Graham's going to find a way to help me.'

I knew it was true. Dad and Pierre were going to sort this together. It was like he'd said – some things we had to simply accept and be grateful for.

I left him my fleece to put over Phil and went back up the slope as fast as I could, following the path we'd made on the way there. I could hear Trish telling Pierre about Mandy's birthday and reckoned he'd kept the short straw for himself.

Gray was waiting for me as I reached the road and I saw that Sunny had called Moonrise and Sophie had already driven down the hill. As Gray and I arrived, she had a fire going and once it was strong, we went to locate Pierre, calling to him, as Sunny pointed her ears in his direction. It took a moment for us to spot the red material he'd tied onto a branch for us, but we heard him reply and then as we were pondering what to do next, Sunny struck out into the water.

She swam strongly across the loch, her bay coat glistening and headed straight towards Pierre. I went over to Gray.

'Come on, lad, we can help, at least,' I said. He stepped away and when I went after him to mount, he swung his head at me, his ears back.

I was shocked and hurt at first. He'd never put his ears back at me before. But then he rubbed his head on me, as if to say 'Sorry, but you still hadn't got the message' and I realised I must wait.

We watched Pierre get Trish up on Sunny's back with difficulty, hearing her protests and squeals, but then he got up behind her and Sunny was on her way again. It was a long distance and carrying two people while she swam was hard going for her, but when Pierre tried to swim alongside, Trish had a fit of hysteria, being frightened of horses at the best of times. As they reached the shore, Pierre jumped down, hauling Trish after him and carried her the last few yards, splashing through the shallows, while Sunny stood with her head down, panting hard. I rushed with blankets for Pierre and Trish, then as Sophie got them to the fire, I went to rub Sunny down and help her in too.

Pierre was blue but he was fired with determination to get back to Phil and hardly took a moment to warm himself up. He took the long sticks I'd trimmed for him to use as a splint and both my belt and his, as well as some rope.

He clasped my shoulder a moment then stooped to kiss Sophie. 'Don't worry. Keep Trish warm.'

He was about to swim back as Sunny was clearly spent, but then Gray pushed forward, nudging at him. Pierre glanced at me and I nodded, then he sprang up onto my horse, who was smaller than Sunny so his great long legs hung ridiculously like puppet limbs.

No-one had ever ridden Gray but me, and I was torn between dismay and pride at seeing my horse launch himself into the lake with a new rider. But pride won because his willingness to carry Pierre back was life-saving, conserving Pierre's own strength for the worst task.

As I watched Gray smoothly swimming across the loch, the strangest thing happened. After a moment of dizziness, I felt I was back alongside Phil. I pulled the blanket up higher and put his hands, which were cold and twitching, back beneath it. Even though I was standing on the shore, Sophie beside me and Trish twittering about microwave cookery in the background, I was also on my knees across the loch, feeling the twigs and rocks through my cargos and the cold chill of the air on my wet hands.

Phil was in a bad way. I rubbed his chest and hands because his lips were blue and his fleshy face looked as though the skin was sloughing off, leaving strong bones and dark hollows under his eyes. I managed to roll him a little to one side and then to the other so I could tuck the blanket underneath his body. His leg looked grim, at a sickening angle, even though Pierre had done what he could with it. We needed Misha. But, on instinct, I put my hands on his shoulders and felt as though I'd handed over something, some of my youth and strength, the resilience I'd developed since Dad died, since the world ended. I gave him some of that, and a slight hint of colour touched his cheeks. He stirred uneasily, muttering, 'A fucking waste of space' and I began to laugh, perhaps a little hysterically.

'I feel better now,' I told him, not caring if he could hear. 'We're miles from help, Pierre's in danger, I'm in two places at the same time and dishing out energy like a faith healer, but you're still a tosser – even while you're kicking at death's door with a broken leg. That's reassuring – thanks. I needed something to rely on.'

My head whirled as I watched Gray swimming away from and towards me at the same time, then I lost the shore completely and I was alone with Phil, my horse surging out of the deep water to stagger on the rocky edges as Pierre slid off his back.

'Well done, Gray. Go back now,' he said, then he turned to me. 'Can you take these?'

That shook me – where was I? Pierre looked right at me, showing no surprise, and I took the sticks, belts and rope from him as he hauled himself up towards me. Gray went into reverse until he hit the deep water, then slowly swam a small circle and headed back.

Pierre knelt beside Phil, who continued muttering insults at him, though I wasn't sure if he knew Pierre was actually there. He laid his hands on the broken leg a moment, tuning in to some intuitive level of knowledge, then nodded to himself and quickly made a splint, binding both legs together all the way down.

Then, between us, as carefully as we could, we half-dragged, half-carried Phil into the water. It was bitterly cold, yet I didn't feel it. I simply knew it was cold. Pierre pushed himself out, then we manoeuvred Phil so Pierre could get an arm around his neck. He began to swim backwards, dragging Phil's prone body with him, though the bound legs didn't help. So I followed, wading along to help lift Phil's legs and seemed to keep contact with the floor of the lake, even though the cold told me it was plunging far below me. But I kept going, feeling a calm and centred sort of strength that was both familiar and alien. Pierre was working far harder than I was, swimming strongly, but Phil was heavy and it wasn't easy. More than once, I thought he was going under but all I could do was keep Phil's legs up. I wasn't sure why I couldn't swim alongside him or do anything more useful, but I kept up the dreamy wading along, one hand below the bound ankles, keeping them balanced near the surface.

I wasn't sure how long the endless journey had taken when I started shifting back and forth between the shore and the rescue again, dizzily disorientated. I focused simply on doing what was needed and, aside from a brief moment when I found myself back at the foot of the cliff, seeing Pierre struggling with the unconscious body and Sophie watching on the distant shore, I managed to keep my attention on Phil's feet. They weren't inspiring, but they gave me something to focus on.

Then Pierre looked at me, directly at me, and said, 'Thank you Zhoel; thank you Graham.'

Something whirling happened in my head and I staggered back against the pick-up, Sophie lunging to stop me falling,

'Joel,' she cried, 'what's wrong?'

I caught myself, balanced between her outstretched hand and the solid side of the vehicle.

'Whoa!' I said, fighting an urge to be sick. 'What happened then? Where's Pierre?'

'Nearly here,' she said. 'We can wade out and help him in a moment.' She peered at me. 'Are you faint?'

I shook my head. 'Where've I been since Gray swam out with your dad?'

She frowned. 'What do you mean? You've been here with me, watching, of course.'

Gray ambled over to me, his coat wet from his swim, but I wasn't wet, aside from the ankles of my cargos, where I'd waded along the water's edge earlier.

I turned my attention to Pierre's final efforts to bring Phil to safety, splashing into the water with Sophie to help him. He was on his hands and knees for a moment after we took Phil from him, spluttering and gasping, then he rallied and hauled himself onto his feet. He scooped Phil up like a baby, even though he was a big man and a dead weight, his legs strapped together for good measure. Pierre carried him to the back of the pickup and laid him flat, rubbing him dry. Trish came round to help but the girls, who'd woken up like princesses after a hundred year sleep, bemused and fractious, started to cry. So we sent her to take care of them while the three of us rubbed Phil down, manoeuvring the pick-up as close to the fire as we could and rigging up a makeshift tent over him.

Once Phil was warm, Sophie and I chivvied Pierre out of his wet clothes. I'd never seen him naked before and I was startled that he had so little hairy flesh stretched over so many long bones. He rubbed himself down and quickly dressed again.

'You don't eat enough,' I said, holding out a coat for him. He put it on then turned to me and wrapped me in one of the big hugs I liked.

'Thank you,' he said, 'you and your father. Thank you.'

I looked up at him, he was still a good head and a bit taller than me. 'Was I with you? I'm not sure what happened then. I felt as though I was with you.'

'You were both with me. Don't question, Zho, my friend. Just be thankful.'

He smiled at me again and I saw a flicker of Dad at the corner of my eye. I saw something else too – a peace in Pierre I'd never really seen before.

'We'd better make Trish some tea,' I suggested and he grinned at me. 'I think we all need some.'

CHAPTER 24

C learly, we still had problems to cope with but we persuaded Pierre to rest for half an hour, curled up in the passenger seat of the pick-up, while Sophie and I weighed them up.

'Phil's in a bad way.' Starting with the obvious helped me get hold of a problem. 'Trish's lost the plot and the kids are both in shock.'

Sophie nodded. 'But we're still a day and a half at the very least from home. By car it would be much quicker going back to the new place, except that we need Misha.'

We were making sandwiches, production-line style, and Sophie slapped me to get my attention as she handed me the next one. 'I'm doing some key thinking here,' I protested and she rolled her eyes. 'You're a boy. You don't know how to do key thinking.'

'Well, come up with a better plan than this – if you can – you and I go home at high speed cross-country on Moon and Gray while your dad takes Phil and co. back to the village. We'll do it in a day if we get a shift on.'

Sophie nodded. 'Janet and the others will be able to take care of them till Nemisha gets there.'

'I reckon they're suffering from exposure so being inside is probably the most important thing.' I threw a dishcloth at her head. 'Told you it was a good plan.'

She gave me a very French shrug. '*La chance,*' she said.

Gray and Moon set off with a will, but Sunny seemed in two minds as to whether she was going with us or Pierre. She followed us, changed her mind and went after the car but soon caught up with us again. Then she suddenly called aloud and careered off into the distance. I'd learned to pay attention to Sunny after the day's events so I said to Sophie, 'Hang on – we're off.'

I let Gray set the pace and we were most definitely off. He stretched himself along the ground until he was almost flat and tears streamed from my eyes as the cold bite of the wind honed my face down to the bones. Moonrise was right alongside us and anyone watching from a distance would have seen two wisps of cloud storm-driven up the valley.

As we reached the top of the long climb, Sunny had already plunged over the other side onto open moorland, heading for a shape we recognised at once as Flicka with Nemisha. While she adored Flicka and had learned to ride well enough, lack of faith in any natural ability on horseback meant Nemisha didn't take as much pleasure from riding as the rest of us. To see her on Flicka, out alone on the moors, meant something significant was going on so panic for my family set my stomach plunging. I urged Gray on and we hurtled over the springy moorland grass to where Sunny was enjoying a noisy reunion with Flicka. Gray was panting as we flew up to her, though he was still ready to run on and I could feel energy gathering in him even as we slowed.

'What's wrong?' Misha's greeting bewildered me.

'What d'you mean? Why are you out here? Is everything all right at home?'

'Yes, everyone's fine. But the horses got agitated and Flicka wouldn't settle until I tacked her up and set off. Only I didn't know where I was going.'

I could see that this was the ultimate test for her – to place her faith entirely in her horse. She was pale with strain and I wasn't surprised. Flicka had struck out off the way to the new place to find us after our own detour and Misha was completely lost.

'It's all right,' I said. 'You're needed at Eilean wots-its-name. Phil and his family are in trouble. It's a long story but he's got a broken leg and they've had a night in the open. Have you got your stuff with you?'

She nodded. 'I guessed someone was hurt. I thought it was one of you.' She hesitated. 'Will you or Sophie come with me?' She shook her head. 'I'd be fine on foot but, much as I love her, I'm very nervous on Flicka.'

'I'll come with you,' said Sophie. 'Joel can go back to Moth.'

So I made my way home alone and now that the big crisis was out of my hands, I enjoyed the quiet of me and Gray. I knew Moth would be anxious so we kept plodding on though we were both tired. I walked part of the way and nodded in the saddle when I couldn't keep my eyes open any longer. When I worked it out, I realised that the horses must have alerted Misha before we found Phil.

It was past dawn when we got in, tired and cold, but there was a light in the kitchen and Moth and Ginny came out to meet me, both too anxious to sleep since Misha left. Once I'd got Gray rubbed down, fed and watered, I was glad to get in the house and collapse on the couch to tell them the whole story.

Then I fell asleep where I sat and woke a couple of hours later, stiff and groggy, to find Moth was still sitting there, dozing in a chair. She stirred and got up, ruffling my hair wordlessly, before disappearing into the kitchen to return with two mugs of tea.

'You smell dreadful,' she said and I nodded acceptance.

'Thanks. It's sweat, damp, fear and the same clothes for three days. I've kept my shoes on for your protection.'

'I appreciate that. I'll run you a bath before we all die.' She stayed sitting by me though, offensive as I was. 'Tell me, Jo, did anything else happen that you haven't told us?'

I glanced at her. 'What like?'

'Well, yesterday, around mid-morning, Ginny came in and said that Dad and you were helping Pierre with the swimming.' She sipped her tea. 'I get the swimming bit now, but what about you and Dad?'

I told her about the strange sensation I'd had of being in two places at once and Pierre's perception that both Dad and I had been there to help him. She listened in silence, then said, 'You've grown very fond of Pierre, haven't you?'

I nodded. 'Is that okay?'

'Of course it is. He's a good man, in his own troubled way. I'm just – well, I don't know – I feel that Dad's letting you know it's okay too, and maybe letting Pierre know. I think Pierre's concerned that you might think he's trying to take Dad's place, because he'd like to, well, be in that place without taking it over, if you see what I mean.'

I did see. I'd given this some thought on the journey back with Gray.

'No one will ever take Dad's place. But Dad's not here and I miss him, even when he does his corner-of-the-eye hovering thing. If Pierre wants to be a sort of surrogate dad, I don't mind…' I stopped with the last word half-spoken, and changed the sentence. 'Moth, I'd be glad.'

She smiled at me. 'I think that's yours for the asking, love.'

'How do I ask?'

'Well, you don't need to. Act as though it is and it will be.'

When Pierre came back, we picked up the moments of connection we'd made since the first time he returned from the new place and put them together without a word. I was glad of it as we carried on with the move. Phil was recovering, though Nemisha stayed for a week, while Janet and Maureen helped Trish and the girls settle into the cottage Janet had ready. I should have guessed it was for them. The rest of us packed and transported everything we needed to take in the cart, the cars and the caravan, squabbling about what should go where to cover up the wrench of leaving. It was a chaotic process, needing all Sophie's organisational skills, though she was in her element, of course.

But she was showing signs of anxiety herself as during one day of packing we were airline staff, loading goods on to a cargo plane, thinly disguised as Poppa Horse and the cart. Another day, we were medieval farmers herding our stock to market. We were experts at role-playing by now and Pierre's impression of 'ye olde English' country accent was a treat, keeping us in fits of laughter. Sophie's games served a real purpose as fun bonding-exercises, but only some of us understood that they also helped Sophie regain a hold when she felt life hurtling out of control. She revelled in her role as project manager for the move but she'd found safety at Tir na Croabh and reunion with her father and I knew she was uneasy.

As we were getting near ready to go, she found me talking to Gray by Dad's grave. She was very quiet for a moment before she said,

'I'm afraid of leaving, Joel.'

'Me too,' I said. 'We've had some good times here.'

'But it is too small, isn't it? And Tianavaig is beautiful?'

I looked at her dark eyes, noting that she was a little hollow above the cheekbones as though she'd not been sleeping. The resemblance to Pierre was startling. I often saw the mirror image of his personality in her obsessive need for order but I'd not seen it echoed in her face before.

'It will be a real home, Soph. We'll have enough space and enough land, even if more people come. We won't have this treading water feeling of wondering what happens next.' I tried to look reassuring. 'And your dad's made up with it – the boats and the metal working shop. I've never seen him so happy.' That cheered her up.

'He's much better, isn't he?'

'He is.' I gave her a nudge to soften what I was going to say. 'You could lighten up on him a bit, you know, Soph.'

She shook her head. 'He has you for a friend. He'll only be my father if I demand it of him.'

'Is that what you think? I don't think you're right. He's working hard at being a great father and he's doing more than okay.'

Sophie nodded. 'But it's not habit yet.'

I didn't have an answer to that because I saw what she meant. Neither she nor Pierre could relax into the idea that he was just a guy, a dad, yet. He was still too newly returned from the edge.

'He'll be okay, Sophie. We all will. It's like Ginn says, we have to trust the horses and Sunny thinks he's cool.'

'Well, if he's good enough for Sunny,' she said, smiling, and the small hovering cloud lifted from over her head to sail away over Dad's grave. I saw Moonrise, grazing not far away, raise her head to watch it pass, then she wandered over to Sophie. As she reached out smiling to her horse, I caught a glimpse of the woman Sophie would grow into, then she grinned at me, because Moon made her happy, and she was a girl again.

So the packing continued and the last few days at Tir na Croabh, with every now and then someone needing reassurance and someone else providing it. There was an unspoken agreement that Moth, Ginny, Christopher and I would be the last ones to leave, so we could make our farewells to the place Dad was buried. We weren't looking forward to that.

On the final morning, Laurent supervised the loading of his indignant, squawking poultry into boxes made for the journey. I think that less fuss was lavished on Christopher than those chickens, but eventually it was done.

Pierre called me while Sophie was doing a final inventory check with Moth and Ginny. 'Come with me, Zho.'

We walked the boundaries together for the last time, stopping at the top of the hill to admire the view. Then he glanced at me sidelong. 'You okay?'

'I think so.'

Pierre nodded, looking out over our small world. 'Any time you want, Zho, we'll come back here and stay a day or two.'

'That's a good idea. I'd like that.'

'Sure. We'll keep an eye on the place, until it offers shelter to someone else. We can pass the gift on, you know?'

I looked up at him. He was impossibly tall and angular. With his chaotic hair and beard like an escaped madman, despite his earnest attempts at neatness he still looked as wild as the landscape. But I knew differently now. It was the time for saying things that might never be said again.

'When Dad died,' I began, 'I thought I'd be lonely for him my whole life. And in a way, I know I will be. But he's around – you've got to know him although you've never met him.'

Pierre moved to sit on the stile, watching me carefully. 'Yes. I number him among my friends.'

If I hadn't loved him already, I'd have loved him for that.

'Well, I think he numbers you among his. And you know I do, don't you? Pierre, I miss my Dad something dreadful but when I'm with

222

you, well, it's a lot better.' I hesitated. 'I just wanted to… make sure you know that, before we go.'

I couldn't say anything else but it seemed to be enough. He smiled at me, a gentle, ramshackle smile that lit his worn face like the soft glow of sunlight on old wood.

'Dear Zho,' he said. 'I couldn't have found myself again without you.'

We stayed like that for a moment, watching each other, then he extended a great long arm around my shoulders and we wandered back to where Sophie was arguing with Laurent, who was determined to ride in the back with the feathery crates.

Pierre grinned at me and scooped up his son to hang over his shoulder, Laurent's favourite place, saying, 'Hit the road, Jack.'

Ginny took up his cue for a song and we joined in a rousing chorus displaying very little singing ability but excellent lung capacity. That got the three of them in the pick-up and on the move, with a few tears and kisses and some hugs and lots of waving. As they disappeared from view, we could hear Souris barking and the indignant protests of flustered poultry. Then there was only the four of us.

We wandered around once more, doing a top to bottom check, cupboards, boxes, drawers, workshops, to make sure we'd not left anything. I heard Ginn calling the horses down and went out to greet Gray. To my surprise, it wasn't only him, Poppa, Misty and Whiskers. They were all there, all eleven of them, waiting in a neat line by the cart, even though Beauty, Momma, Smoke and Flicka were supposed to be at the new place, and the other three had left a couple of hours earlier with Pierre's gang. Now, they were all there, back as we'd started, just us and them.

'Oh guys,' Moth said. 'Thank you for coming.'

We worked our way down the receiving line they made, giving them each a hug, then set off to do what we didn't want to do – say goodbye to Dad.

Moth gave Christopher to me and I carried him in the crook of my arm so he could dribble happily down my shoulder, gurgling at Whiskers. Then Moth and I each gave Ginny a hand and we walked down the field in a line, the way we'd done the day Dad died. But now we had

Chris, too, and the eleven horses following. They fell into file, Poppa, Momma, then the others in a graded height arrangement so comical that we had to keep turning to laugh at them.

We were so busy looking backwards as we stumbled along that we reached the gate before we expected to and stopped, startled in an odd way, feeling something had changed.

'It's a year today,' Moth said, moving from Ginny, to me, to Chris, to take our faces in her hands and kiss us on the forehead. 'A year today since we lost him and the horses came.'

My eyes filled with tears as I looked at them, my family and the horses. Had it been as short – or as long – as a year? Surely Gray'd been with me all my life. Surely it was only a few days since Dad last said, 'Fancy a quick walk, Jo?' then trekked me ten miles before tea.

Ginny was sobbing but she was smiling too, as she told our little brother, 'Daddy sent the horses to take care of us. And now they're going to see us to our new house.'

Moth went to open the gate and lead the way into the field, then she stopped, staring at Dad's grave.

'What's up?' I asked, but Ginny was already running past her. 'Where's Daddy?' she said, turning wide blue eyes on us.

The grave had gone. The round stone too. There was no sign that anything had been there for the past year, not the small mound of earth, the little garden or the path worn as we walked to sit on the bench. The bench, of course, that wasn't there either. The few blue and yellow flowers growing where the grave had been were in grass that merged perfectly with the rest of the meadow. But, while the flowers were dotted here and there casually in front of our feet, as our eyes followed the wandering line they made, we realised that there were blue and yellow flowers everywhere, spilling from the quiet corner by the wall, where the grave no longer was, then down the field to spread out over the grass like a floral coverlet on a child's bed.

We stood staring, the horses ranged out behind us, looking over the wall, making me grin. Moth turned to me in bemusement. 'Were those flowers here yesterday?'

I put my arm around her and kissed her loudly on the cheek. 'Moth, they weren't here two hours ago when I walked round with Pierre. Come on, I think we've got the message. Hit the road, Jack – Dad's along for the ride.'

In the centre of the milling group of horses, we made our way back to the house, said goodbye yet again to everything and then I got Poppa hitched to the cart while Ginny tacked up Gray and Misty. Moth came out of the house and closed the door, Christopher in the baby carrier on her chest.

We took a last look round. 'Have we got everything?' I asked and noticed Ginny grinning and nodding. She pointed to the back of the cart so Moth and I went to peer in. Neatly placed in the far corner at the back were the bench and the round stone with Dad's name scratched into it. Moth looked at me. 'You? Pierre?'

Then, with me and Ginny grinning, she dismissed her own question with a wave of her hand and swung herself up into Misty's saddle.

CHAPTER 25

For the first two days of our journey, we had a full horse escort. Then we woke after our second night away from Tir na Croabh to find that all but our four had gone on ahead. As we drew near to Eilean Tianavaig, we spotted Beauty on look-out duty and, by the time we arrived, there was a house-warming party waiting for us. It was a fine welcome. While the place wasn't home yet, the people were our people, chosen as we were by the horses, and for the first time we were all together with enough room to sit round and talk in comfort. That was a good night. There was plenty to eat and a special sort of punch to drink which, even though it was alcohol-free, seemed to make everyone very happy. Pierre played the guitar and Janet played the flute, while Donald was amazing on a bodrhan he'd found somewhere. We sang and even got some dancing going. Phil and Trish were a quiet presence in the corner, him on crutches, her on the edge, but Paula and Mandy enjoyed themselves.

It set the pattern for the future and soon Eilean Tianavaig started to become home. Living in the big house suited us well. It wasn't so huge we rattled round it but we had plenty of room and could put Pierre to sleep where no-one was disturbed by his snoring. Laurent wanted the chickens and Souris to have rooms of their own, but we scotched that by saying the horses would need one each too then we'd run short and have to move again. The huge kitchen became our little community's meeting place where we made our plans, worked, bickered, fell out occasionally, shared chaotic meals, laughed often, cried from time to time, and lived.

Phil and Trish stayed distant from the horses, though he recovered and she slowly returned to being no more deranged than she was prior to the accident. I'd like to say we became better people and put our differences behind us to live in perfect harmony. I'd like to say that having his life saved by Pierre humbled Phil so that he accepted the great shambles and valued him as he deserved. Sadly, this didn't happen. They didn't often drop into the big kitchen and there was still a certain amount of tension whenever Phil was around. He carried on referring to Pierre as a waste of space, deflecting any protest by saying it was a joke. But Janet, who loved everyone, got on well with Trish, while Maureen loved the little girls, so on an everyday basis, the situation was fairly relaxed.

The first year passed and while Trish and Phil always looked about to leave, they never got around it. Poppa Horse backed off somewhat, but it was clear that the stallion had his eye on Phil. Yet Phil seemed to respect this in a way he never could respect Pierre's quiet presence. Momma Horse had another foal and so did Beauty and while Paula and Mandy were quite taken with these newcomers, they didn't make any special bond with them. Trish actually became an asset because she took a real pride in the domestic details, making clothes and curtains and though I still found her fluffy and irritating, I learned to tolerate her. Moth never got over the feeling that she was after Chris, but Trish was happy enough to have Janet as her friend, so Moth's enforced girly chats were over at least. Phil worked well with Donald and started developing a soft spot for Laurent, though he never got on with Misha. We learned a lot about tolerance that year as we had to live and let live, agree to differ, make sure we didn't live in glass houses and throw stones, walked several miles in each other's moccasins – enough clichés to gladden Phil's heart. When we got it right, it worked very well indeed.

We fished often and everyone learned to sail a boat, even the kids. Paula and Mandy showed a natural skill and Pierre rigged up two little racing dinghies for them. Once Trish had stopped worrying about them getting dirty or ruining their hands, they both thrived. The spark of character I'd noted in Paula found an outlet in an active life and she turned into a bold and adventurous child. Though Mandy was more like her mother, she still showed far more sprit than I'd have ever expected, especially when it came to sailing.

I started charting the sea and coastal life, picking up my interest in marine biology. When it emerged that there were books in the wonderful library of the big house that Janet hadn't realised were there, my group nodded knowingly and added our horse books to the collection. I became the official scribe almost at once, keeping a community journal and the records of everything from the vegetable rotation to the farm plans – whatever we did, I kept a record on it. Sophie was in charge of the planning, I recorded the results and slowly we built up a life that worked, one we could sustain and build on.

Pierre and I sailed round to Corrycreag fairly soon after we moved. Phil hadn't done half as much damage as he liked to think, fortunately, as his fire had burned itself out before it got too far. Once we'd established it was worth the trip, everyone went regularly, gleaning plenty of useful materials on our visits, and gathering a number of cats, as well as a big lollopy dog who adored Donald and was immediately named Robbie Burns by Ginny. Corrycreag made a significant difference to our supplies, especially of clothes and fuel, medicines, building materials, books and other non-perishables, but it also made us feel better that the town wasn't mouldering away in its abandoned state. We did a lot of tidying of things we didn't need, Misha neutered any cat that crossed her path and the main street and harbour area started looking neat, ready if anyone should need them. Pierre, little by little, put Smith's and the windows he'd wrecked to rights. It was the one thing he wouldn't let me help him with.

Pierre quickly became the mainstay of our little community. He worked like ten men. He was inventive and clever with his hands, could make anything, adapt anything, and given the time and resources, was artistic too. He and Janet together made some amazing wind sculptures to sing in the breeze and sparkle when the sun was on them. She was happy to have found another artist in the group and her delight in our arrival after her long loneliness never failed.

Pierre soon started looking less like an old wreck, but it wasn't always easy for him and sometimes he'd come to me, and say, 'Bad day, Zho.'

229

'Okay,' I'd say and we'd go off on foot, with Gray and Sunny following maybe, and we'd walk, Pierre's long legs striding out and mine getting longer to keep up with him. We kept walking, pushing ourselves hard till he got past his need for a drink. There was drink close by, of course, in Corrycreag and even Tianavaig. Phil always had some and I was pretty sure Donald kept a bottle tucked away discreetly. But Pierre wouldn't let me try to persuade them to get rid of it. He chose to face up to its presence and we admired him for that, so no-one said anything when he and I went out trekking over the hills, to return only when we were both crawling with exhaustion but he'd stopped shaking.

Donald, Maureen and Janet seemed very content. They had enough company, enough to do but plenty of young help and spent their time passing on their skills to the rest of us. Phil was always the most restless. He'd prowl around looking for someone to criticise and talking about how he'd soon be heading south to start a new government or set up a sales team or something. Nemisha, perhaps the most driven and forward-thinking of us, was committed to our community but she started getting restless fairly soon too, and I overheard her half-joking with Moth about her biological clock. The imbalances in our little group were obvious. Pierre was the only unattached adult male, but the flicker between them never so much as glimmered again.

Moth and Pierre were another matter. An understanding seemed to grow between them that began with the decision that we'd share the big house – one which I don't think was ever questioned or discussed, but simply accepted as the right choice. They started raising their children together at Tianavaig and, while Sophie and Laurent chose to call Moth 'Moth', one of the first words Chris said was 'Papa' and he never called Pierre anything else. Any stranger who wandered in would have assumed they were seeing a couple, though if they'd picked up on the contented presence of Dad around, they might have thought something unusual was going on, especially as another early word from Chris was 'Dad'. But Dad was part of the unusual family we'd become, though we understood that he wouldn't be around forever. He was waiting for the right moment to move on and so, perhaps, were Moth and Pierre, though I never doubted that they had his blessing. When I caught that quiet smile between them, I saw a potential future I'd never anticipated.

But aside from our group, imbalanced and short of human breeding stock, we remained alone. I kept an eye open for the girls' volleyball team but they didn't turn up. While I began to think I was destined to die a virgin, I could have died four years earlier with the rest of the world. Moth was right about a bond between me and Sophie and in a way we had the same sort of understanding she shared with Pierre. Our awareness that we were the next obvious couple was silently acknowledged as a future possibility. Maybe Moth put something in our tea, but my worries that I'd never be kissed by anyone outside my family settled with the knowledge that whatever Sophie and I became as she grew up, then we'd be forever. We couldn't afford to get it wrong.

So we lived: riding and fishing and growing food, pursuing our own hobbies and doing what the group needed. But there was a sense of waiting for more people to arrive, though Ginny was quick to tell us off when we started worrying that we were the only ones.

'Trust the horses,' she said, 'they'll let us know when more people are coming.'

So one morning, I set off with Pierre to go and have a head count of the sheep because it was coming up to lambing time. As we were leaving, Moth said, 'We'll come too. Come on Christopher.'

She picked my toddling little brother up and put him on my back and Laurent, who'd become the cat-as-well-as chicken-master, trailed along behind with his feathered and feline friends, who tolerated one another pretty well.

Sophie called, 'Wait for me,' and came tearing after us.

She'd suddenly got tall like her dad, though thankfully not as ugly, and I called, 'Come on, Longshanks, we've not got all day.'

'Why? You do nothing anyhow,' she replied, pulling a face at me and sharing the toast she was eating with Christopher, which made me complain because he dropped scratchy crumbs down my neck.

We trekked up the hill in a gang to Dad's bench, with the round stone alongside. We called it the Lookout, where we watched the sea and our land and the changing of tide and weather. It was a favourite place for most of us. Out of habit, on reaching the top, we turned to look at the sea, the foamy waves rippling up on the sand in the brisk breeze.

Down in our little village, I saw Misha striding out with purpose from her cottage. She waved and I waved back then spotted Maureen with Paula and Mandy, while Donald and Ginn were up to something, heads together. They were always up to something, those two, Donald being an incorrigible practical joker. Ginny looked up, saw us and shouted something. Trish was cleaning the windows of their cottage while Phil sat in the sun, reading a five-year-old paper and not looking at anyone, even though Ginny was shouting excitedly.

She hurtled along the path leading to the Lookout and we waited patiently, sitting on the bench or on the ground. It was a fantastic day with the sea very blue and sparkling, the grass fresh green and sun-yellow buttercups all around.

Ginn rushed up to us, gasping and breathless. 'I told you, I told you,' she said. 'Daddy says it's time.'

Pierre, sitting behind me, touched my shoulder, pushing me lightly forward so he could get up and I scrambled up from the ground too. We turned, following Ginny's pointing arm – Pierre, Moth, Sophie, Christopher, Laurent and me – while Dad smiled at the corner of my eye. We turned as our horses, grazing on the hill behind us, swung their heads up, ears pricked, manes swaying, in one movement, looking out over the ridge that marked the edge of Eilean Tianavaig. Poppa Horse called out, and every one of them was tense, alert, poised ready to fly.

'What's going on?' Moth asked, unsteadily and I noticed that while she and Pierre were not exactly holding hands, their fingertips were lightly touching. I nudged Sophie, nodding at them and she grinned, then the horses were on the move and we were running to get a better view as they surged down the hill. No-one ever tired of seeing them gallop. They tore along in a herd, a wave of grey and chestnut, bay and black, hooves pounding on the dry road as they crossed it and disappeared up into the trees on the other side.

'Any moment!' Ginny was jumping up and down, hugging herself with glee. 'Any moment!'

Everyone had joined us by then, the whole of our little community, even Phil, with a face like a slapped arse, I thought, then realised it was also a face I'd grown quite fond of in a grudging way. We were all there, waiting to see why the horses had gone hurtling off over the top of the ridge, heading into the distance. We heard the hoof beats receding and Misha said, 'Where are they off to in such a hurry?'

Ginny was still doing an impression of a jumping bean.

'They'll be back,' she said, so wound up with excitement that she could hardly speak – and a moment later they were.

The hoof beats were getting closer until we could see a cloud of dust as they headed back along the edge of the ridge, thundering down the road that wound towards our harbour. I saw them a moment later, Poppa, then Gray, felt the pounding heartbeats, smelt the sweat. I was in there with them, in the press and adrenalin rush of the herd, the stampede, the joy of running together. I remembered the moment I first saw them and felt tears prickle at the back of my eyes.

The people around me were beginning to see what was happening. Pierre started to laugh, Moth had a hand over her mouth, Ginny was beside herself, while Donald came out with some fine old Scottish exclamations. Laurent was jumping up and down on the bench, clapping his hands while the dogs barked their heads off and Sophie, standing on the bench too, balanced herself on my shoulders. We were all there, laughing and delighted, as Poppa Horse led his herd back to their grazing ground.

They spilled off the ridge, our familiar friends, my beloved Gray, gentle Misty, independent Beauty and wise Momma with their foals, skittish Whiskers, Flicka, Smoke, Moonrise, Sunset and Daybreak – all named by my little sister. But Ginny had her work cut out now because they were only the first, and the new horses galloped steadily along after them, new colours, palominos, duns, some amazing black and white spotted, more bays, greys – all wonderful – foals and adults and half-grown youngsters. They ran below us, a river of muscle and energy, the smell of their sweat rising on the morning air, the thrill of the gallop still on them. Then Poppa lead them down to the beach, thirty or forty of them, rolling and splashing, snorting and playing in the waves.

We watched, laughing and hugging each other, and it was at that moment that Dad touched my shoulder in farewell. Ginny and Moth turned to look at me, loss on their faces, while Christopher suddenly let out a bewildered wail. Then everyone felt it and the ripple of Dad's leaving spread round the group, freezing us in the midst of our enjoyment. But even as my heart threatened to plunge with abandonment, I steadied myself. Dad had stayed until we were secure, until our future was assured. He'd never leave – but he'd be with us in a different way from that moment.

The horses came the day my father died. That was the worst day and yet also the best. He always said that loss and gain went hand in hand. We'd learned through him and them that it was true – now it was time for him to move on. After a moment when the sadness washed over us, we began to smile and laugh, saying goodbye to him aloud – Gray, Graham, Daddy, Dad. His names floated out onto the morning air over the huge herd of horses and every one of them looked up to watch the sense of him drift over the sparkling sea. Then they set off again, galloping along the shore, splashing in the shallows. They wheeled round at the far end, to turn once more and follow Poppa Horse back. Then, catching their breath, they headed for the grazing slopes, to settle in and wait for their people to arrive.

ACKNOWLEDGEMENTS

I would like to acknowledge the influence of Edwin Muir's poem, 'The Horses', in the original idea for this novel and the assistance of the Academi Mentoring Scheme in its development. I would also like to thank Dr. Jane Packard at the Department of Wildlife and Fisheries Sciences, Texas, for her advice on the behaviour of wolves and Alison Layland, M.I.T.I., for checking my French.

ABOUT THE AUTHOR

ELAINE WALKER lives in North Wales, UK. Her publications include fiction, poetry and non-fiction. She is also a singer/songwriter and musician. As a fiction writer, she is particularly interested in magical realism and storytelling that is not bounded by reality. She has a doctorate in English Literature and her academic work on early modern horsemanship manuals crosses into her interest in the fantastic in the lives and writing of the first Duke and Duchess of Newcastle. She offers a consultancy service on the horse in cultural history and has worked for English Heritage, Royal Mail and Atacama Films, among others. Her website, www.elaine-walker.com, has more on her work and links to her social media pages.

ROLLING OLIVE PRESS LIBRARY
Available at www.XenophonPress.com

Memoir of a Death Angel, Anagnost 2014
Hymn to the Chesapeake, Arthur 2015
The Horses, Walker 2016
Physical Education, Holladay 2016

XENOPHON PRESS LIBRARY
Available at www.XenophonPress.com

Xenophon Press is dedicated to the preservation of classical equestrian literature. We bring both new and old works to English-speaking riders.

30 Years with Master Nuno Oliveira, Henriquet 2011
A New Method to Dress Horses, Cavendish 2015
A Rider's Survival from Tyranny, de Kunffy 2012
Another Horsemanship, Racinet 1994
Art of the Lusitano, Yglesias de Oliveira 2012
Austrian Art of Riding, Poscharnigg 2015
Baucher and His School, Decarpentry 2011
Breaking and Riding, Fillis 2015
Classic Show Jumping: the de Nemethy Method, de Nemethy 2016
Divide and Conquer, Lemaire de Ruffieu 2016
Dressage in the French Tradition, Diogo de Bragança 2011
Dressage Principles Illuminated, Expanded Edition, de Kunffy 2016
École de Cavalerie Part II, Robichon de la Guérinière 1992, 2015
Equine Osteopathy: What the Horses Have Told Me, Giniaux 2014
François Baucher: The Man and His Method, Baucher/Nelson 2013
Great Horsewomen of the 19th Century in the Circus, Nelson 2015
Gymnastic Exercises for Horses Volume II, Russell 2013
H. Dv. 12 Cavalry Manual of Horsemanship, Reinhold 2014
Handbook of Jumping Essentials, Lemaire de Ruffieu 1997
Handbook of Riding Essentials, Lemaire de Ruffieu 2015
Healing Hands, Giniaux, DVM 1998
Horse Training: Outdoors and High School, Beudant 2014

Learning to Ride, Santini 2016
Legacy of Master Nuno Oliveira, Millham 2013
Methodical Dressage of the Riding Horse, Faverot de Kerbrech 2010
Principles of Dressage and Equitation, Fillis 2016
Racinet Explains Baucher, Racinet 1997
Science and Art of Riding in Lightness, Stodulka 2015
The Art of Riding a Horse or Description of Modern Manege,
D'Eisenberg 2015
The Art of Traditional Dressage, Volume I DVD, de Kunffy 2013
The Ethics and Passions of Dressage Expanded Ed., de Kunffy 2013
The Forward Impulse, Santini 2016
The Gymnasium of the Horse, Steinbrecht 2011
The Italian Tradition of Equestrian Art, Tomassini 2014
The Maneige Royal, de Pluvinel 2010, 2015
The Portuguese School of Equestrian Art, de Oliveira/da Costa 2012
The Spanish Riding School & Piaffe and Passage, Decarpentry 2013
To Amaze the People with Pleasure and Delight, Walker 2015
Total Horsemanship, Racinet 1999
Training with Master Nuno Oliveira double DVD set, Russell 2016
Truth in the Teaching of Master Nuno Oliveira, Russell 2015
Wisdom of Master Nuno Oliveira, de Coux 2012
Total Horsemanship, Jean-Claude Racinet 1999
Wisdom of Master Nuno Oliveira, Antoine de Coux 2012

Lightning Source UK Ltd.
Milton Keynes UK
UKHW011811260120
357634UK00001B/3